Sarah Mahar,

Beyond the 14th Floor

Enjoy!

Melaney Bossaer

FriesenPress

Suite 300 - 990 Fort St
Victoria, BC, V8V 3K2
Canada

www.friesenpress.com

Copyright © 2019 by Melaney Bossaer
First Edition — 2019

Author photo by Warne Noyce, Warne Photography.
Cover art —Tia Bossaer

All rights reserved.

No part of this publication may be reproduced in any form, or by any means, electronic or mechanical, including photocopying, recording, or any information browsing, storage, or retrieval system, without permission in writing from FriesenPress.

ISBN
978-1-5255-5387-5 (Hardcover)
978-1-5255-5388-2 (Paperback)
978-1-5255-5389-9 (eBook)

1. FICTION, COMING OF AGE

Distributed to the trade by The Ingram Book Company

Dedicated to my people:
who support me,
love me,
make me laugh,
and make me proud.

Chapter One

Sunday, November 10, 10:30 am

The 911 call came in around 2:30 am. An elderly couple thought they'd heard cries for help and banging coming from the walls of their bedroom. At first, they dismissed the sounds as street noise, but in the silence of the power outage, there was no denying someone was in distress in the building. They listened carefully, proceeding into the apartment hallway in their bathrobes, clutching their emergency flashlight, trying to trace the sounds. The beams of light gleamed against the silver door of the elevator and as they walked closer, the sound grew louder. They took turns putting their ears against the cold metal, confirming the source.

The operator logged the call and assured the couple that help would be sent as soon as possible, but the storm had been severe and emergency crews were overwhelmed across the city of Philadelphia.

#

The firefighter looked at his watch as he approached the apartment building. He rubbed his eyes and stretched as his partner pulled to a stop. "When did this call come in?"

His partner glanced at the screen. "About 2:30 am. We're going to have some pretty unhappy campers. They've been in there for a long time."

The firefighter nodded. "It's been a long night. Only two more hours until shift change." He grabbed his tool bag and gloves. "Let's do this."

They found the control box and managed to power up the system. As the carriage began to move, the occupants' screaming and banging echoed down the shaft. The carriage descended slowly from the fourteenth floor where it had stalled, lighting each number on its way down.

When the elevator reached the ground floor, the doors remained closed, so they took a crow bar and pried them open with a pop. The rank smell and shrieking hit them in a wave, assaulting their senses. The scene was frantic. A tearful blond woman in a sleeveless, floral dress cried for them to help as she moved out of the way, revealing a brown-haired teenage girl on her hands and knees doing CPR on an older man. "Our friend needs help. We've been trapped for over sixteen hours. He's diabetic and he doesn't have a pulse."

"It's okay, Ma'am, we're here to help. We'll look after him." The firefighter knelt beside the girl, who was frantically pumping the man's chest. He slipped off his helmet, asking her to stop. He checked for a pulse and looked back at his partner. "Get the defibrillator off the truck."

"Great work, Miss. We'll take over." The girl rose to her

feet as tears slipped down her cheeks, tired arms hanging limply by her sides.

A paramedic joined the firefighters and the woman and girl clung to one another, weeping, each silently praying for the old man stretched out on the elevator floor.

Chapter Two

Saturday, November 9, 2010 6:00 pm

The skies darkened overhead as the storm closed in on the city.

The elderly black man made his way down the busy sidewalk with determination, hitching one leg along as he walked. A bag in one hand, the other went up to wipe his brow, sweaty with exertion.

The air was heavy with the approaching storm closing in. Litter tumbled along the sidewalks and danced in the air as the wind began to pick up. *Almost there*, he thought as he passed store owners closing up for the day. They shuttered their metal-gated storefronts.

He'd seen many storms in his lifetime and the dark churning clouds looked ominous. He hoped it wouldn't be difficult getting home later.

#

Horns blaring all around her, Jill Jones' progress crawled in the slow-moving traffic. Muttering under her breath, she flicked on the radio as she finally began to inch ahead. The Q102 radio announcer punctuated the space between songs with warnings of the approaching storm. Jill craned to look up at the sky between the buildings. *It sure looks dark. I should be getting close. This might be a bad idea...*

Unfamiliar with the area, she scanned the building numbers as she drove. She pulled a business card from her purse and rechecked the address. Satisfied, she tucked it back in beside the wallet she was planning to return. Parking in Philly was impossible. As if she had won a lottery, there was a space open near the entrance of the apartment complex she was looking for.

A teenager strode along in her plaid shirt and jeans, her long, dark, hair whipping around her face. Backpack slung on her back, only the top of her head appeared visible to anyone approaching her. She was absorbed with her cell phone. People weaved around her as she walked until suddenly, she stopped and looked up. She studied the building and then her phone. Yes, this was the place.

Jill parked her car and strode with purpose to the entrance. As she walked through the lobby, she found the elevator. The older man was waiting for the door to open and he acknowledged her arrival with a polite nod. She smiled in return. The silver doors popped open and he waved her in first. He shuffled in after and reached over and pressed button for the sixteenth floor.

As the doors began to close, an arm shot through the opening, causing them to bounce back. The teenage girl scrambled into the elevator out of breath. She was surprised to see others inside. She nodded to them and her backpack dropped to the floor with a thud as she pulled the wind-blown hair away from her face.

"Wow, it's getting pretty stormy out there," Jill said to the girl.

"Yeah, it's crazy. It really looks like it's cuttin' loose across the city already."

Jill's finger hovered above the panel. "What floor?"

"Eighteen."

"That's the same as me," said Jill as she tapped the glowing button.

The doors closed with a thud and the elevator groaned and rocked a bit as it began its ascent. The lights flashed as the elevator seemed to struggle and slow down. They glanced at one another, searching for an explanation. They turned to watch the panel and stared transfixed as each number lit up—ten, eleven, twelve, no thirteen (as that was superstitious), and then fourteen.

The lights flickered again and suddenly the elevator screeched to a halt. They gasped in surprise as their hands shot out to grab the walls to steady themselves. The elevator plunged into momentary darkness. Emergency lights hesitated and then illuminated the space in a sickly yellow glow.

"'What happened? Why isn't it moving?" the girl asked, her face flushed. "This is weird."

"I don't know," replied Jill. She repeatedly pushed the buttons on the panel, causing no reaction.

"Seems like the power went out, probably on account'a the storm," said the man, showing tobacco-stained teeth that were several shades lighter than his skin. He peered up at the lights. "Those look like emergency lights. See the box they're mounted on? That's a battery backup. We're lucky; a lot of elevators don't have 'em."

They sat in silence for a moment, pondering the situation. "What do we do now?" asked the girl, turning around and looking at the ceiling.

They turned again to the unlit elevator panel. "Okay, here's the emergency button, let's give 'er a try," said the old man. He pressed the red button, causing a bell to ring loudly in the elevator. "Hopefully somebody can hear and realize we need help."

He let go of the button, they held their breath, and listened. There was nothing but silence.

A shiver of panic tingled down Jill's spine and she mentally pushed the feeling away. *Great, I really need this now.* She reached past the man and pressed the red alarm button again and held it. It jangled loudly and when she lifted her finger off, her ears still rang with the echo. Silence.

"There must be a number we can call," said Jill. She dug through her purse and pulled out her phone. "Look on the panel. There must be a help-line or maintenance person's number." The other two occupants leaned over to scan the panel.

"Okay, this actually says *emergency number*." The girl recited a string of numbers as Jill keyed them into her phone. She put it on speaker-phone so they could hear. Nothing happened. Call failed. She looked at the other two, shaking her head.

"I can't believe it," said Jill. "What good are emergency numbers if cell phones don't have service in the elevator?"

They stood looking at one another, not knowing what to do next. "Maybe my phone has service," offered the girl, tapping in the numbers. "Nothing. Fuck." Her eyes widened. "Sorry."

Jill went to the panel and pressed the numbers, and then rang the emergency bell again. They listened. Nothing. She slouched against the wall and slid into a sitting position on the floor. "I'm not sure what to do."

The man nodded. "Even if the power comes back on, chances are they'll still be needin' someone to restart it. It's a safety thing most elevators have."

His weathered fingers pressed a few buttons on the dark panel. He shook his head. "Nope," he said. Minutes passed as they assessed their situation.

Without warning, the girl lunged forward, startling them both as she banged on the doors. "Help, help, we're trapped in the elevator. Can anyone hear me?" Her fists flailed against the metal doors. The other two watched helplessly. Lord knows, they both felt the same way.

Futility replaced the frenzy as she turned to them in disbelief. "I can't believe this is happening, this has been the shittiest week of my life." Her face wrinkled with despair as she slumped against the wall and sank to the floor joining Jill.

"Unfortunately, there ain't much we can do," said the man with resignation. He looked around the elevator. "Even if we pried the doors open, if we're between floors we'd just be lookin' at a wall."

The girl fought back tears as her composure slipped away. She was spent. She wanted to be home but hadn't been there for a few days. She had been on the streets, like a homeless person. Hot tears trickled down the end of her nose and dripped onto the elevator floor between her scuffed running shoes as she hid her face in her hands.

"We gotta' think if there is anythin' else," said the man. They looked up at the ceiling and around the elevator, searching for an escape. "No roof hatch like you see in the movies."

"I'm not sure who could even help us. A friend of mine got stuck in an elevator once and the technicians needed the fire department to help. They got out, but it took six hours." Jill sighed. "We may be here for the long haul."

"I've worked maintenance in a school for over forty years. We have one elevator. Somethin' goes wrong, we call the elevator folks." He shrugged and shook his head. "Do either of you live here?"

The girl shook her head, keeping her face buried. Her mom didn't know where she was, and her dad didn't even know she existed, and certainly wasn't expecting her.

Jill also shook her head. "Nope."

"I don't either. I was going to my daughter's place, but she's not home." He shrugged and sighed. "That sitting looks like a good idea." He smiled at the girl. "I'm just worried about gettin' up again. I might be needin' your help." He lowered himself to the floor with great effort as he tried to stabilize his descent with hands firmly braced against the walls. His eyes squeezed shut against the sharp stabbing pain from his hip. Involuntarily, a groan escaped his mouth and he panted at the effort as he settled into one of the corners.

"Wow, what happened to your leg? Did you hurt it?" the girl asked.

"Or is it your back? That sure looks painful," Jill added.

"I've got a worn-out hip. I shoulda' got it fixed a year or two ago. A replacement, they say I need."

"That sucks. How do they replace your hip?"

"My aunt had her hip replaced. They operate and take out the damaged joint and they replace it with an artificial one. She needed it really badly by the time she was finally able to get it done. You seem like you're in a lot of pain right now." She stretched her hand out to him. "I'm Jill Jones."

"Martin, Martin Sanderson." He held out a rough, weathered hand and shook Jill's, then the girl's hand.

"Leah Armstrong. Why haven't you gotten it done yet? It must be hard to get around like that."

Martin nodded. "Yup, it's bin singin' pretty loud today. I'm kickin' myself. I forgot to take my pain meds, or as I call them, my magic pills, at dinner time. That usually calms it down a lot." He shrugged. "I shoulda' fixed it already, but it costs a lotta' money and, truth be told, I'm a bit scared. I ain't had no operations in my life, 'cept tonsils when I was twelve."

"It took my aunt about six weeks to recover. She was glad though, she said it was worth it. It gave her some freedom back. I stayed with her for a while to help her."

"That's the other thing. I be needin' someone to help me once I get home. My Phyllis passed away on me 'bout five years ago now. Came home one night and all the lights was out, place was dark. I don't know how you know it, but in my gut, I knew somethin' was wrong. Every night, my home was lit up and Phyllis greeted me. I opened the door and called out to her." His voice softened. "Well, I found her. She was in her favorite chair with her book open in her lap. She looked like she had dozed off right there, but I knew."

"What happened?" Leah asked softly.

"We never saw it comin'. Rosa, my daughter, and me. Massive heart attack. So, I've bin livin' alone for a while now." After fifty-five years of marriage, he felt lost without her. Every day waking up without her felt unfinished. He cherished her and never expected she would die first. She had looked after him, cooking favorite meals, laying out fresh clothes every day, and rubbing liniment on his aching body. He missed things a married couple do for one another as naturally as breathing air. All the conversations he wanted to have piled up inside his head. Some remained unspoken and some were whispered to her as he lay alone in bed at night.

"Can't your daughter help look after you?"

Martin shook his head. "Nah, I don't wanna' ask. She would, she's a good girl, but she's got a busy job and a family of her own. As a matter of fact, I was on my way to check on her cats and feed them. She's away on business."

He lifted the white grocery bag to show them. His daughter named her cats after some of his favorite musicians and music she grew up surrounded by: Sam Cooke and Ray Charles. They would have gotten a kick out of it if they had still been alive to see the two fluffy cats upstairs named after them. He had planned to feed them and steal a nap on his daughter's couch before he headed home.

Beyond the 14th Floor

They settled into a stillness once again.

He stole a glance at Leah and Jill out of the corner of his eye. He wished he'd been alone when the elevator stopped. He could have made a picnic on the floor and then dozed until rescuers arrived. Instead, he was confined here with the two women. He shifted, trying to pull his legs in. Pain rocketed down his leg and up his back, so he left his legs stretched out awkwardly in the middle of the cramped space. Just as he was beginning to doze, a voice jarred him awake.

"Okay, let's figure this out. We have two cell phones. We should limit our use to save our batteries. Maybe we'll get a signal at some point. So please don't use it unless you have to." Jill looked at her phone. "I'm at 46%. That should give us some time." She glanced at Leah. "What about you?"

"Only 8%." She frowned.

"Martin, when will your daughter be coming home?" Jill asked.

"Not for a few days."

"Do you have any other family that would be missing you?"

"No, it's just my daughter. She was adopted. It's a long story. I don't wanna' bore you."

"Well, we're stuck in this miserable box and we need some entertainment. Please tell us." Leah crossed her legs and cradled her chin on her hands, giving Martin her full attention.

He chuckled. "Are you sure? I don't wanna' bore you, but you've got a point. It looks like we've got some time on our hands." He shifted to a more upright position and glanced to Jill, who nodded.

"Well, I can't tell you how we became parents without telling you about my Phyllis first."

#

"I married Phyllis in 1960. Shoulda' bin sooner, but it took me a while to get up the courage to ask. She was a fine woman, fierce yet soft at the same time. I met her at my dad's restaurant, where I was working."

"Was that before you worked at the school?" Jill asked.

"Well, for a time I was workin' at both places. Maybe that's what she saw in me, that I would be a good provider." Martin chuckled with twinkling eyes. "I never dated much, not enough time to woo someone. I wasn't ready. A late bloomer, I guess. Phyllis, she was different. I never said a word to her; she was always surrounded by her friends, but she always dazzled me with her beautiful smile and a wave or a nod when she came to my pop's restaurant.

"Late one evening, Phyllis came into the restaurant with a man. 'Bout her age, I was guessin'. They were laughin', and to me, it seemed they was on a date. She was wearing a lilac sweater and her hair was pulled back in a tight bun. You might think it's strange that I can tell you that, but I remember it like yesterday.

"Her lovely face was glowing as she was with this man. You coulda' knocked me over with a feather, she looked so fine. The pit of my stomach turned to stone seein' them together. The bell rang behind me, snappin' me out of it, as my pop put up another meal to be delivered.

"My pop had sent the rest of the waiters home and I

was the only one left to take their order. So, I goes to their table and wait while Phyllis's date finished the story he was tellin'. She giggled politely at the end, even though in my opinion, the story wasn't funny at all.

"She looked me square in the eyes as she placed her order; made me feel like the only person in the room. I was wishin' that I was the guy sittin' across from her. Instead, I went back to the kitchen to put the order in. A few minutes later, there was a commotion in the dining area. I heard a chair clatter to the floor. I swung the door open and saw Phyllis had jumped to her feet. She was mad as a hornet. She grabbed the full glass of ice water I just brought 'em and tossed it right smack into Mr. Know-it-All's lap. He was furious." Martin chuckled and shook his head.

"This guy yells at Phyllis, 'Wait a minute! Woman, what's the matter wit' you? You is one crazy…' Well, I won't say what he said, but it was downright rude. My Phyllis looked at him like he was something she just stepped in and wanted to scrape off her shoe. She waved him away. 'Just go,' she said. 'My momma didn't raise her girls to put up with that.' She was so angry, I was almost afraid to approach her, but I did and asked, 'Miss, you okay?'

"The man shot daggers at us and shoved his chair in so hard the silverware clattered on the table. 'You've made a mistake, Phyllis. You woulda' bin lucky to be with me. Not anymore.' I stepped in front of Phyllis to protect her and nodded in the direction the door. I would have hit him, if I'da had to. My pop always said, 'The strength of a man is defined by how he treats a woman,' and no woman in my presence was gonna' be disrespected.

"Well, he stormed out the restaurant in a huff. He slammed the doors so hard the bells on the door almost played a full song before they stopped movin'. I turned to Phyllis and saw her mouth tremble. My heart ached. It was all I could do not to take her in my arms. I picked up the chair and then the bell rang, her order was ready. So, I look over at the counter where two steamin' plates waited. I ask her, 'Miss, can I buy your meal for you? If you are still wantin' to stay, that is.'

"Phyllis squared her shoulders and smiled. 'Yes, but only if I don't have to eat alone.' I looked around the restaurant before realizin' she meant me. I felt like I had won the prize. 'Yes, Miss, I'd like that. I'd like that a whole lot.'"

Leah clapped her hands with glee. "Way to go, Martin. Was that the moment you knew she was the 'one'?"

"Well, yes, I think that was the moment. It took a little longer for her, I think, and we dated for a while. She was a strong woman, so she was determined to have a career. She had seen her aunt struggle with three kids after her uncle had died. With no trainin', her aunt only could get low-paying jobs that barely supported them."

"Good for Phyllis. What career did she have?" asked Jill.

"She worked at a hospice, you know, carin' for people that don't have much time left. She had such a great way wit' people."

"It takes special people to do that kind of work, it's so sad," Jill said.

"So, you convinced her to marry you?" Leah asked.

Martin nodded and laughed. "Yes. There I was, a thirty-two-year-old bachelor in a little Philadelphia brownstone on my knee proposin', and do you know what she said?"

"What?" Leah's eyes widened.

"Instead of saying 'yes,' she said 'FINALLY!' I guess she was waitin' for me to ask for some time and I was too afraid to hear what her answer would be." The ladies filled the elevator with laughter.

They paused for a moment to stretch their arms above their heads and move around a bit. Jill shrugged her jacket off as her body broke out in a sweat. A wave of heat rolled over her as the nausea rose in her stomach. The walls of the elevator felt closer than ever before and the faint smell of body odor filled her nostrils.

The three each sprawled in their corners. Everyone had shed any extra sweaters, jackets, and even shoes. The air felt heavy and the shiny metal walls became dull with moisture.

"Our dog ate my engagement ring," Jill said, breaking the silence.

"What? No way. How did that happen?" Leah exclaimed.

"After a year of living together, my boyfriend, Brad, proposed—kind of. I got home from work one afternoon and heard a ruckus in the back yard. Brad was yelling at his dog and wrestling with him to get something out of his mouth. I was surprised at how determined Brad was. He seemed pretty distraught.

I asked, 'Brad, what's wrong?'

This was just the distraction Buck, his dog, needed. As Brad paused to look at me, Buck did a satisfied gulp, like someone eating the last bite of pie at the Thanksgiving table. Gone.

"Brad rolled over onto his back in the grass with an

agonized groan and Buck bolted across the yard to hide under a tree. I was so confused. I was worried that he had gotten into poison or something. I was beginning to freak out and asked, 'What did he eat?'

"Brad lifted his head and said, 'Your engagement ring.'

"I couldn't believe it. The situation was so ridiculous. Poor Brad didn't know what to do. It definitely didn't go the way he had planned. He tells me that he was planning to propose, and he was showing Buck the ring, mainly because he loves me as much as Brad does, and BOOM, he snatched it out of Brad's hand. He thought it was a treat or something. He had spent ten minutes chasing him around the yard before I got home. Then Buck goes and swallows it. I was laughing so hard, but I felt so bad. Brad told me he wouldn't propose until he had a ring to put on my finger."

"That dog sounds like quite a character." Martin grinned.

"Oh, is he ever. I asked Brad, 'How are you going to get it from Buck now?' After a few calls to an amused vet, we got advice on how to get the ring back. Expensive surgery or poop patrol were the two options. For the next few days, Brad followed Buck around like a lab technician, investigating everything that went through the dog." Jill shook her head, smiling at the memory.

"Oh, that's so gross! I wouldn't want the ring after that," said Leah, wrinkling her nose.

"On the second morning, there was a whoop from the back yard as I was getting ready for work. By the time I came out to the kitchen for my morning coffee, Brad was waiting with the black lab sitting behind him sporting a silly grin.

Brad gave me a quick squeeze and got down on one knee with the newly polished ring and asked me to marry him. Of course, I said yes. My ring was beautiful, despite Buck's involvement in the process."

"Wow, I've never heard a proposal story like that one," said Leah.

"Yep, that's a good one," Martin said. He cringed as he shifted, and a jolt went down his leg. He sighed, lifted his wrist to check the time, sighed again, and folded his arms across his chest.

The elevator was silent with the occasional creak. Leah thought she had heard voices at one point, and they pounded and hollered again, but to no avail.

Leah put her hand to her neck. "My throat is getting sore from all this yelling."

"I know. I feel like I've been to an all-night concert."

"Maybe we should try something different." Martin reached beside him and grabbed Jill's shoe. He firmly banged the heel against the elevator wall in a regular pattern. He continued the sequence three times. Leah put her hands to her ears as she observed. Jill smiled.

When he stopped, Leah piped up. "The devil himself will hear us, banging that loud."

"Do you know what I just did?"

"It seemed like some kind of rythym."

"I think Martin was doing an SOS signal: three short, three long, three short." Jill nodded with approval. "That noise should really carry—and save our throats as well."

"Yup, I'm hopin' someone will hear and understand our message." He wiped his sweaty forehead. "How long have we bin in here now?"

"Forever," said Leah.

Jill checked her phone. "About three hours. I'm getting really thirsty. What do we each have for food or water?" She pulled her purse onto her lap.

They rummaged around in their belongings and placed assorted food items on the floor in the middle of them. Martin pulled meat sticks and a bottle of iced tea from his grocery bag. Leah found a bag of Skittles and a half bottle of orange soda in her bulging backpack.

"Wow, you've got a lot of stuff in there," Jill observed. "That's it for food?" They both nodded. Jill rummaged in her purse and came out with a pack of gum and a granola bar.

Leah picked up the granola bar and read the package. "We can't eat this. I'm severely allergic to peanuts. Even the smell could kill me, and I didn't bring my epi-pen."

"That's terrible. We won't even consider it." Jill removed the bar from the pile and tucked it back in her purse.

"I sometimes even forget myself. Schools are always 'peanut aware.'" Leah did air quotes and dropped her hands back to her lap.

"Okay, we'll try to pace ourselves and share our resources. This could be a long night." Jill sighed and slumped back against the wall. Her stomach was heavy and feeling gurgly. Every inhale filled her nostrils with the stale elevator smell. She began to fan herself and tug at the neckline of her shirt like she was loosening a noose.

"Are you okay, Jill?" Leah asked.

"Guys, I'm sorry, but I think I'm gonna' be sick. Martin,

gimme that grocery bag." Her hand flew up to her mouth. No sooner had she snatched it from Martin than she turned and retched into the bag.

A sour odor filled the elevator. "Oh no, I'm so sorry," Jill said weakly through watery eyes, her face flushed. "I have been feeling so awful lately. I'm pregnant."

"That sucks!" said Leah, then immediately backtracked. "Not that you are pregnant, I mean, that you are sick."

Martin nodded. "That's pretty tough."

"It was sure a big surprise for me. I didn't think I'd ever have kids," said Jill.

"That reminds me, Martin, we haven't found out how you got your daughter yet," said Leah.

"Oh yes, our little Rosa. What a special surprise she was." Martin's face lit up. "Well, babies were supposed to follow the weddin', but it was hard. Real hard. My poor Phyll, got pregnant no problem, but her body had a hard time keepin' 'em. Each time began with hope but ended with her cryin' on the bathroom floor. Sometimes even a trip to the hospital. So hard. I acted strong for her and she didn't know how much it affected me too. Each time my heart hurt so bad for her and the child we'd lost."

Jill sniffled loudly. "Oh my gosh, Martin. I am not very far along, but the thought of losing my baby, even at this stage... I don't know what I would do."

"Yes, it was really difficult for both of us. Our marriage struggled along, we talked less, and Phyllis wanted to be alone more. It came to a point where we were almost afraid to try again. We didn't talk about it. I don't know if she felt that way, but I sure did. It gutted me to see her go through that loss, but then one day, it all changed."

"Phyllis came home from the hospice late in the evening and said, 'Martin, we gotta' talk.' I woulda' bin worried, but her beautiful brown eyes had a sparkle that I hadn't seen in a long time. We sat on the back stoop of our little brownstone. Phyllis was shakin' like a leaf as she tried to find the right words to tell me her news.

"'Martin, you know I have bin talkin' about a young mother that's dyin' of cancer. I really got to know her. She doesn't have a husband and her new baby, the poor wee one, is being looked after by neighbours.' I just sat there quietly soaking it all in. I knew my wife's heart and what she was askin' as she sat there wringin' her hands.

"'Martin, she wants us to have her girl! She knows she won't be on this blessed earth for much longer.' I hadn't much thought about having a child that wasn't my own flesh and blood, and here was a chance for somethin' we never thought could be possible. I looked into Phyllis's eyes and I saw the spark of renewed hope for the first time in a while. I smiled and reached for her and she knew my answer before I even said it.

"Well then, I guess we're havin' a baby.

"My Phyllis had somethin' special with Ellen, Rosa's mother. That was her way; she knew just what to do that would help people to be comfortable. We took the request to adopt Rosa very seriously. This woman trustin' us to have her baby, well, it just gets me right here," Martin said, patting his chest over his heart. "Phyllis had long talks with Rosa's mom, 'bout what she wanted for her girl's future.

"We decided that Phyllis would focus on work and

lookin' after Ellen in the short time she had left. The neighbors would continue to watch Rosa until Ellen passed. Phyllis would stop work then and be home with little Rosa. Was hard to wait, but at the same time it was hard to see little Rosa's mom slippin' away."

"Phyllis and Ellen worked together to create a memory box for Rosa with letters Ellen dictated to Phyllis. It tore Phyllis's heart out as they put Ellen's whispered messages onto paper. The box was filled with a few pieces of jewelry, some photos, and other things she wanted Rosa to have. When she felt prepared that she was leaving Rosa in the best hands, she said to Phyllis, "Always tell my baby that I loved her with all my heart." Not long after that, Ellen lost consciousness and on a warm spring mornin', she passed away.

"Our new life began with this little one. We couldna' bin happier."

"What a great story. You gave a little baby a home, and for that mother to know she was going to be in good hands must have meant everything to her," said Jill, blowing her nose.

Leah said, "You and Brad must be excited about your baby coming."

A mixture of emotion flitted across Jill's flushed face. "It's kind of complicated, but it's not Brad's baby." Her hands moved to her tummy. "He passed away over a year ago."

Martin and Leah's eyes met in surprise. Awkward silence filled the elevator, heavy with emotion.

"So sorry to hear that," murmured Martin. Leah nodded in agreement

Chapter Three

That was a conversation killer. A mutual silence permeated the stifling elevator. They shifted around trying to find comfortable positions to rest. Jill closed her eyes and tried to divert her thoughts from her queasy stomach. Guilty feelings gnawed at her: how do you explain that your husband is dead and that you are already knocked up by someone else? Her mind drifted to Brad and his lopsided grin. She had been having so many better days where she could handle his loss without coming apart thinking about him. She pulled a tissue from her purse and quietly sniffled in her corner, knees pulled up to her chest.

On the day she met Brad, she was holding an open house. Several families came to the showing, along with a few nosy neighbors. A guy in a ball cap and a Yankees jersey showed up. He clearly didn't fit her profile for someone wanting to buy the property.

After most of the agents and people had left, she approached him and introduced herself. "Hi, I'm Jill Jones from Integrity Realty. You're pretty brave wearing a Yankees jersey in Philly." She smiled and shook his hand.

His eyes twinkled and he chuckled. "I drove in from New York, so I was on point this morning." He held the open house leaflet in his hand. "I am looking for a place and don't seem to find the time to get organized. I was driving back to my apartment when I saw the Open House sign. On a whim I pulled in."

"Are you interested in this house?" She raised her eyebrows.

"No, not really my style." He laughed, looking at the all-white interior with white shag rug running wall to wall. "I need a place for my dog as well."

She gathered her papers and they walked out to the driveway. In the truck outside, an excited black lab began barking as soon as his owner came into view.

"Buck, it's okay. She's fine," he called. Placated, he settled down and patiently watched them from the passenger seat with his drippy tongue hanging out as he panted.

"I am done with apartments and sharing houses. I just want a place of my own. Buck needs a yard." He gestured to the truck, where the dog began wagging with excitement at the mention of his name. They exchanged business cards and she was surprised to see he was a freelance sports writer. Had she been interested in sports, she might have realized he was well-known.

She took him on as a client and was quickly surprised that he had good taste. The properties she had originally picked to show him weren't up to the standards he was looking for.

By the eighth showing, she was getting impatient. She still hadn't found anything he liked. Despite this, she began to look forward to meeting up with him every few weeks to view another property.

They met for lunch a few times, and although she always planned on paying, he would sneak the bill from the waitress and settle up before she had a chance. He would often open her car door for her as well. She had never experienced such chivalry before. They had a natural, lighthearted rapport with one another. A bystander would think they were a couple walking through the different homes, joking about the horrendous artwork or odd decorating choices people would make.

Jill had sold lots of homes but didn't often have clients as tough as Brad. She finally stumbled upon a listing that seemed to check all his boxes. She tried to reach him, but he was away on business and it took her two weeks to book a showing with him.

They strolled through the home and she beamed with pride at his remarks. This was the one. It was more expensive than what he had planned, but it was perfect.

"I guess Buck and I may need to eat hotdogs for a while, because this is really nice," Brad said. His grin widened. "I think it's time to make an offer."

"That's great. I was really excited when I saw this one. I couldn't wait for you to get a look at it." Jill beamed. She grabbed her phone and stepped out onto the back patio to call the listing agent with an offer. After a short discussion, she stepped back into the house. "They said we should hear back today."

They took another walk around the property, making mental notes of any small repairs or changes Brad would make if he got the house. The backyard was quite large with lots of grass for Buck. There was even a small pool off the patio.

Just as they were walking him out and down the front driveway, Jill's phone rang. They looked at each other and Jill checked her phone. "This is the listing agent calling. I hope it's good news. They've come back so quickly." He crossed his fingers and she walked a few steps away and answered the call.

Brad paced and watched her as she nodded and waved her hands as she was talking. She ended the call and came walking back with a frown.

"They turned us down, didn't they?" Brad asked, kicking a stone on the driveway out of disappointment.

"Wellllll, they have a few conditions, but I don't think anything they've asked for will be a problem." Jill broke into a huge grin and thrust out her hand. "Nothing is official until we get the paperwork done, but if you want it, you've got the house. Congratulations."

Spontaneously, Brad let out a whoop, picked her up in a bear hug, and swung her around. Buck, watching from the nearby pickup, couldn't contain himself and leapt out of the truck to join them in jumping on the driveway. Brad set Jill down and stepped back, pumping his fist in the air with a whoop.

She laughed and crouched down to pet Buck, who covered her face in sloppy kisses. "I think Buck is happy with this house too. Look at him." She chuckled and patted his back. "I'll put the papers together." She looked at her watch. "Could you come to my office tomorrow to sign your life away?"

"You bet. I'm pretty happy with this one. I can really see myself living here."

"I was beginning to think you might give up on me. I'm glad I was able to find you something." Brad had been pickier than most clients Jill had dealt with and specifically wanted move-in ready. He admitted he wasn't handy at fixing things.

Two months after the sale, Jill couldn't help but miss their interactions. They often joked around, even flirted a little. She wanted to ensure she remained professional with him, but it became more difficult every time she saw him. Jill caught herself sitting at her desk thinking about him. She began paying more attention to the sports section, looking for articles he had written.

The possession date arrived, and she set up a time to meet Brad at his new home to pass on the keys. When she drove up, she could see his truck parked in the winding driveway. Buck was racing all over the yard and jumped up and down at the base of a tree. She giggled. *Buck has discovered that squirrels live here.*

She found Brad sitting on the front step wearing an Armani suit with a tie hanging loosely from his neck. She was taken aback. *Whoa, he's handsome.* He usually wore jeans and a t-shirt, so this was a side she'd never seen.

"Hey, thanks for coming. Good thing I bought the place, I might not get Bucky to leave now." They both turned to see the frantic dog racing around the tree. The squirrel taunted him and raced up and down the branches. They both laughed as they walked into the empty house.

Brad pulled off his jacket and tie, tossing them both onto the kitchen counter.

They toured the property, reviewing the operating instructions left by the previous owners for different things, like the furnace and the pool heater. As they were bending over looking at the heater, Buck bolted through the patio doors and launched himself into the pool like a spring breaker, splashing them with a tidal wave. Jill shrieked and recoiled at the icy shower. "Crap, I'm so sorry, Jill." He was mortified and then broke out into a deep laughter.

Jill stood and paused, pushing the wet hair out of her face. There was no way to try to look calm and collected. Buck was oblivious and proudly leapt out of the pool to chase a bird across the yard. Her dress clung to her body. *Lucky I didn't wear white today, or we'd have a real show on our hands.*

"Your dog is an asshole." She tried looking angry, but a smile twitched at the corner of her mouth.

"I'm sorry, he can be a real dick sometimes." He grinned, raked his fingers through his wet hair and peeled off his dress shirt to hand it on a tree branch near the pool. He was in great shape; he obviously spent time at the gym.

"Typical guy," she said and winked at him. "I'd better get going. I need to get some dry clothes on." She turned to leave and just as they were at the front door, she paused. "Shoot, I forgot. I have something in the car for you."

"Okay, I'm just going to go back to check on Buck. He is going to wreck this house before I even move in."

Jill returned carrying a bottle of champagne and two glasses. "I always bring a gift for my new home owners to celebrate their move. I know it's not beer, if you don't like it, perhaps you can save it for guests."

"That's perfect; you're my first guest." He grabbed the bottle and before she could protest, he popped the cork. Champagne bubbled over, filling the two glasses.

She smiled and looked at her watch. "I don't have any more appointments today, so I guess I could have a glass."

With nowhere to sit, he gestured to the pool edge, where they slipped off their shoes and tentatively dangled their feet in the water. "Yup, still cold," gasped Jill. She pulled her feet out quickly. "You've got to get the pool heater switched on." Brad didn't seem to mind and rolled up his pant legs to dangle his feet in the cold water. Buck was now relaxing on the patio in the sun, letting out an occasional snore as his feet kicked idly in the air.

They fell into easy conversation. Brad was a farm boy who grew up with a love of sports. He earned a football scholarship, but injuries sidelined him, and he discovered sports journalism could be a way to stay involved.

Jill explained that she had grown up in the city. Her parents had her in their late thirties. Being an only child, they doted on her. She told Brad she had lost them suddenly in a tragic highway accident when she was twelve. As she talked, the memories of her parents came flooding back: weekend camping trips, skating, slumber parties on the living room floor, and the birthday cakes her mother made for her.

Brad leaned over and rubbed her arm. "I'm so sorry. That's pretty rough, no matter what age you lose your parents at."

"It makes you realize how you shouldn't take anything for granted, because in a moment, everything can change." Jill shivered as Brad's warm hand left her arm.

The sun had set, and a cool breeze had come up. "I should get going, I'm getting cold." Brad got up from the poolside and reached down for Jill's hand, helping her to her feet.

He continued to hold her hand and gently pulled her closer to him. He let her decide where this would go, and she met his gaze and raised her face to his as their lips met. She shivered again. He let out a soft chuckle and put his warm arms around her. She was feeling so cold but was comforted by the warmth of his bare skin. Her body tingled under his touch.

Her hands slid up his back and her fingers curled in the hair at the base of his neck. He gently pressed his body against the length of hers as they kissed. It was apparent they had both thought about this moment. Jill nibbled his lower lip and Brad's tongue teased hers.

Reluctantly, they pulled apart. Jill wrapped her arms around herself, suddenly self-conscious of her thin dress and obvious arousal.

Brad laughed softly. "This has been a nice house warming party." He gently smoothed her damp hair behind her ear. "I'd like to do this again, once I get settled in."

"I think so. I'm going to miss seeing Buck." Jill winked and smiled.

It seemed natural for Jill to help Brad pick out furniture and decorate his new home. They complemented one another in their tastes, beliefs, ambition, and their mutual love of Buck, who thrived under Jill's attention.

One sunny Sunday afternoon, Jill grabbed her overnight bag and was leaving to go back to her apartment. Brad grabbed her hand. "Buck and I miss you when you aren't here. All we do is spend our time driving back and forth, and most times, you stay here because I can't leave Buck for that long. Move in with us." It was more of a statement than a question. As if on cue, Buck came over and looked up at Jill, barking and wagging his tail as if waiting for an answer.

She laughed and shook her head. "You two have a pretty comfortable thing going on here. Adding a girl to the mix might cramp your style." She hugged Brad and whispered in his ear, "I'll think about it, but I don't think your closet is big enough for all my shoes." He picked her up and slung her over his shoulder, holding her there until she begged to be put down.

Brad didn't mention it again; he didn't want to pressure her. After his offer, every time she left for her condo in the bustling center of the city, it became more difficult to leave his comfortable home in the suburbs. Brad's place was a little bit farther from her office, but it seemed like the right thing to do. She had helped him decorate his place, so it already had her touch. Also, Buck had become so attached to her they joked that he liked her more than Brad.

Sitting among the last few boxes in her empty apartment, she felt both fear and excitement. All the years of being on her own were in the past, and perhaps a family of her own awaited. She was ready to move on to a new chapter in her life.

Chapter Four

The vomit bag sat in one corner and it was evident there was a small hole in it as a trickle began to make its way across the floor. The pop bottle was filled with urine, as they'd had no choice but to relieve themselves as the others turned their backs for privacy in the confined space. They had become accustomed to the fetid odour; there was no escaping it.

Occasionally, they would hear noises. They weren't sure if it was rescuers or one of the residents. They took turns pounding and yelling until they were depleted.

"Are we ever going to get out of here?" moaned Leah. She swayed between angry and weepy, but now she was mostly quiet.

"I sure hope so," said Jill with a weak smile. "I have a manicure next week I don't want to miss." They all chuckled. They passed around the iced tea, taking turns until the last gulp trickled down Martin's throat.

The elevator walls continued to sweat in the humid environment and the heat in the elevator felt almost unbearable. They continued to shift around, standing for a bit, sitting, and then lying down on the floor, even though there wasn't much room.

"I think we should try our cell phones, again just in case," said Leah. She pulled hers out and tapped it in frustration. "It's dead."

Jill picked her phone up from the floor. "I still have battery life, but no signal." She shook her head. "I hope someone comes soon, this sucks." Her eyes watered a bit. Wisps of hair stuck to her damp cheeks.

Leah raked her fingers through her tangled hair. "I'd give anything to have a shower. It's been two days and now this…"

"Leah, what happened with you? Who were you coming to see?" Jill asked.

"Maybe my dad. I don't know." She shrugged.

"That sounds pretty vague."

"I thought my dad was dead. That's what my mom always told me, but I found out recently that he's alive. I'm trying to find him."

Leah looked to Martin, who hadn't said anything for a while. He didn't look right to her. Despite the heat in the elevator, he seemed to be shaking a bit. It was subtle, but having spent nine hours in the elevator together, she knew something was off.

"Martin, you okay?" Leah asked, tapping his shoe with her foot.

He seemed groggy. Jill crawled over beside him and gave his shoulder a little shake.

"Martin, what's the matter?" asked Jill. "Are you okay? Martin?" She looked worried as she checked his pulse. It was really slow. She felt his forehead. Despite his trembling, he was sweaty.

He mumbled something and they both leaned closer to hear him. Leah came to his other side and they both tried to help him sit up.

"Diabetic," Martin mumbled.

"Oh my. Martin! We've got to get some sugar in you before you crash." Jill reached back into their food supply. She grabbed the bag of Skittles and the package ripped, spilling the contents all over the dirty elevator floor. She scrambled to grab a handful. "Crap. Sorry, Martin. I guess we go with the five-second rule."

They helped him eat the candies and Leah gave him some sips from her bottle of orange pop. Jill looked at her watch. "Hang in there. You should feel better in about fifteen minutes. We've got you." He smiled weakly and squeezed Jill's hand.

Leah and Jill sat watching Martin. "How did you know what to do?" asked Leah. "How can you make someone who is sick better with candies?" She put her hands up. "Not that I'm arguing, it's a pretty sweet deal to me."

"No pun intended," said Jill with a wink. Leah smiled.

"My uncle had diabetes. Martin, do you have any medication with you?"

Martin understood what she was saying and shook his head. You could almost see a cloud lifting from him as the candies did their job.

"If my uncle skipped a meal, or got too busy to take a break, or forgot to take his insulin, his blood sugar level would drop and he would get into trouble," Jill explained.

"Diabetes isn't fun. We've been in here long enough that Martin's eating routine is all off." Soon, Martin became more alert.

He shook his gray head. "I'm sorry. I don't want you to have to take care of me along with us being stuck in here." He put his hand to his forehead and rubbed his eyes, blinking to focus properly.

"Don't worry about it. We're in this together, like the Three Musketeers," Leah said, trying to lighten the mood.

He smiled and patted her arm. "Maybe we need to have a picnic. I need to eat so I can keep my wits about me. Grab those sausages."

Martin dug in his pocket for his jack knife and unfolded it. The well-worn blade was dirty from everything else he had cut with it. He pulled bits of pocket lint off of it and wiped it on his pants. He cut each of the women a couple of pieces of sausage and took a few for himself.

"Wow, this is so good," said Leah, chewing carefully. "I didn't realize I was so hungry."

"Hey Mart, do you have a crust, sauce, and cheese to go with it? I am kind of craving a pizza now," Jill said straight-faced. They all laughed.

"I would pay a thousand dollars for IHOP pancakes right now." Leah grinned.

"Ah, with some strawberries and that whipped cream. I can almost taste it," Martin agreed.

"Normally, I would say a large Starbucks coffee, but with this nausea, I haven't been interested in coffee."

"I'd be havin' a big cuppa' Earl Grey tea."

"When you can't have it, you seem to want it so much

more, hey?" Jill said. "I guess I should ask if anyone else has any other medical conditions. I mean, that we should know of—in case you need help."

Martin said, "No, Ma'am. Strong as an ox otherwise. Doc said he wished his ticker was as healthy as mine." He shifted his position and winced. "The hip needs work, of course."

"I'm good," said Leah, giving a thumbs-up. "Just allergic to peanuts."

"I don't have anything, just pregnant with all-day morning sickness." Jill grimaced and rubbed her tummy, although she was hardly showing yet.

Once they had finished eating, Leah rested her head against the elevator wall and imagined a home-cooked meal and her comfortable bed. At this point, she didn't know what to do. She had left in such haste she hadn't had time to put a proper plan together. All she could think about was getting out of the dismal elevator. She wasn't sure if she could go home yet.

She hadn't wanted to disappoint her mother, Lydia. Even as a young girl, Leah sensed her mother always had sadness lingering under the surface. Sometimes the weight of that feeling hung on like a real burden, but at the same time, it pushed Leah to excel at things to make her mother happy.

Lydia had plenty of rules for Leah: No dating. No makeup. No dances. Those were mostly okay. She didn't care much for any of those things anyway. She wasn't interested in dressing "girly," much less wearing makeup. No worry about that.

Starting at a young age, she gravitated not to girl things, but to girls. She felt so confused. She couldn't understand. She had friends but often found she developed little crushes on them. Nothing ever happened, but she seemed to like them more than boys. She never told anyone, especially not her mother, who was worried about being judged by everyone.

Leah had never met her own dad. If people asked, Lydia would tell them Leah's father had died before she was born. If Leah tried to ask questions, her mother would grow quiet and end the conversation.

Leah had a small circle of friends. They were neither popular nor outcasts. As they entered high school, a lot of them moved in different directions as they pursued other activities like sports, cheer team, and dance. She felt safe, but never confided in anyone. Her friends laughed and talked about boys and she would go along with it.

One day a new girl, who looked shy and nervous, showed up at school. Leah was intrigued. She was the most beautiful girl Leah had ever seen. Leah arrived early for band practice and there in the middle of the empty room, with her cascading red hair, was Stephanie Haskell practicing the flute.

Leah stopped in the doorway, staring. Stephanie looked up and smiled shyly. Leah stared and then smiled back. She stepped forward, offering her sweaty hand. She felt giddy, her heart pounding, and hardly knew what to say.

"Hi, I'm Leah."

"Hey, I'm Steph. I'm new." She gestured to the chair beside her.

"I know," Leah said. "I noticed you in the hall." Leah blushed and looked down at her music case.

Stephanie laughed, grabbed a lock of her red hair, and flipped it. "Gingers tend to stick out in a crowd."

That seemed to break the ice. Leah felt more relaxed and filled Stephanie in on their eccentric music teacher and gave her advice on some of the school rules. They were having a great conversation, hardly noticing as the room around them filled with students. Class was ready to begin. The teacher entered sporting a wildly patterned sweater that looked like a thrift shop purchase. They exchanged a glance and giggled.

The girls really hit it off and began to spend a lot of time together. They didn't have many of the same classes, but always ate lunch in the cafeteria together and studied for exams at either of their homes. Stephanie was gorgeous and rarely bothered with makeup. The boys didn't seem to care. They ogled her and flirted with her at school all the time. She would just sigh and roll her eyes with indifference and continue her conversation with Leah.

Lydia was pleased to see Leah had a good friend, and Stephanie seemed like a decent girl. Leah was so happy. She looked forward to their private jokes and camaraderie. Leah had begun to wonder if Stephanie was like her. Stephanie never seemed interested in boys either. She was dismissive of any attention from them. Leah felt ready to confide in someone.

After school one day, they agreed to hang out together. Stephanie was acting really weird and excited. "I have something to tell you!" Stephanie gushed. "I have been wanting to tell you for a while!"

Stephanie kept smiling at her all the way to Leah's house. Leah put together a snack for them and they went and sat on the couch together. Leah's heart fluttered when Stephanie took her hands and faced her. *Could this be coming true? Does Stephanie feel the same way about me as I do about her?*

Leah smiled back at her and waited to hear the big announcement.

"I know we've been really close for the past several months," she began, "so I feel bad that I have been keeping this from you." She trailed off and looked down, a bit embarrassed.

"Steph, you can tell me anything," said Leah, giving her hands a reassuring squeeze.

Stephanie inhaled and then exhaled in a big breath. Then she blurted out, "James asked me out!" She grinned from ear to ear.

Leah felt like someone had punched her in the stomach. She blinked and shook her head to clear her ears. "Who's James?" she asked in disbelief. She pulled her hands back into her own lap like she had been burned by a hot iron.

Stephanie jumped up and started pacing the carpet. "I know, it's crazy. Most guys at school are so immature. Mr. Clancy put us together as lab partners." She hugged herself and squealed. "He has the bluest eyes!"

Leah still couldn't find words and sat there crestfallen. Her world had just stopped. What was happening?

"Leah, what's wrong? Please don't be mad. I just didn't want to say anything. I didn't even really think he liked me back." She sat back on the couch and faced Leah. "I'm not ditching you. We're still best friends, right?"

Leah looked down, fighting back tears. They heard the rattle of keys as the front door swung open. Her mother arrived home from work. Stephanie turned to Leah. "I should go. See you tomorrow, right?" She hugged her. On the way out, Leah could hear Stephanie and her mother making small talk, and then Stephanie left.

"Hey Leah, what should we have for supper, meatloaf or spaghetti?"

"I'm not feeling well. I think I am just going to go lie down."

Lydia grabbed her arm and put her hand on Leah's forehead. "Not hot, I don't think you have a fever. Is it your stomach?"

Leah nodded. "Yes, I have a stomach ache. I am just going to go rest."

She curled in a ball and quietly cried until she eventually fell asleep. Everything was different now. Her heart was broken.

Leah could tell Stephanie was making an effort to include her, but she slipped into third wheel position. James was nice to her, but it was becoming awkward. They would hold hands or give each other a peck, then look at Leah. She began to decline their invitations. Leah and Stephanie still ate lunch together and Stephanie would tell Leah all about the things her and James would do together. She nodded and commented where appropriate, but jealousy and sadness diminished any joy she might have felt for her friend.

"James said we're going to do something special this Saturday. He won't give me any hints," Stephanie said.

Leah shrugged. "There is a concert in town on Saturday. Maybe he got you tickets."

Stephanie's eyes grew wide. "That's probably it!" she said, slapping her leg. "I'll have to pretend I don't know what he's up to." Her eyes gleamed. "I'm so excited!"

Leah looked away so Stephanie couldn't see her face. *I should be going with Stephanie,* she thought.

Saturday arrived and Stephanie kept texting pictures of the outfits she wanted to wear to get Leah's advice. Leah just wanted the day to be over. She was tired of hearing about it.

Leah had dinner with her mother then settled in to watch TV and work on some homework. She glanced up at the clock periodically and wondered about Stephanie. At about 10:00 pm her cell phone rang, showing Stephanie's number.

"Hey," answered Leah. "How's the concert?"

Stephanie was sniffling and tearful on the other end. "I'm down the block from your house at the bus stop. Come meet me."

Leah tried to keep calm so her mother wouldn't suspect anything. She talked quietly into the phone, "Steph, are you hurt? Why are you crying?"

"I'm not hurt, just come," she sobbed.

She snatched her jacket from the kitchen chair and headed to the door.

"Mom, I'm just going out for a walk, I'll be back in a bit."

"At this time of the night?"

"Yes, studying is giving me a headache. I just need some fresh air," she called over her shoulder as she slipped out the door.

She found Stephanie at the end of the street sitting in the bus shelter. Tears streamed down her face and she hugged Leah. She cried for a few minutes and then pulled back. They sat on the bench as Stephanie collected herself, wiping her nose.

"What happened at the concert?" asked Leah, rubbing her arms.

"That's the problem. We didn't go to a concert. The big surprise was he wanted to have sex. He said we had fooled around enough, and it was time." Stephanie shrugged and put her face in her hands sobbing. "I said no, and he called me a tease. He's been so nice the past two months, but tonight he got so angry. I just grabbed my stuff and ran out of his house."

"What a jerk!" said Leah, her fists balling up.

"I don't ever want to see him again. I should have never dated him. Hanging out with you is way better." She shrugged and looked at Leah. "I am so sorry I let some dumb guy get between us."

Leah kept a straight face but inside she was jumping for joy. Stephanie hugged her. They held onto each other for a while. Leah felt overcome with emotion and could smell the freshly shampooed hair and soft perfume Stephanie was wearing. Thoughts ran through her head. As they clung to one another, she closed her eyes as her senses took over. She turned her face and gently kissed Stephanie's neck.

She felt Stephanie stiffen and then quickly pull away from her. Stephanie looked confused. "What are you doing?"

Leah snapped to attention. What had she just done? Like someone had poured cold water on her, she jumped back. "I'm sorry. I...I didn't mean to." Stephanie's eyes narrowed.

"Leah, what was that?" she demanded with hands on her hips.

Leah blushed with embarrassment and couldn't answer her or return Stephanie's gaze. She felt her bare soul would tumble forth.

"James asked me about you. He thinks you're gay. I said, 'No, if my best friend were gay, I would know it.' Every time he would spot something about the way you acted, he would throw it in my face. I defended you. I wouldn't have cared if you were, but now you're hitting on me!"

Leah shook her head and began to cry, still unable to say anything. Her silence spoke volumes.

"This is the fucking worst night of my life!" Stephanie let out an agonized wail. "I lose my boyfriend and best friend in the same night." She grabbed her bag and strode away down the dark street.

"Steph, wait. I'm sorry. Please don't go. It was a mistake. I didn't mean to." Leah tried to walk after her, but Stephanie spun around and stabbed a finger in her face.

"Leave me alone. Don't follow me." Leah backed off and let her go.

She stayed in the shelter for a while longer until she could compose herself enough to go back to the apartment.

Beyond the 14th Floor

Luckily, her mother had already gone to sleep, so she quietly shut off the rest of the lights, shivered, and crawled into bed with tears wetting her pillow.

For the rest of the weekend, Leah hardly slept and could barely eat. She sent a couple of texts to Stephanie but didn't get a reply. On Monday at school, Stephanie sat apart from her in class and didn't come to the cafeteria at lunch.

Leah knew she had to give Stephanie some space. People were whispering about her and conversations fell silent when she entered the classroom. She found a note on her seat that said "Lezzie." She quickly picked it up and crumpled it in her hand, hoping no one had seen her. Snickers from the back of the class confirmed the guilty people. She glanced over and caught Stephanie staring at her, then quickly turned back to face the front of the class with her chin thrust forward.

Her face was hot, and her heart was pounding. It was too difficult to focus, so she went home sick, unable to face the rest of the day. She was in this all alone. People knew and she had no one to talk to. Her best friend was gone.

#

"How was school going for you?" Jill asked Leah.

Leah shrugged, "Not great, I am just trying to make it to graduation." Her voice dropped to a whisper, "I kinda' don't really have many friends, so that's hard."

"I'm sorry that you've had a rough time, school wasn't that great for me either." Jill offered. "Kids can be so cruel."

"Yup. I seen lotta' good things and some really bad things workin' at the school."

"Like what, bullying?" Leah asked.

"Uh huh. As a janitor, I might as well be a fly on the wall. Kids ignore you, and, well, you see everything. It's pretty hard on kids when they become a target. I wish I could help more but sometimes I'll tell the school counsellors if I see somethin' not right. So sad. Kids can be so mean."

"I'm glad that you do that, Martin. When I had no one to talk to, I went to our school counsellor. She was nice."

"Were you bullied?" Jill asked, concern furrowing her brow.

Leah shifted self-consciously. "I wasn't really bullied, but I just wasn't fitting in. I kinda' felt alone. My best friend found out that I was gay and she freaked out, then others found out. I didn't even know for sure myself." She threw her hands up. "I'm still not sure. I'm so confused. Everyone hates me or is mad at me."

"I'm sorry you had to go through that, but you said that the school counsellor helped you. What did she do?" Jill asked.

"She was cool with it all. I pretty much sat there and cried when I dropped my bombshell. I was so scared and nervous, I wanted to throw up. I had never actually told anyone how I'd felt before."

"That was so brave of you," Jill offered.

Leah shrugged. "Not really. I had been called to the office because my grades suck and I was dropping out of stuff like band. I thought I was really in deep trouble, but she was so kind to me. I just unloaded on her." She reached for her scruffy stuffed backpack and unzipped the outer pocket. She pulled a tattered folded paper from the pocket.

"She gave me this." She handed the paper to Jill.

Jill unfolded it and held it out into the direct light to read aloud. "Teen Gay Alliance Group, meetings every Thursday, basement of Philly Perk in the Washington Square area. Confused? Scared? We offer safe, non-judgemental support to those discovering their truth. All welcome." Martin nodded and she folded it and handed it back to Leah. "That sounds really positive. Did you go?"

"At first I was so scared and I didn't. School was still so tough, and I couldn't talk to my mom about it. She woulda' pulled out the Bible and had me saying prayers or something about 'my condition.'" Leah rolled her eyes. "I lied to her and told her I had a club group for something, I can't even remember what, and I went to the meeting."

"What'd ya' think of it?" Martin asked.

Her demeanor changed as she thought for a moment. "I arrived at this trendy little coffee shop and saw the Gay Alliance sign pointing downstairs for the meeting. No one pointed or whispered, and several other people were going downstairs. It was really cozy, with old couches and posters. It kinda' looked like someone's living room. A girl met me at the bottom of the stairs and took me over to get a cup of coffee before I sat down. Everyone was so cool. No one was being treated like a freak or anything. I was sweating buckets, but no one noticed that either." She grinned and rolled her eyes again.

"That's good." Martin smiled.

"That's where I met my friend. He was one of the speakers. He understood what I was going through."

"It's great when you can find someone."

"He was such a good person. Even though he was young, he was so smart. When I went to that first meeting, I listened to several people speak, but it was his *way* that really drew me to him. He felt the same way about things that I did." She could see him standing at the front of the room that first night, captivating everyone with his good-natured banter.

#

A teenager about her age approached the podium with confidence, pushing his glasses and squaring his shoulders. He grabbed the sides of the podium and spoke loudly into the microphone.

"Hi, I'm Scott. I'm gay." That startled everyone to attention. He continued. "Not really what my parents had planned for me." The audience chuckled and he smirked. "Most of you know me; some of you are new tonight." He paused and looked at the new faces in the crowd, making eye contact with each, including Leah.

"We come to these meetings to help one another. Some people don't have other support or don't know where to go. For some of you, your family knows about you, but many others don't. Some of you haven't been able to tell your families. Maybe we can help you."

He went on to describe more about the group. There were a couple of other speakers who shared their experiences. Leah relaxed as the meeting went on. These people weren't going to judge or make fun of her. She could take the time to figure out who she was, because she wasn't really sure.

Beyond the 14th Floor

The young man was the last at the podium. "Hey all, thanks for coming tonight. I'm glad to see our group growing as more people find out about us. I'm going to pass out an information leaflet for you. You'll notice my name on the bottom with my phone number. If you ever need someone to talk to or are in trouble, if I can't help, I will find someone for you to talk to. Good night!"

Leah looked down at the green leaflet. It listed websites, chat groups, and counsellors in the community. She carefully folded it and tucked it in her bag. As the room emptied, the young man came over to her.

"Hey, Newbie." He offered his hand.

She wiped her sweaty hand on her pants and shook his hand. Her cheeks flushed. "I guess you could call me that."

"This is your first time with us, isn't it? You looked like you are ready to run for the exit."

"Yes, I've never been anywhere like this before. I'm really nervous," she said, biting her bottom lip.

"What did you think?" He pushed his glasses up his nose and ran a hand through his wavy hair.

"Um, I thought it was good. It was interesting to see who was here and to hear what the speakers said. It's nice to know I'm not alone."

"Yes, it is nice to be in a room with people who might be going through the same things you're going through. I helped start this group about a year ago." He smiled and nodded as people walked past. "I got a lot of flak from people who knew me, especially my parents."

"Your parents know?"

"Yes, they do. They weren't thrilled to have their oldest

son be a 'flaming queer,' but slowly they accepted it. I think they always knew but didn't want to believe it. Do your parents know?"

"No. No, she doesn't. It's just my mother. She wouldn't understand. She thinks it's a sin. That's why this is really hard."

"Oh, sweetie. Since starting this club, I've heard a lot of really bad stuff. Kids getting bullied and tormented. Families treating them terribly. There are even kids that are afraid they're mentally ill. This is a hard thing to do, but it's so worth it to live your truth. I personally know two members that felt like they had nowhere to go. They were thinking about suicide. Suicide." He repeated with emphasis. He shook his head. "We offered support, acceptance, and helped them find resources. We've saved lives. So, this is worth it."

"Wow. That's amazing. I'm really glad I came tonight."

"What's your name?"

"Leah Anderson."

"Hey, I have to get going, but if you need anything or someone to talk to, my number is on the sheet." He walked Leah to the door. "I hope to see you back here."

"Yes, I think I'll be back. Thanks." Leah took the bus home, slipping in before her mother arrived. She felt calm, understood, and accepted—a feeling she hadn't experienced in a long time.

Over the next few weeks, Leah looked forward to her meetings. She would lie to her mother and say it was a new club she joined at school. She wanted to go out without a bunch of questions. She felt terrible lying, but she wasn't ready to tell her mother her secret. In fact, she didn't know if she would ever tell.

Despite the fact the young man was around her age, at their weekly meetings he seemed older and so sure of himself. His confidence was inspiring. He seemed to be a role model for several participants.

"Next week, we're going to talk about religion and being gay. Should be interesting." He left the podium and mingled around the room, laughing and visiting with a few of the members.

Leah had made some acquaintances and was beginning to see familiar faces every week. They made small talk and she got to know them through the sharing of some of their stories at the different meetings. She hadn't yet had the courage to share hers.

She also began to understand her own feelings more as people shared their own experiences of discovery. She knew she was attracted to girls. She just hadn't felt comfortable or safe enough to meet anyone. She was attracted to Scott, but mostly because he was a dynamic person, not because he was male. He was gay anyway.

She got up the courage to approach him. "Hey, thanks for the good meeting tonight."

He nodded. "Thanks, the support helps you to know your own truth. How've things been going for you?"

"Okay. I feel a little better at school. At home is the same. My mom believes homosexuality is a sin and that I will need to be exorcised or something if she finds out." She rolled her eyes and he laughed.

"That's a tough go. It's hard when your parents aren't

supportive. Do you have grandparents or an auntie, or some you trust for support?"

"No, my mom doesn't talk to her family. She has never told me why. I feel like it is something to do with my dad, even though he died before I was born." Leah shrugged.

He looked at his watch. "Hey, I've got bit of time. Do you want to go for a quick coffee? Obviously not a date!" He looked at her in mock horror and they both chuckled.

"Yes, I would love to go for not-a-date coffee with you."

They went upstairs to the café and stayed for an hour longer, telling each other more about themselves. He talked about how confused he was when he was younger. He knew he didn't fit in with the boys and was often bullied for spending recesses skipping with the girls instead of playing the rough and tumble sports with the boys.

"I cried a lot back then. I never felt comfortable. One day my grandma was visiting. I will never know for sure if she knew I was gay. She squeezed my hand and told me, 'Don't be afraid to be who you are. There is strength in being true to yourself.' It kind of blew my mind then, but it also gave me confidence to be comfortable in how I was feeling and to stand up to the bullies."

"That's really amazing. You assume older generations wouldn't understand homosexuality."

"She was a really cool woman," he said, taking a sip of his cappuccino. "I think I'm ready to launch a pride club at school. I have talked to the principal. He wasn't overly supportive, but he would allow me to do it. *Allow* me. What an asshole. Does he think my plan is to convert everyone?!"

Leah laughed. "Good luck with that!"

Beyond the 14th Floor

"I know, right? Hey, I gotta' go. Let's do this again next week. This was good." They left the coffee shop and walked their separate ways to get home.

As their friendship formed, they had coffee after meetings almost every week. She looked forward to a time when she could be herself with him without any agenda. She confided in him about her childhood with just her mom in her life.

Why did her mom not talk to her parents anymore? When she got home, her mom was already there. Emboldened by her new friendship, she wondered what advice he would give handling the situation with her mom.

She was in the kitchen sitting at the sewing machine hemming a pair of pants. "Hey, Sweetheart. How was the club meeting?" She looked over her glasses at Leah.

A lie rolled out with ease. "Oh, it was good. We're planning a spirit week at the school for next month." She had hoped it sounded reasonable enough.

"That sounds fun. Is all of your homework done?"

"Yes, I'm caught up. I got my biology exam back, I got 78%."

"Great! I'm glad to see things are improving now that you're focusing on your studies more." Lydia looked up and smiled.

"Thanks, Mom." Her stomach churned from keeping her secret. She wasn't ready to say anything yet. Things seemed to be going so well right now, she didn't want to rock the boat—hell, sink the boat! She did have something on her mind that she wanted to bring up.

Leah slid into the chair across the table.

"Mom, I know you don't like talking about this," she could see her mom subtly stiffen, "but when friends ask me about my dad, I don't know what to say. I tell them he's dead, but I don't know how he died. You won't even tell me is name. Why don't we ever go to his grave? Didn't you love him? Where did you get married?" The questions tumbled out. She had already crossed the line as tension crept into the room.

Her mother's mouth pursed, and she looked down at the pants she was sewing. "He died from pneumonia before you were born. He got sick and three days later, he was dead. He was cremated. We spread his ashes in a park near where we lived at the time. He was a nice man."

"Why don't you ever talk to your parents, my grandparents? What happened?" Leah asked.

Her mother looked down, focusing on the sewing machine to hide her emotions. "They wanted me to give you up. They didn't want me to be a single mother, but I loved you so much already, I said no."

"I don't understand. You didn't do anything wrong." Leah felt so bad thinking of how difficult it must have been for Lydia. Her mother's face was full of emotion and her lip quivered. Defeated, her mother's shoulders sagged, and she exhaled.

"I have never wanted to tell you this. God give me strength." Her mother's face contorted as she struggled to find the words. "I wasn't married. They wanted me to give you up because I wasn't married!" Lydia burst into tears and leapt up from the table, running to her room. She could hear her mother's bedroom door slam and then sobbing.

She didn't fully understand what her mother just told her.

She sat for a while and then turned out the lights and tiptoed down the hall. She stood by her mother's bedroom door. It was quiet now. She lightly tapped on the door. No answer. "I'm sorry, Mom. I didn't mean to upset you. I'm glad you kept me. I love you. Good night." Silence.

Who was her dad? What had he been like? She knew after this difficult conversation, it was going to be hard to get more information from her mother.

A few days later, Leah got home from school and Lydia was still at work. Leah went to the dresser beside her mother's bed. She sifted through the items until she found a small key. She knew her mother kept papers in a locked file cabinet in the dining room. It held her tax information and bank statements, but perhaps there were other documents that could provide a clue to her dad.

She fumbled with the key. Bingo! It worked right away. She looked at the clock; she had about thirty minutes to look before her mother returned.

Her mom kept all sorts of things: newspaper clippings, bank statements, and a bunch of other papers that were boring and meant nothing to Leah. She combed through the files. At the back of the bottom drawer was a small manila envelope. On it was marked "Leah" in Lydia's handwriting.

Pangs of guilt stabbed at her conscience. This was her mother's private information and she was snooping. She almost closed the cabinet and stopped. She was torn. She glanced at the clock; in ten minutes, her mother would be home. She carefully pulled the documents from the envelope. There were some newspaper clippings. She read through the items. She wasn't sure why her mother would save such strange articles. One was an advertisement for a business, and the other article was an obituary for a woman.

She found her mother's last will and testament. Whatever she had would be left exclusively to her in trust until she was eighteen, heaven forbid something should happen to Lydia before then.

A paper fluttered to the floor. It was her birth certificate. Leah picked it up, scanning it until she came to the line stating the name of her father. She gasped. There in black and white letters was her father's name. The name she had wondered about for years. She sat, stunned at the revelation.

Suddenly, a jolt went through her body and the hair stood up on her arms. She flipped through the papers again and studied the items. The newspaper articles were dated five years ago. Her father was listed as a living son in the obituary. Her father was alive.

Chapter Five

Weariness crept over the occupants as the early morning hours enveloped them. At first when a foot touched another, it was quickly pulled away, not to encroach upon the other's space, those cordialities quickly dispensed as everyone shifted to find a comfortable spot to rest.

It was clear by the continued movements and restlessness that everyone was awake. Leah and Jill helped Martin to a standing position, all stretching and twisting, trying to work out the stiffness of being in the confined quarters.

"I will never complain about sleeping in any bed ever again," said Leah.

"Or being too cool," groaned Jill, her hand rubbing the small of her back. She wiped the sweat from her brow with her other hand.

"How far along is the little one?" Martin asked, his eyes inadvertently glancing toward Jill's torso.

Jill thought for a moment. "By my calculations, almost three months. I'm not going to lie; this baby was a complete surprise to me—but a good one."

"What happened to your husband?" Leah said. "Sorry, is it okay to talk about it?" She got flustered. "I've been wondering since you mentioned that he died. What was he like?"

Martin glanced at Jill to see her response and was relieved to see she wasn't upset.

"No, it's okay for me to talk about him. Each day that passes gets easier for me to handle my emotions about losing Brad. Don't get me wrong, sometimes I will be going about my day and a song, a scent, maybe a memory flits through my mind and it will almost bring me to my knees with sadness. Martin, you must know those feelings."

He nodded. "Every day, but you learn a new normal. I also think 'bout what Phyll would want for me. She'd give me a shake if she saw me mopin' around all day, but nights are the hardest. Too much thinkin'."

"Brad was amazing: handsome, funny, and kind. He appreciated everything, from a quiet walk in the woods to going to a sports game. We had a great marriage. I even sold him his first house."

"You're in real estate?"

"Yes, I'm a real estate agent. That's how I met Brad. I helped him find a house to buy. With all the meetings and showings, we fell in love. Then he proposed, you know that story already, with Bucky eating my ring."

"Yeah, still gross." Leah grimaced.

"We were doing great. Brad was a sports writer and the real estate business was doing well in Philly. A couple of us partners have a real estate office on 20th street, near the old Eastern State Pen."

"I hear that place is haunted," Leah said.

"I've never seen any ghosts hanging around my office." Jill smiled. "Brad used to tease me about that too. He had a great sense of humor, even after he got sick."

"What did he get sick from?" Leah asked.

"Bone cancer."

"I heard that's real painful. No one should ever haf ta' go through that."

"At first, he was doing okay. He wasn't in a huge amount of pain. We kind of found out he had cancer by accident."

"By accident?"

"We were lucky, because we probably had more time, getting diagnosed as early as he did."

"How did you find out?"

"We wanted to have a baby, but nothing was happening, so we went for testing to see if there was anything wrong, and that's when they found the cancer. That was a really hard day. It changed everything. Our future plans and goals changed to treatments, prayers, and tests to see if he could beat it."

"So hard…" Martin agreed.

"Didn't the treatments work?"

"They did at first, but they really needed to remove the tumor. But it was in a spot on his spine that they couldn't operate on without him likely becoming paralyzed. Brad didn't want to live that way, so we made the best of the time we had. We worked on doing what Brad could manage."

"That just sucks. Life can be so unfair."

#

Brad and Jill wanted to start a family but hadn't worried much about it at first. Their lives were so hectic, but they both looked forward to Brad returning from his trips. They would spend their first day in bed for most of the morning having lazy sex and cuddling together.

After months of not using any protection, nothing was happening. Jill felt a sense of urgency because of her age. She consulted her doctor and he sent her for tests.

"Looks like you are all clear. You are mid-thirties, still in your child-bearing years, and you don't seem to have any other health issues that are impacting your fertility. All tests have come back normal for your reproductive health." Dr. Flanigan put the clipboard down and sat back in his chair, the buttons of his dress shirt straining over his round belly.

"We should take a look at Brad. We can do a physical and he can provide a sperm sample. That should give us a better idea of the situation."

Brad wasn't thrilled at the idea of going for a physical, but he was appalled at the idea of providing a sperm sample. "Jill, are you kidding me? I am going to have to go into a little room and whack off to some porno magazines while the nurse waits outside the door?" He was incredulous. Jill was having a bit of fun with it.

"I think they provide movies too—to help get you in the mood." She turned so he couldn't see her smile.

"I have always been able to… you know, perform, but I don't think I can make the magic happen under those conditions," Brad said. Jill strung him along a little bit more and then let him off the hook.

She dug in her hand bag and pulled out a little bottle

and held it out to him. "You're in luck: they also do a home version for you shy types. You just have to get the sample to the clinic within an hour, so the little guys don't die."

When he realized he had been duped, he set the bottle on the counter and turned to her with a mischievous look. He slowly walked toward her. "So, you think that's funny." He lunged at her and Jill let out a squeal. They raced around the house with Buck in hot pursuit, not wanting to miss out on the excitement.

Brad tackled Jill on their bed and began tickling her until she wiggled and gasped. "Stop, stop! I'm sorry." They lay there catching their breath. Buck realized the party was over and he retreated to his bed in the corner.

Jill's hand was on Brad's chest and it slowly crept down to his belly. He raised his eyebrow and smiled. "Perhaps Dr. Jill can assist you with your donation." She smiled slyly while undoing his belt.

"I guess I have to listen to the doctor's orders."

#

Dr. Flanigan's office called and asked for both of them to come in for the results of Brad's tests. Sensing his nervousness, Jill said, "Relax, he's going to tell us that you're fine and we need to drink less coffee, wear looser underwear, have more sex, and dial back our workloads so we can have time to get pregnant."

Brad shrugged and they waited in the office for the doctor to come in. He greeted them, sat behind his desk, and opened the file, reading it for a moment before lowering it to the desk. He cleared his throat.

"Thank you for coming. I know you've both been tested for fertility. Brad, the good news is your sperm count is within the normal levels for a male your age." He looked down at the charts. Jill slid her hand over and squeezed Brad's. "However, we have found something in your blood test that we will be following up on. There seems to be something your body is fighting right now."

Brad and Jill exchanged glances. "What does that mean?"

Dr. Flanigan explained it could mean a number of different things, but they would like to run a few more tests. He closed the file and looked over his glasses.

Emotions flickered over Brad's face. "Doc, I feel fine. My back gets sore from time to time, but I travel a lot. If my body is fighting something, wouldn't I feel sick?

He gave Brad and Jill an encouraging smile. "We'll do more tests and figure out what we're dealing with. You're a strong, healthy man, so hopefully it's something we can treat easily and be done with it."

They found themselves back in the same office a week later. Waiting for results, Brad had cancelled his out of town work for the week to go for more tests. His mind was racing. He had been more tired lately, but they were both so busy all the time. He figured because he was approaching forty, it was just his age.

Jill had been trying to act normal as well, but he caught her staring off into space and she had been distracted all week long. She finally admitted she was worried and just wanted to find out what they were dealing with.

Once again, they were summoned back to the office for

the results. Alarm bells were going off; if it was nothing, wouldn't they have found out over the phone? They braced themselves for the news.

Doctor Flanigan looked uncomfortable. "There is no easy way to say this. I'm sorry, the tests reveal you have bone cancer. There are several spots on your spine, indicating that it's stage three. I have spoken with my colleague and I will be referring you to her. She is an oncologist. The five-year survival rate for this type of cancer is about 70%." Jill couldn't register what he was saying as her mind was racing, she merely watched his lips moving as he spoke. Brad sat beside her, nodding solemnly.

The news was devastating to them. They sought second opinions and consulted leading oncologists on the treatment they should pursue.

They were all in agreement that surgery wouldn't be an option because of the risk of paralysis. Jill said she would rather have him alive, even if he was only able to blink, but it was Brad's choice. They went with the non-surgical options, radiation and chemotherapy.

It was a miserable time for everyone. Brad's family came to the house and took turns staying with Jill to help. They realized how many friends they had, and how many people, even strangers, cared about them during their difficult time. It would have been great if Jill could have just stayed home with Brad, but she needed to work to ensure Brad could receive the best care through their health insurance.

Brad wanted to be treated as normally as possible, and he still tried to get out to sporting events on his good days. He had lost all of his hair and was noticeably thinner, but friends still recognized him and gave him a clap on the shoulder and wished him well with his recovery.

Their house was often filled with Brad's buddies, as it was easier for them to come over to visit. It was exhausting, but she knew it made him feel included and helped take his mind off his situation. Brad's co-workers organized a BBQ to raise some extra money for them, so when Jill needed to take time off, they wouldn't have to worry about finances.

Buck was concerned. He treated Brad differently. Before he would take a running leap at Brad when he walked through the door. Now, he was confused. One day when Brad came home from one of his treatments, Buck came running with his usual vigor only to be yelled at by Jill and Brad. He put his head down and crept away, not understanding what he did wrong. Later, he came to the bedroom and put his big head on the bed by Brad's and looked at him with sad eyes.

"I'm sorry, Bucky. I'm not feeling so good," Brad said, patting the soft black head. Instantly, the black tail thumped against the floor. Brad patted the bed and Buck jumped up, lying beside him as still as a mouse. That became the routine from then on.

Brad went for treatments and received the best care. They tried to maintain hope, but they could see it didn't seem to make a difference. The cancer had spread to his lungs. Drug trials, rounds of chemo, blood tests; the cruel merry-go-round was slowing down as all the options for treatment ran out. Go home and make the most of what time you have left, they said.

It was a gut punch. Brad's quality of life seemed to

diminish a bit each day. Although he still managed most tasks, everything became slower and more painful. Jill was determined to ensure his remaining time would be well-spent. She had to hide her misery and be positive for Brad.

He asked for a paper and pen before Jill left for work. He wanted to have something to show her when she returned home. He could feel how exhausted and discouraged she had become. He wanted to plan something they could focus positive energy on.

Jill arrived after work. "Hey guys, I'm home." She carried a bag of Chinese food for dinner. Buck danced around her with excitement. "Buck, it's not for you." She gave him a little shove with her foot.

Brad came to meet her at the door and gave her a hug. They chatted idly about her day as they unpacked the food in the kitchen. His appetite had disappeared as his illness advanced, but he pushed the food around on his plate, taking reluctant bites for Jill's benefit.

"Hon, can I make you something else? A smoothie or something?"

He reached over and patted her hand. "Maybe some beer and wings." He winked at her.

"Trust me, if I thought you could handle it, they would be sitting in front of you." She knew he was trying to lighten the mood. Every meal time was a test to see what his body would let him handle.

Jill cleared the dishes and changed into her yoga pants and sweater. Brad was interested in hearing about her day. She had sold one house and had a few offers on some others.

He pulled a folded paper out and handed it to her,

giving a sheepish smile "I've been working on something today. I want us to make the most of what we have left. These are the things I would love to see and do before I die, my bucket list." Her eyes welled as she squeezed his hand and smiled. She unfolded the paper and read the items aloud.

"1. Rent a house on the ocean with our family.

2. Go to a last Major League Baseball game with the boys.

3. Get a tattoo.

4. Have lots of sex with my wife.

5. Become a dad."

Her face crumpled and she cried softly as Brad caressed her arm. "I'm sorry, I didn't mean to upset you with this," he whispered, wiping the tears from her cheeks.

"No, no, I'm sorry. This list is wonderful. I'm so glad you made it. I feel helpless and if there is any way I can help make this better for you, that's exactly what I want to do."

The next few weeks, Jill enlisted family and friends to help with some of the items on Brad's list. His sister found a gorgeous beach house on Hackett's Cove in Nova Scotia, near Peggy's Cove. Many of Brad's siblings and parents joined them for a long weekend and they fished and kayaked and enjoyed each other's company. Buck got to come too. Brad would sit on the beach and throw the tennis ball into the water and have Buck fetch it. Buck would have played forever if Brad had the energy.

Brad rested when he needed to, and every evening ended with stories and laughter around the campfire on the dock. His family, understanding the significance of the trip, did their best to be positive and make it special. Jill and

Beyond the 14th Floor

Brad felt surrounded by love.

As a well-known sports journalist, he didn't just get tickets with his buddies to a play-off game; he was asked to throw out the first pitch. Despite having chronic pain, he managed a pretty decent pitch. The audience knew his story and gave him thunderous applause. Brad grinned from ear to ear. Jill's heart was full that night as she helped him to bed. He seemed genuinely happy. His friends made sure he had had a memorable time.

The doctors advised Brad that he shouldn't get a tattoo because of risk of infection, but he didn't care. He wouldn't say what his tattoo was going to be. He was quite mysterious about it. He had never talked about a tattoo before, so this seemed out of character for him. They picked a reputable tattoo parlor and Jill dropped him off; she was told she couldn't stay.

"I'll text you when I am done," he said. He waved goodbye to her through the window.

He texted her three hours later and said he was finished. When she arrived to pick him up, he was tired and drawn. His bicep had a big patch on it, covering the new tattoo. He didn't say much so Jill prompted him. "Well, how did it go?"

"Hurt like hell," he grumbled. He was exhausted when they got home so he went to lie down. She made them some snacks and tea. After a while, he called to her from the bathroom. She arrived to find the patch had been peeled back and he was looking in the mirror at the masterpiece on his arm. It was a beautiful tattoo. It said in script, "My love Jill, every moment with you is a gift." There was a little sprig of Lily of the Valley, Jill's favorite flower, below it.

"Brad, that's so special." Jill hugged him and cried as they rocked back and forth. Brad choked and said with a husky voice, "I just wanted your name to be on me, something I could take with me."

Brad often was too sore or sick to have sex, but occasionally they managed to have a tender lovemaking session, which they both enjoyed. They shared a lot of cuddles and connected in a way which they never would have had time for in their previously busy lives. They enjoyed their quiet Sundays alone. Those were the days with no appointments. Family members were sent home and friends stayed away. It gave them both a time to rest and be together.

As the trees began to lose their leaves, Brad became more limited by his sickness. Jill decreased her work load to be home more. They had agreed, when it became too difficult, they would move Brad into hospice care so he could receive the pain relief and support he needed in his final days.

They had long talks about the best end of life care. They talked about his wish to become a dad and how he was just too sick for it to happen. They both knew it wasn't a possibility for him and Jill was deeply saddened she couldn't give him everything he had asked for.

Brad told her he wanted her to find a decent guy to be with so she wouldn't be alone. "One condition, though," he said in a mock stern voice. "Buck has to approve." Hearing his name, the dog thumped his tail against the floor.

One evening, while Jill was helping Brad to bed, he stumbled and almost fell. She helped him to the edge of the bed, and he sat with his head in his hands and cried. He had been so courageous throughout the difficult journey, but now his spirit was exhausted.

"I'm so sorry, Jill, for all this." He looked up at her, his face clenched with anguish. "We were supposed to have a family and grow old together. This is so shitty. I can't even be alone anymore." He pulled her toward him and held his face against her stomach while she stroked the stubble on his head and gently rubbed his shoulders.

"Shhh, don't be sorry, I wouldn't be anywhere else, than with you. I love you, in sickness and in health, remember? I hate that you're going through this. It's so unfair."

They waited as long as they could manage before moving Brad to the hospice. His illness escalated to where they could no longer provide the pain relief he needed at home. Family could stay with him, so he was never alone. Jill rarely took breaks but managed to slip home to sleep and shower while Brad's family was there. She brought Buck in a few times and he would lick Brad's hand and lie on the floor by his bed.

As the days went on, Brad was increasingly uncomfortable and weak. He slept more than he was awake. Sometimes he was panicky and would clutch Jill's hand like he was drowning. Jill's soul was heavy. She wanted his pain and suffering to end, but at the same time did not want to let him slip away forever.

When the end seemed near, everyone had a private conversation with Brad and then left Jill alone with him.

"Hey, my most amazing love," she whispered. "You've been so strong all this time. I am so proud of you and I love you." She sniffed and silent tears rolled down her cheeks. "Bucky and I will be okay. If you are ready, you can rest now." He opened his eyes and gave a slight nod that he understood her. His once strong body lingered for an hour more before he took a deep gasping breath.

His eyes flickered and he squeezed her hand and mouthed, "I love you." His last words.

He fell into unconsciousness. Jill and his family surrounded his bed as he took his last breath the next afternoon, surrendering to the disease that conquered his body.

The quiet funeral Brad had requested followed four days later. Everyone had stayed throughout his illness, so it was time to return to their own lives and jobs. His parents volunteered to stay with Jill for a few days, but she declined. She needed to shut the world off for a while. Somehow, it still managed to go on despite her terrible loss.

#

Leah blew her nose loudly. "Jill, that's so sad. How do you even get through something like that? I wouldn't be able to do anything but stay in bed and cry all day."

Martin reached over and squeezed Jill's hand.

"I lost my parents to a car accident when I was young, so it was really hard to experience that kind of loss again. I *did* stay in bed and cry all day for a while, but eventually you have to get up and get moving again. As much as your life comes to a halt, the world keeps going on. Brad's family was really supportive. They stayed with me, loved me, and then kicked my butt when I needed it."

"Kicked your butt?" asked Leah. "That seems mean."

"Sometimes you need a little motivation to pull yourself out of your grief. Brad's sister came to visit, and she helped me move forward—her and my broken tap."

They both looked surprised. "A broken tap? That's a new one," said Martin.

Chapter Six

It had been eight months since Brad died. While the world continued around her, Jill's life stood still for some time. A new normal began to develop for Jill, moving forward without Brad. People volunteered to help her sift through Brad's things, but she wasn't ready to face the reality of it. She gave away a few items, like some of his sports memorabilia and his golf clubs. She offered to let his family have any items they would like, and they took a few things.

Jill still slept in his shirts and wore his ball cap on walks with the dog. Buck mourned the loss of Brad as well, moping around after Jill and waiting by the front door every day. Even he had lost weight. Their lives were incomplete and the joy in usual things was missing.

Jill tried to ease back into work. She found it exhausting and too hard to focus. She needed the human interaction because the house was too quiet, but she couldn't make conversation. It didn't make any sense. At the end of her day, Buck would come running and maul her like she had been gone forever. She couldn't be mad at him. He had already lost Brad, and he was probably worried about losing her too.

She would drop her purse at the door, kick off her shoes, and pull on Brad's baggy grey sweats and a t-shirt. She often felt too tired to cook so it was prepackaged salads and an early night most evenings. Friends and family would invite her out, and she would go, but felt hollow without Brad.

The worst was when she ran into people for the first time after Brad had passed. They either avoided her entirely or acted awkward, not knowing what to say or saying something silly. She understood their reactions; she had been there before. She knew now there was nothing right to say, and they meant well.

#

On the one-year anniversary of his death, one of Brad's sisters came for the weekend. It felt familiar with her there, almost like a little piece of Brad, so it was comforting. When Catherine met Jill at the door, her face registered surprise and pity. It was a momentary flicker, but Jill saw it. Jill hadn't coloured her hair in months and her wardrobe was easily a size too large for her body. It was effort enough to get out of bed to go to work and look after Buck, any self-care seemed frivolous.

That night they sat by the fire in the backyard, reminiscing and relaxing. Jill appreciated company that wasn't an effort to have. Jill knew Catherine could see all of the things that had slid since Brad's diagnosis. Lots of little repairs had gone undone. The front window was still cracked from a rock the lawn mower had thrown the summer before, the back patio door kept coming off its track, and the kitchen sink tap was leaking. The pool hadn't been used for a year and was full of green water because the pump wasn't working. It needed to be drained. She hadn't seen it herself until she imagined her home through Catherine's eyes.

In the kitchen, the cupboard still contained an expired case of BOOST and Brad's expired medication. The spare room had been turned into Brad's room with a hospital bed and still housed many of the medical devices he had needed to stay at home as long as he could.

After dinner on the last evening before Catherine left, they were doing the dishes together. Jill began mopping up the water that trickled onto the counter from the leaking tap. She felt Catherine watching her and looked up to meet her eyes.

"It just started leaking last month." Jill shrugged. "I guess I should get it fixed." She turned back to the sink.

"Honey…" Catherine began carefully. "I think there are a few things that need to be fixed around here."

Jill sighed. "I know. I just haven't had the energy." She collapsed on the couch on the brink of tears.

"Sweetie, of course you don't. You have been through hell this last year. These things were the least of your concerns. I can't begin to imagine how overwhelming it is to lose your husband. I miss Brad very much too." She sat beside Jill and rubbed her back. "I wish I could help you with all this. I would have brought my tool box and repaired everything for you." They both looked at each other and laughed.

"I won't wait for that to happen. You can't even change your own lightbulbs," said Jill, shaking her head.

"Would you consider hiring a repairman?"

"I don't know. I haven't really wanted anyone in our space."

"Would you consider it at least? I could help you find someone."

"I'll think about it."

Catherine didn't want to force the idea on her but felt glad she had at least planted a seed.

They hugged goodbye and promised to call each other. Jill thanked her for the company and wistfully watched as Catherine drove away. Jill pulled her sweater around herself and looked around the house. Catherine was right; there were a lot of things that could use some attention.

About a month later, Jill called Catherine, frantic. She couldn't make out what Jill was saying. "Calm down, Hon. What's the matter?"

"There's water everywhere. The kitchen tap came off in my hand tonight. The water was hitting the ceiling like Old Faithful in my kitchen! I didn't know what to do until I remembered there must be a water shut off somewhere. It took me twenty minutes to find it. What a mess. I don't know what to do!" She was weepy and exhausted.

"Aw, that sucks. You poor thing. I wish I was closer; I would come and help you. You'll have to call an emergency plumber for tonight. Maybe they can fix the tap and get your water turned back on for you."

"Man, I am so angry with myself. I should have fixed this."

"Hey, don't be so hard on yourself. Give the plumber a call. Maybe they know of someone who could come and do some of your other repairs too."

Jill let out a huge sigh. "Okay. I'm sorry for bothering you. I just panicked and didn't know who to call. It is nice to hear a supportive voice."

"Hey, no problem. I'm always here for you. Let me know how things work out. Maybe I can come down next weekend if you still need help with things." Jill thanked Catherine and hung up.

She flipped through an old phone book and found a listing for plumbers and called one with a twenty-four-hour emergency line. The guy that answered said he could come in about two hours. He advised her to soak up as much water as she could.

By the time the truck pulled up in front of the house, Jill had rugs hanging outside and most of her towels and mops propped up to dry. She was just throwing another bucket of water out onto the front lawn. A man carrying a tool box came up the front walk.

He extended his hand to Jill with a firm, warm handshake, and smiled. "Hi, you must be the broken kitchen tap?" His blue eyes were friendly.

"Yes, what a mess. My kitchen looked like a broken fire hydrant on a street corner. Now, it's just a dripping mess. Thanks so much for coming tonight." Jill invited him in. Buck came bounding up, barked a couple of times, and then gave the plumber a thorough sniff.

"Buck, stop!" She grabbed his collar and tried tugging him away, but his four feet were firmly planted. "I'm sorry, he is such a lug sometimes."

"Don't worry, I like dogs. All good." He reached down

and scratched behind Buck's ears. The dog's tail thumped the floor. Before Jill could say more, Buck flipped over onto his back, exposing his white belly.

"So much for protecting me from strangers, right?" She rolled her eyes and chuckled, shaking her head in exasperation. "Follow me, the kitchen is this way."

She led him into the soaking kitchen. The smell of wet wood filled their nostrils.

"I couldn't find the shut off valve. My husband is the one who knew where it was, so the water ran for a long time before I turned it off."

"Is he not here right now?" The plumber asked.

"No. He's not." Jill paused. It was still hard to explain to people. "He passed away about ten months ago from cancer."

He looked up at her, surprised. "Oh geez, I'm sorry."

She didn't answer but gave a nod in agreement. He paused for a moment and then looked over his shoulder at her. "That 'C' diagnosis has affected a lot of families. We lost my mom a couple years ago to breast cancer. My pop is still fairly lost without her."

"I'm so sorry for your loss too. Cancer fucking sucks. Pardon my language," Jill said wrapping her arms around herself. He nodded.

He got to work and showed her what had happened to the tap. He was able to put on a temporary one. "It's not as nice as the one you had, but if you pick up a proper replacement, I can change it for you later. The bad news is this might be an insurance claim for you. Water has gotten down behind all of the cabinets along this wall in places you can't reach to mop up. It will likely warp the wood and eventually mold and rot." He shook his head. "You may need all new cabinets." He looked down at the hard wood floors and nodded to them. "And floors too. I see they go under the edge of the cabinets."

Her face fell. "This is the last thing I need right now."

"I have to admit, no one I've met has ever felt it's ever a good time for a flooded kitchen."

"You've got a point," Jill agreed. "I'll give the insurance company a call in the morning and see what they say. If I am getting my kitchen torn out, I'll be needing more than a new tap. Can you recommend someone who does this type of work?"

He mentioned a few names but added, "We're a plumbing company but we also do construction jobs, so I'll leave my card with you. If the insurance company thinks you need the work done, we can give you a quote." He pulled out his wallet and found a worn business card tucked inside. He handed it to her.

"Thanks. What do I owe you for tonight?"

He smiled. "You know what? That was a spare tap from another job. Forty bucks for the call-out is all I need. I'll write up an invoice for you."

"Really? That's so kind. I sure appreciate this."

He went out to his truck to get the paperwork and then he came back to the door. "Here you go, any problems give me a call. Have a nice rest of your evening."

Buck and Jill watched from the door as he waved and drove away. The lights from his work truck disappeared down the road. "How was he for a knight in shining armor,

Buck?" Jill asked. She patted her dog's furry head.

#

"That's all you needed, a flooded kitchen. When it rains, it pours." Martin laughed. "I guess it really did pour."

"Oh, it did. I couldn't believe the mess. There was a silver lining to the whole big disaster though. That's how I met the father of my baby."

#

After getting approval from the insurance company to repair the damage, Jill called the number on the card the plumber had given her.

"Hi, this is Jill Jones. One of your workers made a late-night rescue when my kitchen flooded. I would like to get in touch with him, please. He thought I might be making an insurance claim to repair the water damage and he was right."

"Hey, that was me. You're the woman with the broken tap and the big dog." He chuckled. "It's too bad about the claim, but considering the amount of water, I'm not surprised. So, would you like us to do a quote on the job?"

"Please. I need to get this fixed soon."

"No problem. We can get something back to you right away. We actually have a few openings coming up in our work schedule, so perhaps it could work well for both of us."

Their business had a competitive bid and Jill had felt comfortable with the man, so she called him to arrange the work. Catherine agreed to come help her get the kitchen ready for the renovation. They emptied all the cabinets and moved most of the stuff into the garage. There was a mini kitchenette in Brad's man cave where he and his buddies had watched sports, so that became the temporary kitchen. For the first time, it felt good to be going through things.

On Sunday evening, Jill turned to Catherine and agreed it was time. "I think I'm ready to clean out some things." She looked at the boxes they had put together of extra kitchen items she wanted to give away. "It has actually felt really good to pull apart the kitchen and sort through some things. I think I may be ready to go through Brad's stuff too. Maybe I'll redo the spare room—IF I survive the kitchen reno!"

Catherine hugged her and held her. "I am so glad, Jill. It will be hard, but I think you're ready."

There was a knock at the door the next morning and the plumber was standing on the front step ready to get started on the kitchen.

"Hey." Jill smiled and shook his hand. "You know, I don't remember your name. Since we'll be spending some time together, I should probably call you something other than just The Plumber."

He laughed with his eyes twinkling. "I've been called worse, but Evan should get my attention if you need something. Of course, you're Jill."

She nodded and gestured to the wagging black lab by her feet. "Evan, this is Buck, my best friend and fervent protector."

"Yes, I remember the vicious, territorial Buck from last time," he said. He reached down and gave the appreciative dog a scratch.

They sat at the table for a quick meeting to discuss the timelines for the construction and work schedule. The only thing that worried Jill was how Buck was going to react to the strange men in her house. Her concern quickly disappeared as Buck relaxed around Evan like he was an old friend.

Evan said, "Hey, don't worry; we'll be working here all day. We can let him in and out. You don't have to send him to a kennel." He reached down and gave Buck a pat.

Evan said at certain times he would have a few guys helping him with the work, but for the most part, he would be on his own. He would be there all the time. A construction truck and dumpster were pulling up as Jill was leaving. Demolition day was about to begin.

When Jill returned home at the end of the day, her kitchen looked like a warzone: cupboards were torn out and pipes and wires hung from the wall. Buck came bounding to greet her. He was covered in dust, but happy. It was after five, so the work crew had left for the day. Evan was still there cleaning up.

He smiled when he saw her. "Hey, how was your day?"

"Great! Closed a tough sale and showed two other places." She put her hands on her hips and looked at the mess around her. "Looks like you had a pretty busy day too."

He nodded in agreement. "Yes, we're finished here. This is your new kitchen." He waved his arm like he was making a big presentation. His hair was tousled, and his clothes were dusty.

Jill played along. "Fabulous, is this rustic or shabby chic?"

Beyond the 14th Floor

"Basic low-budget style."

"I guess it's takeout for me going forward. You can join me for chicken nuggets and fries dipped in ketchup," Jill suggested.

He grinned. "That's my favorite anyway."

She left him to finish and could hear him whistling while he packed up his tools.

"See ya' tomorrow!" he called as he walked out the door.

#

It felt odd but nice to have someone there when she got home. She hadn't realized how lonely it had been living by herself again.

As the days went on, Buck became quite excited for the work crews to arrive. He would lay by the front door and excitedly jump up when he heard the trucks drive up. The workers enjoyed Buck too, and he often enjoyed extra treats during lunch and coffee breaks.

One day, Jill ended up working from home because of some repair work being done in her office. She made a cup of tea and set up her laptop in the living room. Evan seemed pleased she was there, and they made small talk throughout the morning as he worked in her kitchen.

From her vantage point in the living room, she could see Evan outside when he was working on the back patio. He was sawing the boards for the kitchen floor. At about 12:30, he put his saw down and looked at his phone. He went to his backpack and pulled out a bag of lunch. Despite the cool weather, he wiped his brow and took off his jacket.

He dug in his lunch bag and pulled out a sandwich. He sniffed it, which made Jill smile, then he took a big bite and set it down on the bench. He turned back to the pile of boards to continue.

She saw Buck get up from the spot by the pool where he had been dozing. He stretched, walking over to the bench and sniffing the air. The smile quickly left her face and her eyes widened. *Don't do it, Buck!* In one quick bite, Evan's bologna sandwich was gone. Buck casually walked away as if nothing had happened and quietly plopped back down under a nearby tree, resuming his nap.

She put her hand over her mouth trying to stop the laughter. She couldn't even go tell him or he would know she had been watching. Soon, Evan put his board down and turned to walk over for another bite of his sandwich. Puzzled, he stopped and looked at the empty spot on the bench. He looked behind the bench and on the ground. As if the notion just came to him, he quickly scanned the yard for Buck, who was sleeping under the tree looking completely innocent. He shook his head and frowned with an annoyed scowl.

He brought the board in to place it on the kitchen floor. As he walked past the door way of the living room, he glanced at Jill. She couldn't help herself any longer; the laughter poured out of her as she held her hand to her mouth. He set the board down and came to the doorway with his hands on his hips. She laughed until she cried, gasping for breath and wiping the tears away at the same time.

"I'm so sorry. That was just so funny. Bucky just

casually stole your sandwich right out from under you. Then the little bugger pretends like nothing happened."

His look of annoyance changed to amusement as she tried to stop laughing. He realized she probably hadn't had many reasons to laugh lately and went along with it.

"Buck is quite the magician."

"You don't know the half of it," laughed Jill. She thought of her engagement ring getting swallowed by Buck. "I guess we owe you one." Jill grabbed her keys and purse. "I was just going to go grab something to eat. I'll bring you back something too. I'm so sorry. Buck can be such a troll sometimes."

"Oh, you don't have to. I probably didn't need it anyway." He laughed and patted his tummy. He was in great shape. Jill noticed he definitely didn't need to lose weight.

"No problem, I'll be back soon."

She returned a short time later with some loaded smoked turkey sandwiches and some cold lemonade. They sat on the back patio and unwrapped the lunch.

"Looks like good ol' Buck did me a favor. I went from a sad, warm bologna sandwich, to delicious deli food. These even have lettuce and whatever this is, on it," he said as he held up an unidentified green string with his fingers.

"Those are bean sprouts. They're good for you."

He plucked a few off and held them out for Buck to sniff. Buck turned up his nose and trotted away. "See? Buck is a smart dog, he doesn't think they're food either."

Jill rolled her eyes and snickered. "He's probably already full, from eating your first lunch."

They sat and ate in silence, enjoying the nice fall afternoon. The trees were dropping leaves making the pool look more like a swamp with a layer of foliage on top.

He gestured over to it. "I guess you haven't used that very much in a while."

"No, I need to get it taken care of. Except for the odd duck Buck chases out of it, I only use it when company is over." She shrugged, "I haven't felt much like company this last year." She looked at the house. "I need quite a few repairs done. Plus, I want to redo the spare room." She paused "Do you think you could add some things on when you're done the kitchen?"

"Yes, I think so. The kitchen is on schedule. I noticed your broken front window. You should get that fixed before the snow flies for sure."

"I know. My sister-in-law has been hoping I'll get some things done around here before I have another crisis and insurance claim."

"It's great your family is around to support you."

"It's mainly Brad's family. I lost my parents in a car accident several years ago. I was an only child. Brad's parents and brother and sister are my family. I'm pretty lucky to have them."

"You're very fortunate to have that. I lost my wife, Sarah, eight years ago. Her family stopped talking to me after she died. Blamed me, I guess." He looked down at his hands and hung his head.

"Blamed you for her death? Why, what happened?" She turned caught herself and lowered her eyes. "I'm sorry, that's private, I didn't mean to pry."

He shifted uncomfortably but went on. "It's always been hard to talk about, but I guess you know what it's like to lose the most important person in your life."

"It's the most difficult thing in the world. It changes you forever." She waited for him to continue.

"We met in college and got married. She was so much fun and so full of energy. I was an athlete, but she could leave me in the dust when we would go for a jog. We wanted to start a family. Sarah got pregnant right away and we were thrilled, but then she miscarried. We tried for a while after that and nothing happened. She got depressed. She stopped jogging or doing any of the things she loved to do." He picked at a loose string on his jeans and gazed off across the yard as he spoke.

"I told her I was worried about her. She said she was fine. Well, we all know when a woman says she is fine, she is anything but." He looked at her with a sad smile. "We tried a lot of different things: counsellors, medication, I took some time off.

"Depression is so hard. There isn't a magic button you can press. Everyone is different too, so what can work for one person, may not for another.

"I thought she was getting better. She even started jogging again. Then she got a bad cold. I came home from work one day and I found her in bed with medicine bottles around her." His voice quivered. "She wasn't breathing.

"The reports came back that it was ruled as a fatal multiple drug intoxication. Depression meds mixed with cold medication. There was no note, so I have always hoped it was accidental and that she didn't really intend to lose her life.

"Her family was so angry. They never said it to my face,

but the unspoken feeling was that I hadn't done enough for Sarah. They have no idea how much it tore my heart out when she died. The most devastating thing was during the autopsy they discovered she was pregnant. It was early, and she likely didn't even know herself." He choked out the words with his face in his hands.

He coughed clearing his throat and stood up abruptly. "I really didn't mean to dump all that on you. I'd better get back to work."

Jill got to her feet and gathered up the wrappers and glasses. "Evan, thank you for telling me about Sarah. As crazy as it sounds, it somehow makes me realize that I'm not the only person that has lost someone they loved. It's easy to feel alone when you've gone through something so hard."

Something in her heart changed that afternoon—a subtle, unexplained connection and understanding of loss. Both were members of the broken hearts club. They trusted that each would tread lightly moving forward in their friendship.

#

Over the next couple of weeks, Jill felt herself watching the clock to see when it was time to go home. Occasionally, she would leave early or pop by during the day to drop off donuts and coffee for the whole crew and ostensibly to check on the progress. It became the norm for Evan to stay a bit later at the end of each day to clean up, have a little visit, and deliver a progress report.

"We're about a week away from having the kitchen

done. Maybe you should make a list of all the other items you need done around here so I can schedule them in." He pulled a well-worn, whittled pencil from behind his ear and grabbed his clipboard.

"I'm getting really excited to finally be able to use the kitchen again and have an actual dishwasher back." Jill said.

"Yes, you'll be pleased when you see those granite counter tops go in. You picked some really nice things."

They walked around the house so Jill could show him all the items that needed repair. "Wow, I'm going to be here until Christmas. This place will be in great shape when I'm done though," Evan said, busily scratching notes down on his clipboard.

"Thanks for all of your hard work. You and the guys have done a great job and really taken good care of my kitchen reno and Buck." She smiled as Buck walked with them to the door.

On Friday when she got home from work, she was sad to see Evan's truck was already gone. Her disappointment turned to elation as she walked in to see a brand new, completed kitchen. The granite gleamed under the pendant lights. She smiled to see a little glass filled with water and a couple of flowers from her yard in the makeshift vase. A note beside the flowers said, "Enjoy your new kitchen. See you next week!" She beamed with happiness.

She had planned to show Catherine how well the repairs had turned out and had invited her for the weekend.

Buck heard Catherine's car pull up before Jill did and he bounded over to the front door, wagging his tail and barking. Jill pulled the door open as Catherine approached.

"Hey, it's so good to see you." Jill enveloped Catherine in a big hug.

"I know, I've missed seeing you. We've both been so busy. I've been looking forward to coming."

They collected Catherine's bags and Jill helped her put her stuff away. Jill pulled her by the hand down the hall to the kitchen.

"You have to see this. You are going to be so surprised. Now, close your eyes." They paused in the door way. Jill pulled Catherine forward into the center of the kitchen. "Okay, open your eyes." Catherine looked around at the new kitchen. "Ta da! I bet it doesn't even look like the same house to you." Jill grinned from ear to ear.

"Wow, what a makeover! Your kitchen looks fantastic," Catherine exclaimed. "I love the cabinets and flooring you picked. They did a great job putting it together."

"Yes, I'm really happy how it turned out, even though I never would have thought it needed to be done!"

Jill made them some tea and they curled up on the couch to visit. The tea turned to wine and they talked for hours. Catherine yawned and then laughed as she looked at her watch. "Oh my, it's 1:00. I can't believe it's so late. No wonder I'm tired."

"I had no idea. I guess we need to get together more often." They made up the sofa bed for Catherine as they discussed the weekend plan.

"I think I'm ready to go through the spare room we used for Brad when he was sick, or at least I want to try to see how it goes. I was hoping you could help me." Jill wrung the pillow case in her hand.

Beyond the 14th Floor

Catherine put her hand on Jill's shoulder and smiled. "Absolutely. We can do as much or as little as you want. I bet it will feel good. You want to remember the best times with Brad, not the most difficult ones."

The next day they were both up early. They emptied out the spare room, donating the hospital bed to a nearby care home. It was difficult, but they carefully went through Brad's things and made donation piles for most of his clothes. Jill kept a few special items like some prized jerseys and his favorite t-shirts, which she now liked to sleep in.

As they stood back observing the empty room, she could see the place really needed to be refreshed. All the dings in the walls from Brad's wheel chair and just normal wear and tear were really obvious. The room needed holes filled and a fresh coat of paint. She was glad she had arranged for Evan to work on it.

When the weekend was over, Catherine quizzed Jill. "You may not realize it, but you've talked a lot about your carpenter, Evan, all weekend. I think you might like him." Jill looked at her in surprise. Catherine could see a flicker of different emotions clouding her face. Jill didn't say anything but her face reddened.

Catherine leaned over and rubbed her arm. "Honey, it's okay. I'm not calling you out on this. It's has almost been a year since you lost Brad. You know he always wanted you to move on. I'm Brad's sister; I know you aren't forgetting him. You and Buck don't have to be alone." She smiled.

"I don't know what I feel. I miss Brad so much. Every day I think about him and ache for him, but at the same time, this really nice guy walks into my life to fix my home.

I look forward to seeing him and don't feel so alone with him around. I enjoy the company." Jill struggled with her feelings as she tried to explain.

"You have all the time in the world. I'm just saying you shouldn't feel guilty if you find someone. I know you'll always love Brad."

As Jill tidied up the kitchen that evening, she paused and looked at the now wilting flowers at the edge of the counter. She stepped out onto the back patio. Cool air swirled around her as she pulled her sweater together. She looked up at the stars twinkling in the sky. *Is this okay, Brad? I don't know if I'm ready to move on yet.*

#

"That's a cool story. I especially love the part about Buck eating the guy's sandwich." Leah snickered.

"Buck is a character," Jill agreed. "I could never have imagined falling in love with the carpenter. I think we both understood what it was like to love again after losing people so important to us. I still love Brad too."

"I don't think people needa' be alone. Matter a' fact, I think it's better when people have a partner. Gets mighty lonely."

How did it happen? She never imagined she could love again. At first, guilt weighed heavily on her as she thought about how her relationship with Evan began. There was no denying that he gave her something to look forward to every day. She had relaxed and let the tiny rays of light gently caress her grieving heart and it had felt good.

#

Beyond the 14th Floor

The following week arrived, and the weather was colder. Evan was working on the odd jobs she needed completed now that the kitchen was done.

She arrived home early after work and opened the door to see a trail of blood droplets down the front hallway. *Oh my God, what's going on?*

"Evan? Evan, are you here? Are you okay?"

She could see a glimpse of him sitting on the edge of the bathtub with the door slightly ajar. She paused and began to push the door open. "Evan?"

"Don't come in here. I'm in my boxers." he called.

"What happened, why are you bleeding?"

"That damn front window of yours. I put the new one in and when I was moving the broken one, a shard splintered out and cut the top of my leg."

"Can I help, are you okay?"

"Yes, I'll be fine. It's almost stopped bleeding."

"Do I need to call 911?"

"Nah, I'm fine. I probably can't put my jeans back on though. Do you have a baggy pair of shorts I could use… that aren't pink?" He chuckled from behind the bathroom door.

She went to her closet and dug through her shelf of clothes. She often wore Brad's loose gym shorts when she was working out. Those would probably work.

She tapped on the door and reached through the opening with the shorts dangling from her fingers. She felt them lift from her hand and then heard fumbling and a few muttered cuss words.

"Okay, good, these should fit." Evan emerged from the

bathroom in a plaid shirt hanging over Brad's gym shorts. His white sock was red at the top where the blood had trickled down. He was holding a work rag against the front of his upper thigh where the cut was.

"Wow, are you sure you don't need stitches? Come sit down."

He limped over to a kitchen chair and lowered himself favoring his injured leg.

"No, I won't need stitches. I think it's more of a scrape, just bled like hell."

She went to the bathroom and dug through her vanity to find the first aid kit. She got a clean washcloth and some peroxide and went back to the kitchen.

He looked up and saw the things in her hand. "No, no, I don't need any of that, I'll be fine." He gently pushed her hands away.

"Really, tough guy? You have a dirty rag pressed against your leg. How hygienic is that?" She knelt on the floor beside him and gently pulled the rag away from the wound. It was still bleeding a bit, but luckily, he was right, it was more of a large scrape than a deep cut, nothing you could really stitch.

She examined the injury and gently dabbed at it with her clean cloth. He grimaced in pain. "Wow, that stings!"

"I'm sorry. This is going to be worse." Before he could object, she poured peroxide on the wound. He grimaced and clenched his jaw.

"Goddamn it, that feels like fire." He squeezed his eyes shut and slapped the table beside him. His eyebrows were knit in consternation and he continued to inhale through his teeth.

"It's okay. Look, see the bubbling? That's killing all the germs, so your leg doesn't get infected and fall off." He opened his eyes and watched her as she set to work wrapping a soft bandage around his muscular thigh. She had never been this close to him before and her body was tingling. She tried to finish quickly. Her heart was beating fast and she felt warm. When she looked up, Evan was gazing at her with his deep blue eyes. She smiled and her cheeks flushed.

"Thank you."

"You're welcome," she whispered. She worked on securing the bandage in place. She cleaned up the supplies and stood, extending a hand to help him up.

He took her hand and hoisted himself to his feet, putting most of his weight on his uninjured leg. Instead of releasing her hand, he continued to hold it and stepped toward her. Their faces were inches apart and he leaned closer to her. She closed her eyes in anticipation and tilted her face to meet his.

All of a sudden, a force from out of no-where hit them, almost knocking them over. Instead of an anticipated kiss, Jill got a long tongue licking her face as Buck jumped up and down beside them.

"Buck, Buck, oh my God, Buck where did you come from?" She laughed. Evan winced and got his sore leg out of the way of the excited dog.

"I'm sorry. Buck, you have zero manners," she said with exasperation. She looked at her watch. "Oh, that's the problem. It's past Buck's supper time." She grabbed him by the collar. "C'mon, you big nut." She took him and went to fill the eager dog's bowl.

Evan began to pack up his tools when he noticed he had left a trail of blood on the tile floor. Jill found him trying to bend over to wipe the marks up when she came back to the kitchen.

"Oh no, Evan, I can do that. You don't want to start bleeding again."

"I didn't realize what a mess I made, and I still have to move the old window outside to the dumpster."

"Don't worry about it tonight. Your poor leg."

"Okay, but don't touch anything, there are glass pieces everywhere, I'll be back tomorrow to clean it up. I don't need you or Buck getting cut as well."

She agreed to close the doors to the front room and not go in. Evan left wearing the shorts with his jeans slung over his shoulder. Jill cleaned the floor, then sat in the chair wondering what might have happened if Buck hadn't interrupted them.

The next week was busy for Jill and she hardly ran into Evan. Most nights, she got home late. In the mornings, she was driving away as he was pulling up. The housing market was unusually busy, so Jill wanted to make the most of it. She was still catching up from the time she took off when Brad was sick.

Friday came along and there was a chill in the air. Jill pulled a warmer rain jacket from her closet for the day. There were weather warnings on the news. She looked up at the sky; it was overcast and cloudy. *Good thing I've got a shorter day today.*

Evan was just pulling up and he rolled down his window.

"Hey, you look pretty bundled. I got here a bit early to bring you a coffee." He reached over and pulled a takeout coffee from the holder and passed it through the window.

"Thanks, that was nice. It's so cold, they're forecasting heavy rainfall today." She wrinkled her nose and grimaced. "Hey, how is your leg doing? I've been meaning to ask you all week."

"It's fine. I've had much worse injuries."

"I'm glad it's better. I was thinking about how uncomfortable you must have been those first few days."

"I'm back to wearing jeans again, so it's all good. I'll be doing the mudding in the spare room today. It's coming along well. What've you been doing this week? I was wondering if Buck was living by himself."

She laughed. "I know, he pretty much runs the place. I've had several showings," she held up two fingers, "and two-house sales. It's been a good week for me."

"That's great. I'm happy for you."

"Hey, listen, I'm going to be home early today. Why don't I pick us up something for supper before you leave tonight?"

"Thanks, I'm sure whatever you make will be better than the can of tomato soup I was planning."

Jill was surprised by how much she was looking forward to their meal. All the work she needed to complete was done by mid-afternoon. The weather had become unseasonably cold. She was stunned as snow swirled in fat flakes. What had started as a regular fall day was beginning to look like winter.

On her way home, she stopped at the market and

picked up some steaks, fresh pasta, and pastries for dessert. She selected a red wine and put two in her basket. On impulse, she added a case of beer. Giddy by her success at work, she was ready to celebrate.

The weather was deteriorating by the hour. She was happy she had finished early. The roads were slippery, and the traffic was noticeably slower. She slid into her spot in the driveway with a sigh, realizing she had been tightly gripping the steering wheel.

"Hey Evan, I'm home." she called as she walked in the door. She kicked off her shoes and carried the groceries to the kitchen with Buck trotting closely behind.

There was no reply, but she could hear music blasting from the spare room. He was sanding the walls and hadn't heard her come in.

She tapped on the door and opened it. "Evan?"

He was in goggles and a mask and was covered in white dust. His dark hair looked light gray. He stopped in surprise and pulled off his mask.

"Hey, wow you're early, what time is it?" He smiled.

"I thought I'd better leave work earlier than I had planned. Can you believe it's snowing out there?"

"Snow? What?" Evan walked over to the window covered in plastic. He lifted the corner to see the flakes outside. "What, when did that happen? It was autumn this morning."

"Yes, it hit really hard right after lunch. It was a bugger driving home."

"I'm sure there'll be lots of accidents as everyone relearns how to drive."

She smiled. "I'm going to start dinner. It will be ready in about an hour. Will that be enough for you to finish up?"

"Yes, that'll work." He looked down at his dusty clothes and patted his chest. Puffs of dust floated in the air. "Do you mind if I have a quick shower? This stuff gets everywhere. I don't want to leave it all over your house."

"Yes, no problem. I'll set out a towel in the spare bath. Do you need clean clothes?" She was thinking she still had some of Brad's things.

"Oh no, I'm good. I always keep some extra stuff in the truck."

She went to the kitchen and began unpacking the groceries. It was so cool out that she started the fireplace and clicked on the radio to listen to any news about the storm. Feeling the heat, Buck sidled over to the fireplace and flopped onto the floor, and soon he was snoring. She could hear Evan moving around in the other part of the house and then the shower turn on.

A short while later, he emerged with his damp hair curling around the collar of a blue plaid shirt, which matched his eyes. He grabbed an empty grocery bag for his dirty clothes and put them at the front door.

"Okay, now I am decent again. What can I do to help?"

Jill smiled and put him to work cutting up vegetables.

They kept hearing reports on how bad the storm was and could hear the wind whistle past the patio window.

"Are you sure you're going to be able to make it home in this weather?"

"My truck is pretty reliable, and it's got good tires. It hasn't let me down yet."

It felt comfortable as they worked side by side in the kitchen. Jill kept thinking about how it used to be with Brad. They would do the same thing when they would have friends over.

A popular Keith Urban song came on the radio and Evan surprised her by reaching over and grabbing her hand. He swung her around the kitchen as they danced. She was surprised by how smoothly he moved.

"Fred Astaire, where did you learn to dance like that?" she teased.

He chuckled. "If you ever want to go to a country bar, you'd better know how to dance." He spun her around and she threw her head back and squealed. They danced for two songs and then realized smoke was seeping through the oven vent.

"Oh crap, the food is burning." They parted and rescued the steaks from the oven. They finished preparing the meal together and sat at the table. Just as they poured a glass of wine the lights flickered, and the power went out. The dim light from outdoors kept the room softly lit.

"That was lucky timing," said Evan as he lifted his wine glass to clink Jill's.

"Yeah, supper is going to be delicious. I hope the power isn't out for too long." Jill rose and using light from her cell phone, dug in the cupboards and came back with a couple of candles. She lit one on the counter and one on the table between them.

The candle light flickered as they ate their somewhat burnt, but delicious steak and drank the wine. They laughed and talked about sports, current news issues, and then their families. Feeling more relaxed after a couple of glasses of wine, Jill was emboldened.

"So, Evan." She leaned forward on her hands and gazed into his blue eyes.

He laughed and mimicked her, leaning forward and resting his face on his hands, inches from her face. "Yes, Jill?"

"Why is a good-looking guy like you still single?" she asked, raising her eyebrow.

He grinned and shook his head somewhat embarrassed by the frank question. "Which excuse would you like? I work too much. Women are complicated. My heart has been broken too many times. I'm allergic to cats. I wear the same pair of socks twice. I like those Turkish Delight bars that everyone hates. I love watching The Price is Right. I sometimes eat pickle and Dorito sandwiches..."

"Stop, stop, enough. Too much information." Jill made an expression of mock horror, holding up her hand. "Turkish delight bars? Really Evan? That's a clear deal breaker for sure."

"What about you?" he asked. "It's been a year. Are you planning to date again sometime?"

Jill paused and answered him honestly. "I'm just not sure if I'm ready yet. I feel guilty and scared at the same time. Brad was realistic about what I should do after he was gone. He encouraged me to find someone and not be alone. It's complicated because my heart still aches for what our future should have been."

He raised his glass to her, and they clinked glasses. "To beautiful broken hearts, may they find someone to nurture them back to one piece again." She smiled and nodded.

He pushed his plate back, looked at his watch, and then out the window. "I'll help you with the dishes and then I'd better get going before the storm really socks me in here."

He helped Jill clear the table and fill the dishwasher. The air was electric as they brushed past one another.

"Hopefully the power won't be out for too long. At least you have your natural gas fireplace for warmth but call me if you need anything." He gathered his clothes and tools and she walked him to the door.

"Thanks for the delicious dinner. My stomach feels spoiled by the home cooking."

"My pleasure, I enjoyed the company." She hesitated and then reached out and gave him a quick hug. He was surprised and her soft perfume filled his nostrils. Before he could react, she was already pulling away.

The wind and rain blew in as he opened the door and then slammed it shut. She watched through the window as his head lights lit up and he slowly drove away.

It was now dark in her house, so she used her cell phone as a flashlight to go from room to room turning off light switches. Just as she was digging more candles out of the cupboards in the kitchen, she heard a loud knock on the door.

The sudden noise made her jump and she wondered who could be there at this time of night in the storm. She looked through the side window of her front door, surprised to see Evan had returned.

She quickly swung the door open and he stumbled in. They pushed the door shut as rain flew off his clothes like a wet dog shaking.

"What happened, are you okay?"

"There's a lot of slush out there and I got my truck stuck at the end of the driveway, also the tire is flat. Double whammy. It looks like I need a tow truck."

"Oh my God. Just stay here tonight. It's too cold and with the power out, you can't see anything. The city will be at a standstill in this weather."

"With how things are going, I should probably take you up on that offer. I was thinking about the chances I would have finding a tow truck in this storm."

"Take your jacket off and come back in."

They moved back to the kitchen table, had another glass of wine, and played some games by candle light. Jill was delighted to find out that Evan played chess and realized they were both very competitive.

"Okay, we'll play one more game. The loser cooks breakfast tomorrow. You know my kitchen well enough to know where everything is." Jill smiled as they set up the board for the third round.

"How do you know I can cook?" he asked with a raised eyebrow.

"I saw you prepare the salads tonight, you know how to cook." She winked.

"Deal," said Evan. "I'll have my eggs over-easy please, and my bacon extra crispy."

"Aren't you cocky, we'll see about that."

They played in silence for the next half hour, carefully concentrating on each move as though their lives depended on it.

Jill's eyes grew wide as she saw the perfect move. She picked up her queen and moved it across the board, plunking it down. "Checkmate."

She looked at Evan triumphantly and his mouth gaped. "I totally did not see that move. Okay, you have earned the title of chess champ, you're the winner. What did you say you wanted for breakfast, Rice Krispies or something?"

She threw a napkin at him and they cleaned up the game. She was surprised to see they had drunk most of the two bottles of wine through the evening.

"I'll grab you some blankets. The couch will have to do."

"Sure, it's good, as long as Buck's snoring doesn't keep me awake all night." They laughed as they looked over at Buck having a doggy dream, kicking his feet and letting out a snort.

She brought a quilt and a pillow from the closet to Evan. She handed him the stack and he put it on the couch.

He turned to Jill and in the dim light, she stood still with a soft smile.

"Jill, you are so beautiful, and funny, and smart, and you have a crazy dog." He said quietly and stepped closer to her. "I would like to be the first to know when you are ready to date again."

She moved into his arms, reached up and planted a soft kiss on his lips. He sighed and pulled her into his embrace. *This feels so right*, he thought. She clung to him and they swayed in the darkness, like a slow dance without music.

She kissed him again, then pulled back and stared into his eyes mesmerized by desire. She grasped his hand and led him as they felt their way down the dark hall to her bedroom. She lit a candle on the dresser. It reflected in the mirror and dimly illuminated the room. Without a word, they stood closely regarding one another almost daring the other to make the first move.

She stood facing him and her hand crept to the top of her blouse and she began to undo the buttons. She slid off her pants and stood in front of him in her bra and panties. He looked into her sparkling eyes and she smiled. His clothes fell from his body into a pile around his feet.

She shivered. "Are you okay?" he whispered as he reached to caress her arm.

"Yes, it's damn cold in here with the power out."

"I hear that cuddling may help, you know, sharing body heat."

"Good idea," said Jill in a husky voice.

"Are you ready for this? I don't want to take advantage of this situation." Evan searched her eyes.

"You know, I am not sure I will ever be ready, but I'm feeling really comfortable with you right now. I feel safe."

"I don't want you to do anything you'll regret."

Her reply was to run her fingers through his hair and pull his mouth to hers. Her body tingled and awakened with sensations it hadn't experienced for a while.

Their skin warmed as they embraced, hands running over each other's bodies. Running fingertips against warm skin, gently nibbling and caressing, they discovered each other, nurturing the passion that ignited between them. They clung together in their cocoon, oblivious to the howling wind and storm that raged outside.

She smiled at him in the darkness. "Wow, that was pretty amazing."

He laid his head against her chest, hearing her heart thumping. "It was. Your heart is beating almost as fast as mine." He clasped her hand and held it against his chest.

"I guess they aren't completely broken after all," Jill said quietly. She averted her face, feeling a sense of peace.

Evan enveloped her and they lay tangled together falling asleep in each other's arms, both more content than they had been in a long time.

Chapter Seven

In the stillness of the elevator, Martin's ears perked up to listen, something had woken him from his slumber. He heard sniffling and quiet crying and he shifted to turn to find the source. Leah, curled in fetal position, was whimpering and weeping in her sleep. He poked the bottom of Jill's foot with his to get her attention. She started and then sat up, rubbing her eyes, wondering what was wrong. Martin nodded to Leah with concern. Jill moved to Leah's side and gently shook her shoulder.

"Sweetie, Leah, wake up. You're having a bad dream."

Her wet eyelashes fluttered open and she looked momentarily lost. Realization of where she was quickly registered, and she burst into full gut-wrenching sobs. Jill rubbed her back, holding back her own tears as Leah continued to cry like a wounded animal.

"It's okay, it's okay," Jill repeated like a meditation mantra. "It's just a bad dream, Leah." Slowly Leah's crying waned and became quiet hiccups.

Jill handed her a tissue, and after wiping her face and nose, she was able to speak. "I'm sorry. I had a dream about my friend, Scott. It just makes me so sad. I feel like there must have been some way that I could have protected him, so that he didn't have to die. It hurts so much."

"How could you have protected him?" Martin asked.

"I knew he was in trouble and I could have told someone, but he insisted that he was okay. He was so smart, and he convinced me that he could handle what was happening."

"Handle what?" Jill asked.

"People were after him."

"Why, what happened?"

"I didn't know what was going on. It was so confusing."

#

It was late when Leah arrived at her meeting, so she slipped into a chair at the back of the room. Scott was at the podium speaking. He wasn't acting like his usual self. She couldn't put her finger on it, but something was wrong. Other speakers took the podium, and earlier than usual the meeting was over. She was surprised because her meetings usually lasted an hour and she was barely there when it was already finished.

She talked to a couple of people and went over to Scott. He saw her coming and quickly looked the other way, acting weird and fiddling with his papers. She waited for him to look up and when he didn't, she spoke to him.

"Um, are you okay? You're acting strange."

"I'm fine," he replied but kept his head down.

"Scott, look at me."

Scott slowly raised his gaze to meet Leah's. Standing

closer to him, she could see his eye was purple with a cut over it and his lip was swollen.

"Oh my God, what happened?"

Embarrassed by the attention, Scott said, "Nothing, it was dark. I didn't see them."

"Someone kicks your ass that bad and you can't explain what happened? How can that be?"

"It was dark, and my glasses got knocked off. Some guys jumped me on the way to my car in the school parking lot. They attacked me from behind. I heard footsteps running up behind me, but before I could turn around, I was already tackled to the ground."

"Are you okay? Did you report it to someone?"

"I'll be fine. Just banged up. I didn't report it."

"Why not? They shouldn't get away with this."

"I finally gotten permission to have Pride meetings at school and I don't want the principal to have any reason to cancel them. The meetings have been going so well."

"I don't understand. How is your attack connected to Pride meetings?"

"They were yelling things like 'queer' and 'gay boy' as they were pounding on me. My parents want me to report it too, but I won't. I owe it to the kids coming to the meeting to show them we can't be controlled by them. Stuff like that is what they're afraid of. If I quit, the assholes win."

He acted so strong, but she could see that he was shaken by it all. He said he had had trouble sleeping because of it. They went for coffee after and he moved as if he was really sore, she wondered if he had cracked ribs or something as well. Leah asked if she could do anything and he said no.

#

"He'd been attacked in the school parking lot and I kept harping on him about getting help, but I could see it was upsetting him more than anything. I changed the subject and told him about discovering that my dad was alive.

"Scott was such a good friend. When I told him that I was going to look for my dad, you know what? He was more worried for me." Leah said. "He just got jumped and he was concerned about me finding my dad. I asked him why he was so worried about it and we actually had a good laugh, joking about who my dad would be. I was angry at my mom for lying to me and he was defending her, saying what if my mom doesn't want me to find him because he's a loser or something…"

"He does have a point. You do need to be careful. What if she had a good reason for keeping him from you?" Jill said.

"I was going to find out today. I think he lives in this building. Then the stupid elevator stops." Leah slapped the wall with frustration. "Now, I'm not sure what to think. Is this some kind of warning for me? What if he's a mean drug dealer or something?"

Martin remained quiet as Leah talked about her friend. As she prattled on about him, he felt a terrible gnawing deep in his stomach. He had a feeling they knew the same person. How could he tell her what Scott had been going through? He hadn't known about him getting jumped in the parking lot. A sickness pervaded his soul as he thought of how strong the young man had been.

Beyond the 14th Floor

\#

"Hey, excuse me," a voice called as Martin was sweeping the hall. He turned around to see a young man, someone he recognized, although he couldn't remember his name. It looked like the boy needed something as he waited by a door.

"Yes, what can I do for you?"

"I'm planning a meeting in this classroom in the next hour and the door is locked." He gave the handle a solid rattle.

"Oh okay, just a minute." Martin pulled out a worn paper that was in his shirt pocket and put his glasses on. He scanned the page for a minute and looked up at the classroom number. "I don't have anything on my list."

The boy shifted uncomfortably. "I got permission from the principal's office to use this room for a meeting today. See, I have been passing out leaflets all day." He showed a piece of paper to Martin. It read, 'PRIDE Meeting, Today at 4:30, Room 324.'

"Oh okay, no worries. I just don't have the updated room booking sheet." Martin pulled out a huge key ring of keys and jingled them until he found the key he was looking for. "I've seen you around, but I don't remember your name, son."

"Scott Tatum. I'm in grade twelve this year. This is my second year here."

"What d'ya think of it here?"

"It's good, better than my last school."

Martin swung the door open and helped Scott arrange some of the tables and chairs to prepare for the meeting.

"Yes, this school is 'bout as good as any. I've enjoyed workin' here."

They finished setting up and Martin pulled a hanky out of his pocket and wiped his face.

"Thanks for the help. If this meeting goes well, we may be having them every week in this classroom," explained Scott.

"What is this meetin', school spirit or somethin'?"

"You could kind of say that." Scott paused trying to find the most tactful way to explain to the old man what Pride was. "This is kind of awkward to explain..."

Martin stopped and looked intently at Scott.

"It's a group that can help kids in this school have a community, a place where they can be safe from being judged or bullied because they are gay." Scott waited for Martin's reaction. If he was going to help start this club in the school, this was the type of conversation he was going to have to have to help educate people. "I want everyone to have the same rights and opportunities regardless of their sexual orientation. It's important for people to learn we're not bad, we just want to feel accepted and safe."

Martin shifted his weight and looked at the floor. He felt the need to respond and Scott looked so earnest.

"Well, I'm gonna' be right with you. I don't understand it. Not at all. Not sure if I agree with it either." He shrugged. "But I am a black man in my seventies. I have seen oppression, racism, and segregation—still do sometimes—so in a sense, I may be able to understand how you might feel. But in a different way, of course."

Scott looked relieved. "Thanks, Mr. Sanderson. I

really appreciate that. It's not easy. Sexual orientation isn't a choice. You're born that way. At least, that's how I've always felt."

Martin nodded. "Good luck to you. I will make sure the door is open next week if you need it."

He walked to the door and as he was leaving Scott said to his back, "I left my last school because I got beat up. They found out I was gay before I was prepared to face it. I'm hoping this time I can help others and it will be better for me too."

"I hope so, I hope so." Martin mumbled, but in his heart, he wasn't sure if their school was ready for this either.

He stopped by later to see how things were going and there were a couple of kids in the room with Scott. They sat together in a small circle and Scott was animatedly explaining something. They all laughed and looked relaxed.

The meeting must have gone well enough to warrant another as the room was booked for the next few weeks. Martin saw a few more kids at each one. They weren't hurting anyone, so he was glad for Scott.

Two weeks later, Martin heard a ruckus in the stairwell. He was just closing up and he limped as quickly as his painful hip would let him. It sounded like kids laughing and banging on things. Just as he got down to the next floor, he could see the door at the end of the hall swing shut. A can of spray paint lay on the floor in the middle of the hall.

Martin walked slowly down the hall and bent over to pick up the can. As he rose, he spotted the writing across the wall and door. 'FAGGOTS' was spray painted in red on the door of Room 324, Scott's meeting room. His heart sank.

He went to the supply room to get the special cleaner and he spent an hour scrubbing and buffing the door until it was almost gone. When he stepped back in the light though, he could clearly see what it said, only instead of red paint, it was a white shadow where he rubbed. He would need to get some more paint tomorrow and touch it up. Meanwhile, he hoped no one would notice it.

The next morning, Martin tapped on the office door. "Good mornin', Principal Schmidt. May I have a word with you?"

Principal Schmidt looked up from his desk over the glasses perched on the end of his long nose. "Why yes, good morning, Martin. How are you?"

"I'm good, thanks." Martin stood in the doorway.

"Have a seat, please." Schmidt gestured to the chairs across his large oak desk. "What's troubling you? You're looking pretty serious and it's not even second semester yet." He chuckled.

Martin shook his head. "No, sir. I'll just stand if you don't mind. This hip has bin giving me a lot of trouble lately and harder to sit than to stay standin'."

"That's too bad. You've worked here a long time. Maybe you should consider retirement to enjoy those grandkids of yours."

"No, sir. My house is quiet without Phyllis. Just as soon keep workin' than spend the day in an empty house."

"So, what's your concern today?"

"There were some vandals in the school last night. They spray painted a doorway."

"Really, did you catch them?"

Beyond the 14th Floor

"No, by the time I got down the stairs they were gone. They were hootin' and hollerin', it sounded like a few boys."

"Was it gang activity? What did they spray paint?"

Martin hesitated uncomfortably. "No, sir. I don't think it was gang activity. They wrote the word 'FAGGOTS' across the door."

Principal Schmidt pursed his lips and brought his palms together in front of him, as if he was praying.

"I was worried about this. Was it the Tatum boy's classroom? You know, the one he holds the gay meetings in?"

"Room 324, yes sir."

"I was worried those meetings might invite trouble. There are a lot of people that have strong feelings about those lifestyles." He frowned and shook his head.

"With all due respect, the kids at the meetin's never wreck anythin'. The classroom is always left neat and tidy. I don't mind unlockin' it for them."

"Yes, I know. They aren't the ones that did the graffiti, but they ask for it."

Martin had to bite his tongue. He liked Scott, he was one of the most mature and respectful students in the school. He was surprised to feel anger rising up inside him. The group of kids at those meetings didn't deserve to be punished for someone else's bad behavior.

"Sir, I've mostly cleaned it off. I'll touch it up with some paint today. No one will know it happened. I'll keep a better watch to make sure no one is wanderin' in the halls."

"Okay. We won't report this to the police, but if anything happens again, this group gets shut down."

The bell rang and Principal Schmidt looked at his

watch. "I've got to go. My son is playing a big game today. I'd better make sure the coach has the roster lined up."

Martin dug around in the supply room and found some extra paint and a brush. Students began milling through the hallway and he was almost finished touching up the door when Scott walked up.

"Hey, Mr. Sanderson. What's up?" He noticed the glistening wet paint and could read the outline of the word. Scott's face paled and his jaw tightened. Martin felt terrible. He had hoped to get this fixed before anyone saw it, especially Scott.

"Nothin', just fixin' some paint chips," he said casually, trying to play it off.

"I can see what it says," Scott said through gritted teeth. "When did this happen?"

Martin pulled his hanky out of his back pocket and rubbed the back of his neck. Scott wasn't stupid. "Last night. Kids came into the school while I was closin' up. I just missed seein' who it was. I'm not as fast as I used to be." He tapped the lid back onto the paint can. "Once this dries it won't show anymore. I'm sorry, I shoulda' bin watchin' better."

"It's not your fault." Scott's nostrils flared as he struggled for control. "Some of the kids in this group are finally feeling safe for the first time, and assholes come along and ruin it for everyone."

"Maybe you could switch to a different classroom?"

"Thanks, Mr. Sanderson, but whoever did this is still here. We could meet somewhere else, but the whole point is to show people we are regular, normal kids and we want to be treated fairly. If we run and hide, they win."

"I'll watch betta' from now on."

"I appreciate that, but it isn't your fault. We just have to catch these cowards."

Sadly, it was just the beginning. Martin kept an eye on Scott, and he began to see boys bullying him. Notes on Scott's locker were the same: "FAGGOT LEAVE." He saw Scott get tripped in the hall by a group of guys. They all laughed as Scott picked up the books that had spilled from his arms while other students walked past averting their eyes. No one helped him. Red faced, he defiantly stood and walked away, ignoring the cat calls.

#

Scott hadn't deserved that treatment, but Martin didn't know what he could have done to help him. He broke from his reverie as Leah exclaimed, "My friend said his group had saved lives, and I believe it."

"I do too," said Jill, reaching out and squeezing her hand. "What a brave person he was."

Martin averted his gaze as he quelled his emotions. The group hadn't saved Scott's life. He closed his eyes in anguish and put his face in his hands, saddened at the realization that he probably should have done something to intervene in what had gone on.

Jill abruptly doubled over with her hand covering her mouth, scrambled to grab her purse, and turned to vomit into it. The smell soured the air and Leah brought her hand to cover her mouth, trying to hide her discomfort. Jill panted for a few moments and wiped her mouth on her sleeve.

"Wow, sorry. That was awful, so much for that purse. I need to get something for this morning sickness. This little baby is really making itself known."

"What does your boyfriend think about becoming a dad?" Leah asked. Her voice was muffled through the shirt sleeve still covering her mouth.

"I don't know. It's complicated. I haven't told him yet, that's why I'm here, I was on my way to his apartment to tell him."

"So, he's waiting for you?"

"Sadly not. I was going to surprise him and tell him the news. He's not expecting me. I'm not sure what he'll say, but he's a good guy, so I think it will go well."

She reflected on how things had gone with their relationship. He would be happy, wouldn't he?

Chapter Eight

Banging dishes in the kitchen awoke Jill from her deep slumber. The smell of bacon had wafted down the hall, tempting her taste buds. She slid out of bed and stretched her arms above her head and smiled, hearing more clatter in the kitchen as cupboard doors opened and closed. She pulled on her robe and slippers and looked in the mirror, grimacing at her unkempt reflection. After a quick trip to the bathroom for some mouthwash and hair brushing, Jill pinched her cheeks and nodded with approval at the minor repairs.

Fresh coffee was perking as she made her way to the kitchen. Evan was quietly whistling at the stove with a flipper. Buck was sitting on the floor beside him, hopeful for any dropped morsels. He turned and smiled as she came into the kitchen. His hair was messy, and his plaid shirt was unbuttoned.

She shook her finger at him. "See, I knew you could cook."

"Unfortunately, I would have starved by myself, so I had to learn." He laughed and walked over to toss some bacon into Buck's bowl. Buck was delighted and gulped it down without chewing.

"Oh, I know Buck loves you, but bacon is seriously cheating." Jill rolled her eyes.

"I know, I kinda' play dirty." He winked at her with a devilish grin.

She peered out the patio doors at the remaining snow melting around the yard as water trickled from the downspouts.

"Wild storm last night, but it's already melting, so early to have a freak snow storm. Tomorrow we won't even believe it happened," said Evan.

"Wild is right. Oh, I guess we still have to fix your truck."

"No worries. I was able to get unstuck because there was barely any slush left this morning. Buck and I already changed the tire."

"Wow, that was fast. I can't believe I slept through it all," said Jill, rubbing her eyes and smoothing her hair. Buck ambled over and put a wet paw on her leg. "Good morning, Buck."

Evan smiled and handed a plate to her with bacon and eggs on it. "Here is my part of the lost bet from last night."

They sat at the table and ate breakfast together in companionable silence. Jill got up and refilled their coffee cups. Evan was thinking how pretty she looked in her robe and no makeup. She curled her feet under her as she sat.

"You know, Jill, I am almost finished all the projects here that you needed done. Your spare room is almost ready; just the painting and it will be complete."

"I can't believe I needed so many things done, I sure

appreciate it. My house is feeling more like a home again. I didn't have the energy to repair anything and the house felt so empty before."

Evan grabbed Jill's hand and stroked her fingers with his thumb. She smiled at him tenderly and squeezed his hand in return. "I'm going to be really honest with you, I'm too old to beat around the bush and play games. I really like you a lot. Last night was amazing. I feel relaxed and happy around you and I haven't felt that way about a woman in a long time." His eyes explored hers as he looked into her soul. "I know you said you may not be ready for a relationship, but what we shared last night wasn't just great sex, it meant something to me too."

She reached out for his other hand and they held hands around their coffee mugs on the table. "I can't deny it felt really good. You have an unfair advantage over me. You see my space and my life every day when you come in the front door. My dog loves you." Jill laughed looking down at Buck lying on the floor with his head on Evan's foot. "I was thinking about it and I hardly know anything about you."

"You know lots about me," Evan said.

"I don't know where you live, I don't know much about your family, or even where you went to school."

"But those things don't matter."

"I don't mean it in a bad way. I am just saying I don't want us to move so fast. We haven't even had a first date."

Evan's face clouded with disappointment and he rose to his feet. He began clearing the table and Jill followed him to the sink. She grabbed his wrist and drew him around to face her.

She looked into his eyes. "I'm not saying no. I really like you too. All I am asking is for us to slow this down. Will you give me that?" She kissed his lips, wrapped her arms around his neck, and laid her face against his chest.

He sighed and enveloped her in a hug. He put his lips to her hair and murmured, "I guess I owe you that much."

"Thank you," Jill whispered.

"So, are you giving me permission to take you on a date?"

Jill looked up at him, her blue eyes twinkling. "Yes, Evan Bates. I will happily go on a date with you."

"Great, well, I'd better get going." He gave her a last hug, gathered his things, and walked out the front door.

Later that week, Evan finished painting the spare room. Jill had ordered furniture and had it delivered. It was a new beginning: no more hospital bed, wheelchairs, or marked-up walls. This room had only reminded Jill of the sadness and sickness, now it was transformed into a lovely guest room again.

"This looks so nice, Evan. It's turned out better than I imagined it could have."

"This is the last day for me," he said, packing up his tools and supplies. "Oh, when I was painting the closet, I found some papers that fell to the back of the shelf." He handed them to Jill.

Jill flipped through them. "These are Brad's," she said quietly. She drew in her breath sharply and looked up at Evan in shock. In her hand was a letter that said 'Jill' on the envelope. Without saying a word, she turned and walked out of the room. Evan wanted to give her privacy, so he continued to pack up his tools.

Jill went to the living room and sat on the couch with the letter in her trembling hands. She exhaled and carefully opened the envelope, slipping the folded paper out. She opened it to see Brad's handwriting. It was dated about one month before he died.

'My darling Jill,

I am so lucky to have had you by my side. This has been the most difficult thing to see you deal with. I thought I might beat this, but I am feeling so tired, I don't know if I will. It devastates me to the core to leave you.

When I was first diagnosed, I made arrangements with Dr. Flanigan to save some of my sperm. I was planning to surprise you when I got better. I knew we couldn't try when I was sick.

I never expected that I might not make it. My wish to become a dad probably isn't going to happen, or at least without me around. It will be your decision if you choose to have our baby on your own or choose to destroy the sperm I have saved. You have my blessing for whatever will make you happy. This is all I have ever wanted to be able to give you.

I will always love you.

Brad

Jill was stunned. She *could* have Brad's baby, something they had wanted and hoped for. She sat quietly with the letter in her lap, absorbing the information. Her heart ached for what could have been. Her eyes welled up and she put her face in her hands. She heard a cough in the doorway as Evan cleared his throat. She looked up startled.

"I'm sorry, I don't mean to interrupt. I wanted to return your key." He pulled out his keys and took her house key off the key chain. He handed it to her. "Are you okay?"

"Yes. It's a letter from Brad. It caught me off guard."

Evan acknowledged the information with a silent nod.

"I'm feeling really confused. This is a huge gift… or not." She shrugged. "I'm not sure what to think of it." Her voice broke. "We'd always planned on having kids and, in this letter, he's telling me that he saved some sperm before his treatments. So technically, I still could have Brad's child. I never imagined it would be a possibility after he got sick."

"Whoa, that's big news."

"Yes, it's a surprise. It's really amazing, if I want to go ahead with it."

Evan didn't know what to say and his heart sank. He wasn't sure how this would affect their growing relationship. In fact, this could be a game changer. He was being selfish. "Will you be okay?"

She nodded and wistful smile played on her face as she wiped her eyes.

"I'm going to go now, then. Please call me if you need anything." She listened to his receding footsteps and then the front door close.

The letter brought memories tumbling back to Jill. She closed her eyes and remembered how Brad would burst in the door after work and give her a big hug, the way he would sit with his newspaper and coffee every morning with Buck curled up on his feet, and his never-ending jokes and laughter. Tears streamed down her cheeks faster than she could wipe them away with her hand. Her heart ached for him, yet he was gone.

She folded the letter, put it back into the envelope and took it to her bedroom placing it in the dresser drawer. She turned to see a towel Evan had dropped on the floor, reminding her of their impromptu night together. Guilt clouded her mind as the image of Brad sick in bed flitted briefly through her mind. She crumpled onto her bed filled with complex emotions as she felt happiness floating out of reach.

#

Evan called a few days later. Jill had to admit it was nice to hear his voice. "How are things?"

"Good. How about you?'

"I'm fine, been busy with some new jobs." He paused and tentatively ventured, "Is everything cool between us?"

Jill paused. "Yes, I think so. I don't regret the other night, but I have a lot on my mind."

They talked about their schedules and the final billing for the work he had completed. Their conversation quickly fell into the comfortable cadence they were used to.

"I was wondering, now that I'm no longer an employee of yours, I would like to ask you to go out with me next Saturday—just hanging out, nothing fancy. Would that be okay?"

"Hmm, I think so. What day is that, the sixth? I'll have

to check my calendar, but I think I'm free."

"Great. I'd like to take you and Buck for the day."

"Buck?" She laughed with surprise. "Our first date and Bucky gets to come? Are you dating me for my dog?"

Evan laughed. "Trust me; he may love it more than you even. Wear jeans and running shoes, oh, and definitely bring a jacket."

"Okay. I'm not sure what you've planned for us, but we'll be ready." It didn't sound too serious, especially if Buck was coming along.

The week was long, and the house was empty and quiet. Buck waited at the door every morning, disappointed that Evan hadn't come back. He moped around, almost in the same way he had after Brad died.

"Okay, Buck, I'm missing Evan too," she admitted. She felt torn. It felt so nice to have someone care about her and to not be alone again. But what about the possibility of having Brad's baby? To have a permanent piece of him, to have his child would be amazing, but was she be prepared to do it on her own? She didn't know. How would it feel to be a single parent? How would another man, perhaps Evan, feel about her having her late husband's baby?

Evan picked them up on Saturday morning and handed her a breakfast sandwich and a coffee for the drive. They headed out for the drive to Lake Absegami. Jill had heard of the lake before but had never been to it. She was always caught up in sports or city life.

As they drove along, the sun came out from behind a cloud making the fall leaves gleam with colour. Evan surprised Jill by singing along to some of the songs on the radio.

"Wow, Evan, you're really good. We have to go to a karaoke night somewhere, you'd win!"

He laughed. "No, I would rather die than sing in front of an audience."

They chatted along the way. Evan offered to answer any questions she had about him.

"Anything?"

"Almost," he said, giving her a suspicious look out of the corner of his eye.

"This is an opportunity." She thought for a moment. "Okay, where did you grow up?"

"In New York City, born and raised."

"Siblings?"

"I have two sisters and one brother. My dad is still alive, and you know my mom died of cancer."

"Serious relationships?"

"I dated some during college, but other than my wife, no other serious relationships."

"Pet peeves?"

"Dishonest people, anyone who uses their authority to hurt someone, and telemarketers."

Jill nodded. "I agree. Favourite thing to do on your day off?"

"You're about to find out first hand, so I am not going to spoil the surprise."

"What did you want to be when you grew up?"

"A pro football player, but I was only average, and I got injured at about the time I should have been really serious about it. I think it's every boy's dream at some point."

Soon they arrived at the lake, the blue water glistened,

and the fall trees were bursting with colour. Evan parked and grabbed some water bottles. Buck jumped out and took off down into the lake after some ducks. They chuckled as the ducks easily escaped as Buck wallowed in the water after them. Realizing how futile it was, he circled back to them, as they got ready to walk to the trail head for a hike.

The weather was warm, so they soon found themselves with jackets tied around their waists. Bird songs echoed through the trees and the earthy smell of the forest was invigorating. Buck ran around sniffing everything and bolting off into the trees chasing mystery creatures.

As they walked, Evan reached for Jill's hand. "I'm glad we came today. I wasn't sure what the weather would be like after that crazy September snow storm we had."

"I'm glad too. This is so gorgeous. Why don't people do this more often? It's so rejuvenating."

"I'd like to do this with you again sometime," he said, squeezing her hand.

"Me too." She jumped in surprise and laughed as Buck came crashing out of the trees with a big stick in his mouth. "Of course, Buck too. He hasn't had this much fun in a long time."

After their hike, they made a campfire and cooked hot dogs and made s'mores. Buck reluctantly hopped into the vehicle as they packed up and headed back to reality. Jill hadn't realized she had dozed off in the warm truck until Evan was gently shaking her shoulder.

"Hey, we're home, Sleeping Beauty."

She jumped and rubbed her eyes. "I'm sorry, I can't believe I dozed off. That fresh air was wonderful."

He walked her and Buck to the door. He plucked a leaf from her hair and hugged her. "What did you think of your first date?"

"It was perfect. Our lives are often so busy, we don't stop to appreciate the peace and tranquility nature provides. You've spoiled us both."

"Good, I enjoyed it too. I'll call you this week. I'm doing a couple of jobs out of town, so I'll have a busy schedule for the next while."

"Bye, thanks again." She reached up and kissed his cheek. Evan hugged her and stepped back. He wanted to keep it low key and not pressure Jill. He was still wondering what she was going to do with the letter Brad left for her. It was so personal that he didn't feel he had the right to ask her yet, but it would affect him if she chose to go ahead with having Brad's baby.

She closed the door behind her and collapsed with Buck on the sofa. "Well, Buck, I think he's pretty nice. If I choose Brad's baby, I will probably lose Evan. I wish you could tell me what to do." Buck's put his head on her leg and let out a big sigh.

#

Evan had been away for two weeks. This gave Jill some room to think about Brad's offer. If she had been alone, without caring for Evan, the decision might have been easier. She probably would have made the decision to have Brad's baby. She had always wanted to have a child and her biological clock was ticking. Now, beginning this relationship with Evan, it would be unfair to expect him to be happy about her becoming pregnant with her dead husband's child. She would have to decide soon, to be fair to them both.

They planned to get together again, and this time Jill planned the outing. Until she made her decision, she needed to figure out how she really felt about Evan.

"Since it's my turn, should I pick you up? I haven't even seen where you live."

"You probably won't want to see my crappy little apartment and I would have to clean it." He chuckled.

"Alright, you are getting back to town around 2:00—can you pick me up at about 5:00 on Sunday?" Jill asked. "My place is probably closer to where we're going."

"You bet. I'll be there at 5:00 sharp. What should I be wear, a tuxedo or swimming trunks?" He chuckled.

"Neither. I wanted to take you to my favorite sporting event, which is a major league baseball game. However, the season is over for the year. Instead, I am taking you to my second favorite, an NFL game. Eagles against the Tennessee Titans."

"Okay, sounds fun. I haven't been to a game in a couple of years."

"What? Are you kidding? Are you even American?" she asked in mock horror.

Evan laughed. "I prefer going to games, but mostly just watch them on TV. It will be great to go."

House sales were going strong, so Jill welcomed the day off to go to the game. Evan pulled up to her house early on Sunday. Buck leapt up and jumped continuously at the door hearing the sound of Evan's truck.

Jill laughed and scratched Buck's head. "Hey, big boy,

Beyond the 14th Floor

your favorite visitor is here." Evan came to the door and she was pleased to see he was wearing an Eagles jersey.

Buck jumped all over him, so Evan spent a few minutes throwing toys and roughhousing before he gave Jill his full attention.

She kissed him on the cheek. "Nice jersey. You look very handsome."

He gave her a wry smile. "You aren't being sarcastic, are you? I wasn't supposed to paint letters on my belly or something?"

She laughed. "No, you'll be just fine. Probably should have dyed your hair green though." She gave him a mischievous wink.

"Crap. I guess this will have to do." He grinned and pointed to his dark curls.

They arrived at Lincoln Financial Field and wove their way through the parking lot. Jill loved the atmosphere of the tailgate parties and the rowdy fans drinking and grilling their food. As they finally got to their seats, the crowd's excitement vibrated through the stadium. They were both starving by the time they got settled so they ordered a footlong hotdog to share and a couple of beers.

Jill hooted and hollered throughout the game, cheering on the Eagles. Evan enjoyed seeing a different side of her.

Evan reached over and squeezed Jill's mittened hand. "Thanks for bringing me to the game. It's so different being here than watching it at home on the TV. The energy of the crowd is awesome, this is so much better.."

She agreed. "You just forgot what you were missing." They laughed at the antics of some drunk fans that were seated near them. She looped her arm through his and hugged his arm. "I'm so glad we came."

By about the third quarter the Eagles were losing, and it was beginning to get cold. Jill wasn't feeling very well. Her stomach was churning and feeling worse by the minute. She was afraid she might throw up.

"Hey, are you okay? You are hardly cheering anymore," Evan asked. He nudged her shoulder. "Are you mad because your team is losing?"

"No, I don't feel very well." She put her hand to her stomach and grimaced. "Must be the stadium food."

"Can I get you anything, or would you rather leave?"

"No, I'll be fine"

After a while, it became clear she wasn't feeling any better. In fact, she was feeling much worse. Evan sensed her discomfort and leaned over to her ear.

"I think we should go, Jill. You aren't even having fun anymore."

"You're probably right. The bonus part is if we leave right now, we won't have to battle the traffic leaving the game." She reluctantly agreed but was relieved at his insistence. She really wanted to be still and lying down.

He put his arm protectively around her and led her through the crowd. He insisted she wait at the entrance on a bench with bottle of water and an empty popcorn bucket while he ran and got the vehicle.

He packed her into the truck, and she nestled into the passenger seat. The next thing she knew, Evan was shaking her shoulder to wake her up again. She opened her eyes to see they had arrived home.

"Oh my, this is ridiculous. Every time you take me out, I fall asleep on you."

"No worries, Sleeping Beauty." He helped her to her door and came in with her. "Are you okay?" He warded off Buck's excited greeting.

A strange look came over Jill's pale face, her hand flew up to her mouth and she pushed past Evan and ran down the hall to the bathroom. He could hear her getting sick to her stomach and he cringed and gave Buck a pat. "That doesn't sound good, hey Buck?"

After about ten minutes, a Jill emerged from the bathroom. Her mascara was smeared, and her hair was tousled. "I don't think I'll be having another hotdog for a while."

"No doubt," Evan agreed. "They go down easy but come back with a vengeance. Can I get you something?"

"A drink of water, please."

Evan put her on the couch with a blanket, let Buck out in the back yard, and brought her a glass of water.

He sat down beside her and put his arm around her, but she shrank away from him. "I'm sorry, I feel so gross." Her eyes watered. "I threw up in my hair…"

He chuckled softly. "Aw, you poor thing. You really got worked over." Despite her declaration, he tucked her under his arm, and she snuggled against him. "Would you like me to stay?"

"No, you don't have to. I'm actually feeling a lot better. I just need to have a shower and go to bed." Her hair hung in a few wisps around her flushed face, and Evan felt his heart flip in his chest as he suddenly realized how much he cared that she wasn't feeling well. "I'm so sorry I ruined the game for you."

"No, no, you didn't. I really had a good time. Our team wasn't winning anyway. This just means that we'll have to go back to another one." Evan stroked her hair and talked about the work projects he had coming up. Soon he wondered why Jill had gone so quiet. He craned his neck to see her face, eyes closed and mouth slightly open. Sleeping Beauty.

He gave her a gentle kiss on the top of her head before carefully removing his arm. She softly moaned in her sleep. He covered her, let Buck in, and quietly let himself out.

Jill was mortified when she woke up about an hour later to realize that Evan had left. She was embarrassed that she had gotten sick, some date she had been. What was the matter with her? She was happier than she had been for a long time, but she was feeling so out-of-sorts.

A realization struck her as she sat up and fumbled for her phone and pulled the calendar up on the screen. She counted with her finger and then counted again. Her eyes widened and the phone fell into her lap. Her period had been really late. *Oh my God. Maybe I'm pregnant!*

Pregnant. An old test in the back of the medicine chest confirmed her symptoms. She sat on the toilet in her bathrobe staring at the positive sign on the stick. It explained why she was feeling so tired and nauseated lately. Buck whined and scratched at the door, impatient she was taking so long.

Wasn't this something she had wanted for a long time? It was the one thing Brad had wanted and together they couldn't make it happen. She wanted to be a mom, but not like this. She really liked Evan, perhaps even loved him. This was just too soon in their fledgling relationship. She thought of Brad's letter. She could have planned to have his baby. She had carefully considered it but was almost certain that she wouldn't. Now she was pregnant with Evan's baby, so that pretty much decided things.

Meanwhile, Evan had texted a couple of times to see how she was feeling. "Much better," she texted back. She had to confirm her result with her doctor before she tipped over the apple cart.

#

"Good morning, Jill. How are you today?" asked Doctor Flanigan as he peered over his glasses, smiling. He patted her arm. "You look well. I know you've had a difficult year," he added.

She felt a twinge of guilt. *I'm great, already knocked up by another guy.*

"I'm doing well. I think I may have an awkward situation on my hands." She looked down at her lap and fidgeted like a nervous school girl. "I think I'm pregnant. We only had sex once." After all the infertility problems with Brad, she felt embarrassed she hadn't been more careful.

"That's all it takes sometimes," said Doctor Flanigan, laughing and patting her shoulder. "I imagine you didn't expect it would come so easy. Let's get a urine sample and we'll know for sure."

Jill nervously waited in the exam room and Doctor Flanigan returned.

"The pregnancy test is positive. Congratulations.

Statistically speaking, 45% of all pregnancies aren't planned, if that makes you feel any better."

"I have no idea what will happen with this relationship, but I will definitely be keeping the baby." She knew that fact from the moment she thought she might be pregnant.

She arranged an appointment for an ultrasound but knew by the dates she was about two months along. She often had irregular periods, which was why she hadn't even realized sooner. It seemed ironic that for several years she didn't use any birth control with Brad because they would have been happy to become pregnant, although they only really began to try in earnest the year before Brad's diagnosis.

Brad. She wished she could have given this to him. Evan, the man who helped her come back to life. The man she was just really beginning to care about, maybe even love. He was really special to her. She wondered if their fragile new beginning could handle big news like this.

Evan was out of town on a project for the next two weeks. This gave Jill some time to think about how she would tell him. She could see him being a good dad. He was funny and sweet. He was caring toward Buck, a great carpenter, and a good cook. She could definitely see a future with him. Could Evan see the same thing with her?

She looked at the invoices he had given her for the work he had done. The plumbing items had the address of Bates Plumbing, but the carpentry work listed an apartment address with his business number. She didn't know how to approach it, but she decided it may be best to tell him in person and on his turf.

She would go to his apartment and tell him, and then she would leave to let him think about it. She was curious about that part of his life anyway. She wanted to see where he lived.

Evan arrived back in town on Tuesday night and called Jill. They talked for a while about what they had done that week. The conversation was easy, and Jill felt more relaxed.

"So, when am I going to see your bachelor pad?" she asked.

"You can see it any time you want. You just aren't allowed to judge my housekeeping skills."

"I'm a realtor; I'm sure I've seen worse. I may stop by and surprise you sometime." she warned.

"I would love that." He laughed. "But meanwhile, why don't I take you to a movie on Friday night? You pick, I am at your mercy. *Titanic, Notebook*—whatever chick flick or movie you'd like to see."

"Deal."

Jill didn't let him off the hook and selected *A Star is Born*. True to his offer, he agreed to go. She was so moved by the movie and with her wild hormones, she wiped away tears a couple of times. Evan smiled, put his arm around her hugging her tighter to him.

Jill was quiet on the way home in deep thought over the circumstances Evan was unknowingly involved in.

"What did you think of the movie?" Evan asked.

"I liked it. It's was amazing, like being at a concert. I knew that the main character was going to die, but I couldn't keep from bawling when he did." She teared up again.

"Awww, you have such a tender heart. I love that about

you." He clasped her hand caressing the back of it with his thumb. "It was a good movie."

They pulled into the driveway and he walked Jill to the door. As usual, Buck was jumping out of his skin at the sound of Evan's truck in the driveway. He bounced all around and Evan threw his jacket to the side and wrestled with him and threw his ball a few times.

"Okay, okay. Wow, buddy. Does your mama not pay enough attention to you anymore?"

They had a cup of tea at the kitchen table and Evan reached over and intertwined his fingers with Jill's. He gently pulled her toward him across the table and their lips met. They kissed with raw intensity. Since their first night together, they had been respectful of Jill's wish to slow things down to get to know one another, but now passion ruled their actions.

He bent down and picked her up in his arms and carried her to the bedroom. He laid her down and they tore each other's clothes off. Jill pulled his shirt and a button popped off, clattering across the floor.

"Oops!" Evan smirked in reply.

Her hands ran up and down his lean body and came to rest on his injured leg. You could still see a red scar in the dim light. She traced it with her fingers, and he groaned at the closeness of her hand to his manhood.

With desire smoldering in his blue eyes, he reached for her. Her eyes met his and she gave him a devilish smirk and grabbed his wrist and in one quick movement, she pulled herself up to straddle his lean body.

She pulled both of his arms above his head and pinned

him to the bed. She leaned forward and kissed him deeply, her tousled hair tickling his face. The scent of his aftershave filled her nostrils and she traced the line along his jawline with kisses until she found his ear. She nibbled his earlobe and her tongue darted into his ear as he groaned with pleasure.

"Woman, you're driving me mad."

Emotion and tenderness drove their passion as they released themselves to one another without the tentativeness of their first encounter. They lay on the bed after sharing a quiet peacefulness.

He reached down and grabbed her hand, then drew it to his lips and gently kissed her knuckles.

"Jill, I think I am falling in love with you."

She smiled and pulled him closer to kiss his forehead. "I love you too," she said. "Almost as much as Buck."

"That must be a lot then." He laughed.

"Evan, I have something to tell you..."

His face grew serious as he looked in her eyes. "What, Babe?"

Jill lost her nerve. This moment was so wonderful, she didn't want it to end. "I'm... I'm scared. This is a big step for me."

"Me too. I never thought I could feel this way for anyone ever again." He wrapped her in his arms. "We don't have to rush anything. We'll take this day by day, as slowly as we need to."

Jill smiled and snuggled into his embrace, enjoying the security of the moment. She didn't want to lose him.

They lay in bed until Evan looked at his watch.

"Oh my God. I've got a really early morning tomorrow. I promised my pop I'd give him a hand, I need to get going."

Evan got dressed and Jill slipped on her bathrobe to walk him to the door.

He observed her with her messy hair in her bathrobe and pulled her into an embrace. "I don't want to leave, I just want to stay in bed with you all day," he said with a hungry growl.

She laughed giving him a lingering kiss and then they reluctantly split apart from one another.

"I'm not sure what time I'll get home tomorrow. Maybe we can get together in the evening, or Sunday."

"That sounds wonderful. Goodnight."

Evan gave tousled Buck's fur and patted his back, with Buck's tail slapping the wall. Jill closed the door behind Evan and leaned against it looking at Buck.

"I know I should have told him. I just couldn't yet. I don't want to risk losing what we have already." Buck tilted his head and looked at her quizzically. "Yes, that's exactly how I feel. Confused."

She tossed and turned all night feeling guilty she hadn't told Evan. She got up early because her nausea had returned. She had a cup of peppermint tea and some crackers and rested on the couch until the feeling passed. Buck pranced around her and kept whining. She got dressed in her sweats and a warm sweater and got Buck's leash.

"Okay, I know. It's time for a walk, isn't it?"

He got excited when he heard the magic word and began racing in circles around her, barking. Jill quickly laced her running shoes and walked to the front door. She was pulling on her jacket when she noticed something on the floor. It was a wallet. She was confused for a moment, before remembering Evan had thrown his jacket down to play with Buck the night before. His wallet must have fallen out.

She picked up the worn brown leather wallet and opened it. Evan's driver's license stared back at her. She smiled and ran her finger over his picture. *How does he manage to have an attractive driver's license picture?*

She set the wallet on the kitchen counter and took Buck for a big walk down the road. When she got back, she gave him a bowl of water and spotted the wallet again. *Hmm, I think I know what I'm going to do with that.*

Chapter Nine

Martin slept fitfully. He struggled with the decision to tell Leah and Jill what happened at the school. He had pains he had never felt before and he was honestly concerned about getting out of the elevator alive. Although his head felt foggy, his memory of the incident came back to him with great clarity.

Martin was closing up classrooms and cleaning on that Tuesday night. Volleyball practice had ended, and he had begun sweeping the gym floor. His hip had been hurting really bad. Glancing at his watch, he was glad to see he would be going home soon.

He pulled the room schedule out of his pocket to see which classrooms he had to close. He took stock, nodded to himself, and shoved the paper into his back pocket. Starting at the top floor and with his big, jingling bunch of keys, he locked a couple of rooms and checked doors.

He thought he'd heard a noise and stood quietly for a moment, listening. Nothing. Just as he began to limp down the hall, he heard it again. Someone was banging on the lockers and yelling. As fast as his hip would let him, he hustled, painfully making his way down the stairwell.

There they were, four guys. They were fighting. His eyes adjusted from the dark stairwell to see down the hall. Wait, no, it was three guys beating a fourth one up.

He started down the hall. Anger welled up inside him. "STOP," he yelled.

One of the boys turned to look at him. He met Martin's eyes and turned back to the boy he was beating. It was Principal Schmidt's son, Sebastian. He had a boy by the front of his shirt pinned against the wall. He pulled his fist back and Martin shouted again, "No, stop!"

His fist rocketed forward and slammed into the other boy's face. The boy's glasses flew off and his head hit the wall. Blood flew and Sebastian released the boy and shouted, "C'mon, let's go." The group ran in the opposite direction as the boy collapsed down the wall and slumped to the floor in a heap.

Martin headed down the hall as fast as his bad hip would allow. He got to the boy and managed to get down on the floor beside him. Badly hurt and covered in blood, the boy groaned and opened his eyes. Martin paused for a moment, a jolt went through him as he recognized the boy. It was Scott. He gingerly shifted Scott onto his back on the floor. Martin pulled off his vest and gently lifted Scott's head to tuck it under. When Martin pulled his hands back, they were covered in blood. He was afraid for Scott.

"Scott, son, you'll be okay. Just take it easy. I'm gonna' get you help." He was in bad shape. Martin frantically looked down the hall for someone to assist. There was a person standing in the far stairwell in a green jacket. Martin

Beyond the 14th Floor

looked down at Scott and looked back up to yell to the person for help, but the person was gone.

Blood was running from Scott's head and pooling on the floor around him. Martin made his way to the closest classroom and fumbled with his keys to open the door. He grabbed the phone on the wall and dialed 911. His heart was pounding.

An operator assured Martin that help was being dispatched and he returned to Scott's side. "Scott, hey Scott. It's Martin. Mr. Sanderson. I'm here, I'm with you." He held the boy's hand. Scott was unable to talk so he just squeezed Martin's hand in reply.

"Hey son, help is on its way. You're gonna' be okay." Martin's face was creased with worry. Scott's bloodied features made him almost unrecognizable. All the boy was able to do was groan and whimper. He was barely moving.

Soon, Martin heard noises. He was relieved to see the police and then paramedics moving down the hall toward them with a stretcher. Martin gave another squeeze and withdrew his hand as he slowly rose and stood back to allow them to attend to Scott.

The paramedic crouched next to Scott with her bag. She leaned in closely and shone a small flashlight into his eyes as she lifted each eyelid. One of the police officers took Martin aside to ask him questions. One of the other officers snapped pictures of the blood on the wall and the smears of blood that had made a macabre pattern on the floor.

By the time Martin's attention had turned back to Scott, he was on a back board wearing a neck brace. They were loading him onto the gurney. Martin followed them down to the door.

The police thanked Martin and handed him a business card. "We will need to talk to you again, Mr. Sanderson. If you have any questions, or remember anything else, just give us a call." Martin nodded and slipped the card into his chest pocket.

Sadness and anger filled his heart as he trudged back up to the third floor. He viewed the mess of empty packages and wrappers the paramedics had dropped on the floor. One of the gurney wheels had run through the blood, making a tire tread line for about five feet down the hall. His work vest was covered in blood, so he carefully slipped it into a clear garbage bag to take home and wash. One of Scott's shoes lay on the floor against the wall, missed in the commotion. Martin picked it up and cradled it to his chest. He took it to the janitor's closet and put it on a shelf, planning to give it back to Scott when he returned to school.

His exhaustion was palpable and caused him to lag as he went to the closet to fill his mop pail with hot water and cleaner. At first, the blood smeared across the floor, but after several passes with the mop, the worn tiles were clean once again. He poured the pink water down the drain and rinsed out the pail. All that trauma washed away with water. If it were only that easy, he knew it wouldn't be that easy for Scott.

When he got home, he made a cup of Earl Grey tea and eased into his chair. He dropped his bloodied vest into the washer and turned it on. While he was physically drained, his mind raced. Slouched in the dim light, he replayed the events in his mind. He was sure it was Sebastian, Principal Schmidt's son, that he saw. The other boys looked somewhat familiar, but he hadn't seen them hit Scott. It was such a racket in the hall and the commotion certainly would have drawn attention. Who had he seen at the end of the hall? It looked like an adult male in the shadows, but just a glimpse and then he was gone. The only detail he could really remember was the green jacket.

He told the police a lot of what happened, but he couldn't bring himself to reveal that he had seen Sebastian. Scott would have seen them all and would tell the police what had happened. It was clear those boys were in the wrong, but he couldn't afford to implicate the principal's son. He had to work for him after, that would be really difficult. Usually Principal Schmidt was fair, but he had seen people in trouble for less.

Martin was a proud man and he couldn't afford to lose his job. He didn't have much tucked away for retirement. He certainly didn't want to be a burden for his daughter. She had worked so hard for what she had. Plus, he probably was going to need hip surgery. He shifted gingerly in his chair and reached for the bottle of pain reliever he kept nearby.

He wouldn't have to say anything about the boys. He would just tell the police about finding Scott and calling for help. He didn't want to get in trouble over this. That was his plan. He sure hoped Sebastian and his thugs got punished for the assault. Did they think they could get away with it?

That poor boy. Sleep escaped Martin as his mind wouldn't shut off. All he could see over and over was Scott's bloody face.

Melaney Bossaer

\#

The trio had managed to sleep for a short time in the cramped quarters of the hot elevator. All of their cell phones had died hours ago. They stirred and one by one, stretched, and sat up.

Jill looked at her watch and grimaced.

"Hey," she said. "Did you both manage to get some shut eye? It's 6:00 am. Hopefully, we shouldn't be here too much longer. Work crews will have better luck getting things going in the daylight, for sure." She tried to sound encouraging.

Martin groaned and Leah rubbed her eyes, making little black mascara smears on her face.

"I feel like I didn't sleep at all, but I must have." Leah stretched her arms up in the air and bent from side to side.

"I musta' slept, but my bones ache and I feel terrible," Martin grumbled. He positioned himself against the wall. "I'm sorry I'm not very peppy. You've both bin very good company durin' this ordeal."

"That's okay. None of us wants to be here. We're all miserable."

Martin had been struggling to sit but after much effort, he straightened up. The food and drinks had long run out and his mouth was parched.

"I don't wanna' scare you or sound dramatic," he croaked, "but I just hafta' tell you somethin' important, so that justice is served. In case somethin' happens to me in here and I don't get out." He looked sickly and weak in the dim light.

"We'll be out soon," Jill said, trying to sound upbeat. "I

Beyond the 14th Floor

know we're all feeling pretty hopeless." Deep down, worry was growing, Martin wasn't looking very well.

"Thanks, Jill. I know you're bein' kind. I needta' get this off my chest and tell someone, if you're willin' to listen?"

They both nodded.

"I bin sittin' here all these hours tryna' sort this out in my head. It's about your friend, the one that died. It seems crazy, but I was wonderin', Leah, if we knew the same boy." He paused and cleared his throat.

"You knew Scott Tatum, my friend?" It was clear that they were talking about the same person by Martin's face.

Martin nodded. "Yes, I knew Scott too. It's kinda' unbelievable, you and me in this elevator in this big city and we know the same person."

"I can't believe it either." She shook her head and Leah teared up. "He was such a special person. He inspired me so much." She pulled a tissue from her bag and blew her nose. "How did you know him?"

Martin cleared his throat and groaned as he shifted himself to get more comfortable. "I work at his school. I knew him because I opened the classroom for his meetin's. He was a fine boy, respectful and kind. I didna' care about the meetin's he was runnin'. He seemed to help other kids, so how can you fault someone for that?" He licked his dry lips and went on. "He got targeted for being different and was picked on. I see a lot when no one knows I'm there. I saw him the night he got beat so badly. I seen who did it." He looked at Leah, shook his head, and rested his face in his hands.

"What? You know who killed Scott? Do the police

know? They murdered him." Leah's questions flew at Martin and he deflected them with his wrinkled, worn hand. When she finally paused, he picked his words carefully.

"The principal's son, Sebastian, punched him. Real hard. Scott's head hit the wall and he fell to the floor." Martin's voice became hoarse. "That poor boy."

"And he died?" Jill asked quietly.

"No, not then. He died two days later in the hospital." Martin put his head in his hands again and let out a sob. Tears rolled down Leah's cheeks. No one spoke and Jill rubbed Leah's leg.

Martin collected himself and pulled a wrinkled hanky from his pocket and blew his nose. "I made a big mistake. "

"What could you have done wrong? You didn't kill Scott," said Jill.

"I lied to the police. I said I didn't see who did it."

"Why, Martin? Why wouldn't you tell them who killed Scott?" Leah's voice was shrill.

"I thought he would get better and be able to tell them. He saw who it was that attacked him. I thought he would be able to tell, and then he died. I can't believe he died." Martin's voice was weak as it trailed off.

"Why couldn't you tell them?"

"It's complicated. I lied to the police about not seein' anyone. That night, there was another person at the end of the hall. I'm sure they saw what happened too. They never came forward, someone wearin' a green jacket."

"Couldn't they ask around the school if anyone saw anything? Maybe that person doesn't know what happened," Jill said.

"I had hoped that too. I prayed and prayed. The day after the attack, I was leavin' for the night and I saw the principal loadin' some things in his car. I grabbed a box to help him. When I put the box in the trunk, I saw the jacket."

"The green jacket?" Jill asked.

Leah let out an incredulous gasp. "It was the principal in the hallway that night and he saw his son beating Scott?"

Martin looked down and nodded. "I'm thinkin' so."

"Oh my God, and he did nothing," Jill whispered. She put her hand to her mouth.

"Why can't you tell now?" asked Leah.

"I don't know what to do. It looks really bad because I lied and if I come forward now, they probably won't believe me." Martin looked at them with tears in his eyes. "I need my job."

"Surely they would listen."

Martin looked at Leah his voice was calm, but his eyes were flashing. "Leah, I am an old, uneducated black man that grew up in Harlem. He is the principal and his son is captain of the football team. Who would you believe?"

It was hard to dispute, and silence was their answer.

"I shouldn'a said anythin' here. There ain't nothin' anyone can do. I just needed to ease my conscience some, I guess."

The condensation trickled down the walls as the temperature rose in the stifling elevator.

Whether it was so, Martin felt a shift in the elevator. Jill and Leah couldn't understand why he didn't just go forward with the truth. It just wasn't that easy.

#

At school the morning after the assault on Scott, it was business as usual, with students horsing around in the halls. He had been struggling, watching the clock to find the best time to talk with Principal Schmidt about the incident. This dilemma resolved itself as a page came over the intercom. "Mr. Sanderson, please report to the office. Mr. Sanderson, please report to the office." *Okay, here it goes.*

He put his janitorial cart in one of the rooms and made his way, with resignation, down to the office. He could see two police officers in the office, talking with Principal Schmidt.

"Hi Martin," said Betty, the secretary. "I guess there was an incident here last night with a student getting hurt." She looked over her shoulder at the police officers in the principal's office. She leaned closer and whispered, "Must be serious. We don't usually get police here."

"Yes, I was the one who called the ambulance. A boy got beat up really bad last night," said Martin, taking a seat. Betty was just going to ask more questions when the office door opened. She quickly looked down at her keyboard and began typing.

"Martin," said Principal Schmidt. "I guess we had something go on here last night. These police officers have some questions for you. I was surprised that I am only hearing about it this morning."

"Sir, I didn't really see anything. I just found the boy. Scott, Scott Tatum. I called for help right away," Martin explained. He didn't want to be in trouble. "I cleaned up the mess after," he offered.

"Come in to my office. The police want to ask about

what you may have seen. I told them the same thing, that you probably hadn't seen anything." Martin wasn't sure what he was picking up in Principal Schmidt's voice, but he understood that he'd better play along.

The officers again questioned Martin. He told them that he heard the noise and came into the hallway where he found Scott all alone, bleeding on the floor. Then he called for help. "Could we get you to write out a statement about what happened?" Martin nodded and sat for a few minutes scratching down the details as best he could put together, still without revealing the perpetrator.

He signed the form and handed it back to the officer. "How's the boy?"

"He sustained a serious head injury. He's in City Hospital. We haven't been able to talk to him. It's a good thing you found him right away, or he might not have made it." The blood drained from Martin's face and he felt cold. *Poor Scott.*

"If you think of anything else or remember something, just give me a call." One of the officers extended his hand with a card. Martin reached for it with his worn fingers and nodded.

"That should be all, Martin. Thanks." Principal Schmidt nodded to the door. Martin walked out past Betty, who perked up and looked at him expectantly, waiting to hear the details. He could see her disappointment as he gave her a nod and continued past her and out the door.

The students were in class, so the halls were empty. His step had quickened as eagerness propelled him. He barely noticed his grinding hip as he arrived at the landing of the third floor. He pulled out his huge ring of keys and jingled through them until he found the right one. He opened the janitor's closet and stepped inside.

He looked up onto the shelf where the Nike running shoe sat. He pulled it down, sat on the bench, and looked at it. He hadn't noticed last night with all the excitement, but there was blood on the top of the shoe and a smear on the side.

He wasn't sure why he hadn't mentioned it. The police hadn't noticed the cast-off shoe, so maybe it wasn't important. He carefully replaced it on the shelf and moved a cleaning bottle in front of it.

As the day wore on, Martin's body vibrated with restlessness. He had to know whether Scott would be okay. By the day's end, some of the pressure had eased as Martin devised a plan of action. Luckily, volleyball practice was cancelled, so he didn't have to hang around to close up, which further added to his relief.

Martin took a city bus to the hospital. He was relieved to see the stop was close by, so he only had to limp for a block. At the front door, he was grateful to see a bench and he sat to catch his breath. Once he had collected himself, he went inside and approached the reception desk.

"Hello, may I help you?" A middle aged, thin woman with a bad perm looked at him over her glasses. Her strong perfume wafted to his nostrils as he glanced with silent amusement at a nearby sign indicating the hospital was a scent-free zone.

"Yes, I am coming to visit someone. I need the room number for Scott Tatum, please," Martin said.

"Okay, let me see." The woman looked down and tapped the keys of her computer. Shook her head and typed some more. She looked puzzled, then her face brightened. "Okay, I found him. I'm sorry, sir, he is in ICU. Only family is allowed to visit and only two at a time." Martin was surprised to hear Scott was in ICU. *He must be in real bad shape*.

She pulled her glasses down on her nose and peered over them. "Are you family?"

His heart stopped momentarily, then he quickly blurted out, "Yes, I'm his grandpa."

The woman gave him a suspicious look, pushed her glasses up, and reached for a piece of scrap paper. She scrawled a number on it, smiled, and handed it to him, "Second floor, west wing. I'll be hoping for a speedy recover for him and I'll send some prayers for your grandson and your family."

Martin thanked the woman and clutched the paper in his hand. He tried to nonchalantly walk away as fast as his bad hip would carry him. He took the elevator to the second floor. When he arrived at the ICU, he could see the medical staff going through a shift change. They were gathered in little clusters reviewing patients' charts. He could see through the door they were at the end of the room deep in conversation.

He squinted and read the names on the nursing station chart that were on the wall. Scott Tatum was in bed six. He could see the doorway to bed six was slightly ajar. He took a deep breath and quietly walked in, casting a side glance at the staff. No one looked up. He peeked into the room. He could see a figure in the bed with tubes and monitors, but no visitors. *Good, this wouldn't take long.*

He slowly approached the side of the bed. Despite the tubes and wires, he could see it was definitely a teenage boy. There was heavy gauze wrapped around the patient's head and one eye swollen shut. Martin noticed the name plate above the bed confirming it was Scott.

Martin leaned over to the boy and gingerly put his hand on Scott's shoulder. "Hey, son. It's me Martin, I mean Mr. Sanderson." He was so nervous and looked back over his shoulder, but no one had come.

Scott's one eye flickered open. He looked at Martin and did a slight nod. Martin felt he had recognized him. Scott tried to speak but his swollen lip barely moved with the effort.

"No, son, it's okay. Don't talk. I just wanted to see if you were okay. Did you see who did this to you?"

Scott's eye watered as he tried to keep looking at Martin. Martin felt bad doing this so soon instead of waiting for Scott to recover more. He just had to be sure Scott could let them know who had done this to him. He gave another almost imperceptible nod. *Good, those punks won't get away with this then.*

Martin stood for a moment then reached and gently patted Scott's shoulder. "Son, you take care. You'll get through this and be back at school in no time." Scott blinked and then his eye slowly closed. *Must be on some heavy painkillers, he's really out of it.* "Bye, Scott."

Martin peeked around the corner of the door and slipped back out into the hall. *Whew.* He exhaled without realizing that he had been holding his breath. *At least those punks will pay for it. Scott can tell the police who had beaten him.* Martin wouldn't have to get involved.

The next few days went as usual. He had seen Sebastian Schmidt in the halls but never ran into him directly. He wondered what kind of punishment he and the other boys would get for assaulting Scott.

He walked into the office on the Friday morning to get the schedule. He whistled softly as he checked his mailbox, which was filled with announcements and staff mail. He turned to leave when he noticed Betty was sitting at her desk dabbing her eyes and sniffling. "Betty, what's wrong?" She shook her head and a few more tears squeezed out. She caught her breath, clutching a crumpled tissue to her chin

"Martin, that poor boy, Scott Tatum, you know, the one that got beat up on Tuesday night." Martin's blood ran cold. "He died."

Martin felt the room go white and quiet and he stumbled to grab the counter. He steadied himself, his mind clouded with disbelief. "When?" he croaked.

"I guess last night. His family called this morning. They are obviously upset. They want to know who did this to Scott. They're calling it murder." Betty blew her nose loudly and sniffled.

"Don't they know who did it?" asked Martin incredulously.

"No, that poor boy never revived enough to tell them."

#

"Leah, I'm so sorry. I made a huge mistake. I really liked Scott too. I felt really awful 'bout what happened to him.

He didn't deserve it. Not at all."

Leah's face softened. "It was the worst night of my life, finding out about Scott."

She texted with Scott frequently. They chatted about school and how hard Leah had found it before finding the support group. She was determined to get through her last year. To Leah, she was still an outcast, but the kids that had bullied her had since found other targets, so they left her alone. Stephanie transferred to a different school, so she didn't even see her anymore. Scott kept her motivated and had been a good friend.

It had been a couple of weeks since Leah had been at the Gay Alliance meeting. She went to the meeting early. She had wondered why she hadn't heard from Scott all week. It was odd; she had even phoned and there was no answer. She was worried about all sorts of things. Had she said something wrong? She looked through all of their texts and didn't find anything that would have made him angry with her.

As people arrived, several were crying, and Leah had no idea what had happened. A guy sat beside her and leaned over to ask, "What's going on, why is everyone so upset?"

She looked at him and just shook her head. She had no idea. When she had a chance, she would ask Scott. He would know.

She carefully scanned the room as it filled, still not seeing any sign of Scott. One of the usual presenters took the podium and cleared his throat. His eyes looked red and puffy. *This must be pretty bad.*

"This is really difficult for me to say." His face contorted and he paused for a moment. "We have lost a very special person. Scott Tatum was beaten up at school last week. They took him to the hospital with a bleed on his brain. His parents confirmed he died on Thursday night. It is difficult to understand who would have done this to Scott and we hope they find the pathetic criminals responsible." He wiped tears with the back of his hand and kept talking about a funeral service.

Leah's body went cold, and she felt dizzy. She jumped up and pushed past other people who were also in stunned shock. She ran out onto the street, collapsing onto a nearby bench. She let out choking sobs. Scott was so kind. All he wanted to do was help other people, even if it meant making himself a target. How could this happen?

She couldn't bother with the bus, so she zipped her jacket and slowly walked the streets across town to her neighborhood. Some people she passed asked if she needed help as tears freely flowed down her cheeks. She resolutely shook her head and kept walking.

She got home around 10:30 pm, which was late for her on meeting nights. She was disappointed to see the kitchen lights on. She didn't have the strength for a confrontation with her mother.

She quietly let herself in and her mom called to her from the living room.

"Leah, is that you? Why are you so late? I was getting worried." Her mother was sitting in a chair reading. She looked up as Leah entered the living room. When she saw her puffy, red eyes and tear-streaked face, she jumped to her feet and took her by the shoulders. "Leah, what's wrong? Why are you so upset? Are you okay?" Lydia pulled Leah into her embrace, hugging her.

Leah sagged against her and cried like she never had before. They stood and rocked together until Leah's sobbing became sniffles and the odd hiccup. Her mother wiped tears from her own face. She grabbed Leah's hand and led her over to the couch.

"What's wrong, honey? I've never seen you so upset."

"I just found out a friend of mine died." She managed to squeak out. Her voice sounded so small.

Her mother grabbed her hands and rubbed her arms. "Oh honey, I'm so sorry. What happened?"

"He got beat up really bad and… and…" She burst into tears again. Her face contorted with anguish, "and he died!"

Her mother rubbed her back. "That's terrible. Where was he? How did he get beat up?"

"He was really nice, he was always helping people. He got beat up at school after a meeting."

"That's terrible. What was his name? You've never talked about a boy before."

"Scott Tatum"

"Poor boy. Did you like him? You weren't dating him, were you?"

"No Mom, it wasn't like that. He was my friend. He doesn't even go to my school."

"How did you know him then?"

"He is at the meetings I go to every Tuesday. He helps kids. He has even saved a couple of kids from committing suicide. He was my friend."

"What happened? Why would someone do that to him?"

Leah hesitated and then forged ahead. "He was gay. He tried having Pride meetings at his school and he got bullied and beat up, more than once." She looked down at her lap and stifled a sob. "The last time, …it killed him."

Lydia lifted Leah's chin to look into her eyes. "I guess people aren't ready for that. Everywhere you turn nowadays—media, TV, everywhere—they are trying to push it on people. With the right help, I'm sure these kids could find their way out of it. If they turned to God, they would see it's wrong and with His love, they could be healed."

Leah stiffened. "What?" She was in disbelief. She searched her mother's eyes for understanding.

"Do you think it's a choice?" Anger welled up inside Leah. "Do you think people choose to be gay so they will be ridiculed, left out, bullied, and shamed? Do you think it's easy when people do come out and then all of a sudden their friends won't talk to them anymore?"

"No, I think some kids are lost and think it's what they want. Maybe they're experimenting. Maybe their parents exposed them to bad things when they were growing up. They need better role models and counselling to control their urges. They just don't know any better."

Leah clenched her fists and tears of anger fell from her eyes. Frustration and disappointment bubbled over.

"Mom, how come you haven't asked how I know Scott?"

"You said he goes to the same school meetings as you." Lydia looked puzzled.

"Mom, they are GAY ALLIANCE meetings!" Leah could see her mother's confusion as she tried to process the information.

"But… but… why would you…" Her mother put her hand to her mouth as realization began to sink in.

"Bingo, Mom. I was going to the meetings because," she paused, "I'm pretty sure that I'm gay." Her voice became flat. Leah was exhausted. She was so done with the lies, the hiding her feelings, tiptoeing around her mother's feelings. Done.

"Oh my God. Oh my God. Oh my God." Her mother kept chanting and shaking her head. "What did I do wrong? It's all my fault. I shouldn't have left the church. I didn't teach you enough about God. Now God is punishing me!"

"What? What are you saying?"

"I had sex one time and got pregnant. One time. It was a big mistake, I gave into my urges. My family wanted me to give you up. I left the church so I wouldn't embarrass my family and now God is punishing me. I thought I could do better without them, now…THIS."

"You think that me being gay is God punishing YOU?" Leah turned on her heel, went to her room, and grabbed her backpack off the floor. She began stuffing it with clothes and anything she could get her hands on.

"What are you doing?" her mother demanded in a shrill voice as she followed her.

Leah turned to face her. "You think I'm a punishment to you from God. How is that supposed to make me feel, Mom? Don't you understand? I didn't choose to feel the way I feel. I fought feelings I've had for a long time. I don't know what to do."

"I didn't mean it that way. We'll get you help. No one needs to know about this. You will not go back to those meetings." Her mother's voice shook with anger.

"For the first time in my life, I feel like I fit in. I feel like people understand me. I feel like I have friends. I won't give it up. NO WAY!"

Leah did not expect it, but a stinging slap landed on her left cheek. Shock was quickly replaced by anger. Leah was ready to explode.

"Maybe I am a punishment. Maybe you should have told me about my dad so I wouldn't have been so lost my whole life. Why, Mom? Why couldn't you tell me about him?"

Lydia looked like she had been the one struck. She stepped back. "He wasn't in our lives because he died. I was protecting you."

"Protecting me. I know your secret. He's still alive. You've lied to me. He *is* still alive, isn't he? Does he even know about me?"

"Why do you think he's still alive?"

"I found your newspaper clippings and my birth certificate. My dad is alive. Why hasn't he wanted me in his life? Have I ever met him?"

"He doesn't even know I had you. He didn't know I got pregnant."

"Was he some loser you didn't want to be with?"

"No, it wasn't like that. He was nice."

"Why didn't you at least give him a chance to know about me?"

"I was scared, Leah. You don't understand how it was. My parents were so angry and ashamed of me. I was so embarrassed. I didn't tell him and then he left to go to school. I didn't know what to do."

"Where is he now, do you know?"

Her mother collapsed on the couch and put her head in her hands. "I haven't checked for a long time, but I think he lives in Philadelphia."

"He lives *here*? I could have bumped into him on a sidewalk or ran into him, but I never even looked for him because I thought he was DEAD. I am going to find him. He deserves to know about me, and I deserve to meet him." Her backpack slung over her shoulder, Leah tried pushing past Lydia to leave.

"Haven't I loved you enough? You don't need him. You have me. I've made sure you had everything you needed all these years."

"I feel so lost all the time," Leah cried in anguish. "Maybe if I can put some pieces together, I will find out how to feel like a whole person for the first time." She turned and started to the door.

Her mother's face fell and then darkened. She began shrieking, "Why are you doing this to me? Why? I don't want him to know." She grabbed at Leah's arms, pulling her back. Leah squirmed and twisted out of her grasp. Lydia stalked to the door after Leah and tried dragging her back inside the house.

"You can't do this to me, Leah. Please. Don't go."

They struggled together and Lydia grabbed Leah's arms, pinning her to the door. Leah once again pulled out of her grip. She was not a child anymore. She shoved Lydia with all of her might and raced out the door into the night. She ran and ran until she leaned over heaving and catching her breath.

Beyond the 14th Floor

For several hours she walked trying to determine what to do, a chill set in and she began to shiver. An angry blister mocked every step as her damp sneakers tore at her feet. She had nothing left, no emotions anymore, just numbness. She looked up to see a subway entrance down the block. She walked down through the turnstile with her pass and the stale smell of the underground filled her nostrils. She climbed aboard the subway in amongst the blend of people coming and going. Her tired, aching body relaxed, and she leaned her head against the seat. The rocking of the train put her to sleep.

Chapter Ten

It was ten in the morning. They dozed on and off in the cramped space. Moving was difficult as their stiff muscles cried out in displeasure. Leah felt dizzy, she was so thirsty. Jill felt panic rising and she closed her eyes, counted to ten, and took some deep breaths. She looked over at Leah, who was awake now as well.

"What are you going to do when we get out of here?" asked Jill.

"Drink five gallons of ice-cold water and eat some tacos. I feel like shit," Leah groaned.

"I agree. I'm so thirsty. I had a dream about being in the desert and having a popsicle floating beyond my reach." Jill rubbed her eyes. "What I meant was, what are you going to do about your mom when we get out of here?"

"I found an address for someone with my dad's name in this building. I was going to see if I could find him, to see if it was him. I was on my way, then… this."

"Yes, this," said Jill.

"I can tell you something though, I won't be going to meet my dad like this. I feel so disgusting." She gestured to the empty drink containers they had used to relieve themselves in the corner, along with the vomit bag. "This elevator is a cesspool."

Jill nodded. She tried to avoid breathing through her nose; it made her feel like vomiting again.

"Leah, if you have nowhere to go, you could come to my house. Not to stay, but to clean up, wash your clothes, and call your mom."

"I'm not calling my mom."

"I'm not going to say she handled your situation very well, but she must be going crazy worrying about you. You don't have to go back to her, just call her to let her know you're okay. She has probably called the police looking for you. I would have if I were her."

Leah didn't answer. Jill understood by her silence that she agreed with the assumption.

Martin hadn't said anything for a while. He seemed like he was in a deep sleep. Leah slid her foot over and tapped the bottom of his shoe. "Hey Martin, how're you doing?"

He stirred but wasn't very responsive.

Oh no. This isn't good. Jill crawled to his side and felt his forehead. He was sweaty and beginning to shake. She squeezed his arms and propped him up into a better sitting position.

"Leah, look for some Skittles. Maybe we missed one." They both knew the answer, but Leah lifted their things looking on the floor of the elevator for any of the Skittles that had spilled earlier. They had already found the last one hours ago.

"Hey Martin, wake up buddy. It won't be much longer."

"Don't feel so... so good," he mumbled with his eyes closed.

"I know you need your insulin. Martin, can you give me some information? Can you tell me your daughter's name?" Jill was worried about him and thought she'd better find out who she could call if anything happened.

"Rosa," he mumbled.

"What's her last name?"

"Jackson."

She reached down and grabbed his wrist to feel for his pulse. It was racing despite the fact he had been lying still. *This isn't good. We haven't moved in fifteen hours.* Jill didn't want to scare Leah, so she kept her concern to herself.

"Hey buddy, stay with me. Hang in there." She squeezed his hand and his weak reply made Jill's panic increase.

Jill was afraid of what would happen. Martin needed medical attention, and soon. He was in deep trouble.

Martin suddenly grimaced and his hand jerked from Jill's. He pulled at his collar like he was being strangled. He began to gasp and pant, searching for air.

"Oh my God. Martin, what's going on?" Jill shrieked, trying to hold him steady. Leah grabbed her jacket and began flapping it in his face to give him some air.

"C'mon Martin, you'll be okay. Take it easy, they're coming. Hang in there." Tears escaped down Leah's cheeks as her stomach clenched with fear.

Martin's whole body convulsed and then he went limp. Jill grabbed his wrist her hands shaking and paused. She put her face close to his mouth and shook her head. "He doesn't have a pulse and he's stopped breathing." Jill looked at Leah with stark panic. "Do you know how to do CPR?"

Leah's eyes widened. "We had to take it in high school. I've never done it on a real person before. I don't think I can." She shook her head, looking down at Martin's gaping mouth and tobacco-stained teeth. The thought of putting her mouth on his repulsed her.

"I don't know how, but you're going to have to do this. Martin needs us, we're his only hope."

"I can't remember!"

"Leah, you have to. He will die."

"I'm so scared."

"Do your best, I'm right here."

"I can't." Leah wailed in anguish.

Jill reached across Martin and grabbed Leah by the shoulders and looked squarely into her eyes. "Martin will die unless we are able to do this, we are his only hope. You can do this."

Leah took a deep breath and nodded, wiping her face. Vomit rose in the back of her throat and she swallowed it back. Stress vibrated through her body.

They scrambled to get Martin on his back. They knelt on either side and Leah hesitated and then put her hand under his neck to lift his head. She looked at Jill, who nodded for her to go ahead. Leah reluctantly lowered her mouth to cover Martin's and gave two slow breaths.

Jill saw his chest rise and fall and then Leah put her hands onto Martin's chest, feeling for the correct position. She straightened her elbows and pushed down hard and began pumping his chest up and down.

"That's great. Keep it going. Martin, c'mon buddy,

come back to us."

Time stood still as Leah became a machine, doings breaths and then compressions. Periodically, she would pause, and Jill would take his pulse and shake her head. "Keep going."

The elevator was chaotic. Jill's face was red, and Leah's hair clung to her cheeks as sweat glistened on her face. It had been almost fifteen minutes and Leah cried, "I can't do this anymore. I'm so tired. It's not working." Martin's still body lay between them.

Suddenly, the elevator gave a little jerk. It was a motion they hadn't felt so far. Leah looked at Jill in surprise. Before either could say anything, the elevator jerked again and swayed slightly.

"Keep on, keep on. If we're getting rescued, we've got to keep going. Maybe we can save him," Jill pleaded.

Bang. Bang.

With renewed vigor, Leah continued her pattern of breaths and compressions and Jill jumped to her feet. The lights flickered. The banging echoed down the elevator shaft to them.

Jill screamed and shouted, slapping the walls with her hands.

"Help, help us, we're stuck in the elevator."

The lights came on. With the power back, the panel buttons lit up like a Christmas tree. What an amazing sight to behold. The elevator suddenly, and smoothly, began to descend.

"Oh my God, we're getting rescued!" Jill cried with relief and crouched down with Martin and Leah.

"Martin, hang in there. It's almost over. Help is here." Jill yelled in his face as if the volume would revive him.

The elevator buttons lit up as the elevator made its journey down from the fourteenth floor. Five, four, three, two, one. Ding, ding. Like a magic wand had been waved, the doors opened on the lobby. Fresh, cool air rushed into the stagnant elevator. Fire fighters were waiting on the other side.

"We need help right away. We've been trapped for over sixteen hours. Our friend needs help. He's diabetic and he has no pulse." Jill yelled over her shoulder as Leah continued to work on Martin.

"It's okay, ma'am. We're here to help, we'll look after him." They moved back as the firefighter moved onto the floor beside them. He slipped his helmet off and asked Leah to stop. He checked for a pulse and looked back at his partner.

"Get the defibrillator off the truck."

The firefighter continued CPR and Leah slumped back against the wall. Jill grabbed their bags and helped Leah up and out the door as the firefighter returned, joined by a paramedic.

Cool air rushed around their bodies and they shivered by the elevator door. Leah stood wringing her hands. Jill reached for her and hugged her and rubbed her back as Leah burst into tears.

They could hear the people working on Martin. "Clear. Okay, check for pulse."

"We got a pulse. It's weak, but we've got one. Let's get him loaded."

Jill clutched Leah with relief and began to cry herself. They were both spent.

They loaded Martin on a gurney and wheeled him past to a waiting ambulance. Two more attendants came over to check on Jill and Leah. They were dehydrated and hungry, and Jill's nausea had returned.

She asked the attendant which hospital they were taking Martin to. She wanted to call and make sure he was okay.

#

It was about 10:30 am. Now that power had returned, the city streets were coming back to life. Water ran through the gutters and wind had strewn garbage through the streets. Cars wove through slowly making their way. They spotted a deli up the street.

Jill carefully extracted a few items, her car keys and wallet from the purse she had vomited in and threw the rest into a nearby garbage can. "Ugh, I'm not even going to try to clean it." She wrinkled her nose and gestured to Leah to follow her to the deli. "I know we look terrible and probably smell worse, but let's slip in quick, use the restroom, and grab something to eat and drink."

They refreshed themselves, wetting paper towels to wipe themselves down.

"In everyday life, we really take such basic needs for granted—plumbing, water, a clean bed." Leah shook her head.

They bought sandwiches and a couple of waters and headed to Jill's car. Jill was walking slowly and feeling more terrible with each step.

"Is there any chance you could drive? You have your license, right?" She felt the bile rising at the back of her throat.

Leah shrugged. "Yeah, sure. Are you okay?"

"Yeah, I'm just feeling sick to my stomach again." Jill held onto the car and closed her eyes until the awful feeling subsided.

Jill instructed Leah where to go as they made their way across the city. Signs of the storm were evident, in some places police were directing traffic around debris and broken trees.

Leah proved to be a good driver and Jill relaxed in the passenger seat. The radio provided updates of the storm that had caused so much chaos the night before.

Leah broke the silence. "I really appreciate this, getting to come to your house. I need to figure out what I am going to do."

"Listen, I am willing to help you, but you need to call your mom. We can figure out the rest after. You shouldn't be missing any more school either."

"I know. I've texted her a couple of times since I left so she knows I'm alive. My phone has been dead a lot because I haven't been able to charge it much."

"Where did you stay this week? I mean, you had to sleep somewhere?"

"I slept in the locker room of a twenty-four-hour gym one night; the subway; a bus depot. It's amazing where you can blend in for a while."

"Why didn't you call someone?"

"I don't know. How could I explain why I left? No one really knows I'm gay. I have friends at the Gay Alliance meetings but some of their families don't know about them either, so I didn't want to get them into trouble."

"What're you planning to do?"

"I don't have a real plan. I was just going to find my dad. There are about five people in Philadelphia with his name. I've found two of them. One is living in a nursing home and the other is on Facebook. He's in his first year of university. I have three to go before I run out of options."

Jill motioned to turn up ahead and they pulled into her driveway.

"My poor Buck is probably wondering what happened to me. He's terrified of thunder and lightning." Jill's brow furrowed with worry as she flung open the front door and Buck launched himself at her. He jumped and whined, clawing wildly at Jill.

"Okay Bucky, okay! I'm sorry I didn't come home!" She grabbed his collar and scuttled him to the back door and let him out into the yard. He quickly ran over to a tree and relieved himself.

"I'll have to check for messes. Poor guy was locked inside for a long time."

Leah nodded, looking around at Jill's home. To Jill, she looked like a lost little girl standing in the middle of her living room. She was overwhelmed with a maternal urge to protect and help her.

Jill stepped forward and gently took Leah by the shoulders. "What you did back there was incredible. You're a real hero. If it wasn't for you, Martin might not have had a second chance. You saved his life."

Leah shrugged and her bottom lip quivered. Jill pulled her into her arms and hugged her as she wept. Jill rubbed her back as the tension left her body.

"We're both exhausted. I'll go and get a towel and washcloth for you. I'm sure a warm shower will make us both feel more human." Leah plopped onto the couch as Jill left to rummage in the hall closet.

When she came back to the living room Leah was fast asleep on the sofa. Jill set out towels and shampoo on the floor next to the couch for Leah to see when she awoke. Buck had hopped on the sofa by Leah's feet and looked up at Jill with his big, brown eyes. She smiled to herself. *Bucky, you want to protect her too.*

Her body savoured the warm, soapy water as it caressed her stiff muscles. The sweat and grime from the long night ran down the drain. She slipped on fresh yoga pants and a t-shirt. Her phone had charged enough to make a call.

"Hey, Evan."

"Hey baby, how're you?"

"Better now. I had the worst night ever last night."

"Why? What happened? That storm was crazy. Are you okay?"

"Yes, I am now. I was going to surprise you by bringing your wallet by, but the power was knocked out by the storm and I got stuck in the elevator in your building for sixteen hours."

"Geez, that's terrible. The power was out everywhere. I couldn't get across town, so I slept on my dad's couch. I tried calling and I couldn't get you. Are you okay?"

Jill relayed all the details to Evan about the long night and Leah saving Martin's life. "And I've brought Leah, the runaway, home with me."

"Home with you? Is that safe?"

"Yes, it's fine. Don't worry, she's a nice girl. I feel sorry for her, she's had a tough time. I'll have to explain later. I'll let her stay tonight and then help her find a place to go tomorrow. We're both exhausted from this horrible ordeal."

"Babe, I'm so sorry. I can't believe you went through that. You were coming to see me, and I wasn't even there to help you."

"It's all my fault. I was being impulsive. I should've called first. Apparently, there's a force bigger than me that doesn't want me to see your apartment." She laughed.

"Hey, it's not that bad. I am going to have to come up with something really big to make this up to you."

"I still have your wallet."

"Would it be okay if I stop by to see you and to pick it up tomorrow night?"

"Yeah, that would be great. I may have developed an elevator phobia, so I'm not interested in going back to your place anytime soon."

"Now I'm going to be weirded out too. I live on the eighteenth floor—it's going to mean a lot of stairs for me in the future. I still won't be home until later today. I'll be careful with the elevator."

They hung up and Jill tiptoed out and looked around the corner into the living room. Both Buck and Leah were curled up and dead to the world. *That's just what I need too.* Jill grabbed a cozy blanket, climbed into her soft bed, and fell asleep within moments.

She was dreaming the elevator was filling with water. She was panicking as the water began to splash at her face. She moved her head back and forth, but the water kept coming. Her eyes shot open and Buck's muzzle was inches from her face with his big pink tongue bathing her cheeks.

"Okay, okay, stop. I'm awake, you crazy nut!" She pushed him away as she sat up and rubbed her eyes. In disbelief, she realized that she had slept for three hours. She heard a noise down the hall. Leah was in the shower.

Jill's stomach growled and instead of feeling nauseated, she was starving. She pulled on a sweater and ambled to the kitchen. Buck followed behind as she put out some fresh food and water for him. Jill dug in the fridge for some food to fix for supper.

Leah came out not long after in a clean outfit with her dark hair damp from the shower. "Hey Jill, would you mind if I washed my clothes? I don't have much and I've worn the same thing for three days." Her nose wrinkled. Jill showed her where the laundry room was, and she put a load into the washer.

"So, did you call your mom?"

"Yes, I did. There was no answer. I left a message. I'll call her later tonight."

Leah sat at the kitchen table with a glass of milk while Jill worked at the kitchen counter.

"I was thinking, maybe I could help you search for your dad. I may know of places we could look for information. I also want you to be safe. If you have no idea who he is, maybe there's a reason your mom didn't want him in your life."

Leah nodded. "I've thought of that, but I still don't care. I want to know everything about him." She shrugged. "I need to know."

Jill understood, she'd feel the same way. It would gnaw at her every day. She stepped into the pantry to retrieve the glass salad bowl. "What's his name?"

"Evan Bates."

Chapter Eleven

The salad bowl crashed to the floor and shattered. Jill willed herself not to turn around so the shock on her face wouldn't be revealed. Leah leapt up to the pantry door.

"Jill, are you okay? Did you get cut?" Leah knelt down and began picking up pieces of the shattered bowl. Buck was wary and stayed on the edge of the dining room.

"Yes, I'm okay. It just slipped. I'll get the broom and dustpan." She went to the broom closet; her hand was shaking as she grabbed the cleaning supplies. *Did Evan have a daughter that he wasn't telling her about?* Her mind raced.

She composed herself as they cleaned up the glass together. Dinner was ready and they sat at the table together. Jill evaluated Leah's physical appearance. Although she wore no makeup, she was a natural beauty.

Was she Evan's daughter? She had the same dark hair, although hers wasn't as curly. She had a dimple on her right cheek. Did Evan have a dimple? Jill tried not to stare.

Through dinner, Jill told Leah about Brad, going through cancer, and how difficult it was to lose him. For the first time in ages, she was able to talk about it without breaking down. Leah was flattered that Jill felt comfortable sharing her emotional memories.

"Tell me more about you."

Leah paused as she decided where to begin. Her lip trembled and she took a deep breath. "It's always been my mom and me. She would never talk about my dad except to say he'd died before I was born. I could never ask questions, or she would freak out on me. No graveyard to visit, or anyone to talk to about him. When I was a baby, my mom had a big fight with her family, so I don't know them either. That's always really hard because most people have family they visit and talk about, but I never had that.

"Don't get me wrong; my mom isn't a complete ogre. She's made a lot of sacrifices for me. I know she wants the best for me. She's always worried about what other people are thinking though, so when I kept wondering why I felt different, I didn't want to share it with her because I didn't think she'd take it well. She had had enough disappointments in her life, I didn't want to add to it.

"In the middle of struggling with how I felt about being gay, I found my birth certificate in my mom's things. It had my father's name on it—Evan Bates. I was excited to find out his name, but there were newspaper clippings in the folder as well. Even though she always told me he was dead, the clippings had his name all through them. I even saw his mom's obituary; she died from cancer. He's not dead. They were all dated within the last five years."

"That's a lot to handle. I wonder why your mom wasn't able to tell you the truth."

"I was totally freaking out. My dad is out there

somewhere, but my mom won't talk about him. On the night I ran away, I had just found out about my friend Scott dying. I left is such a hurry, I didn't really have a plan on what I was going to do. After I thought about it, I decided that I would find my dad before I go home. Maybe I could live with him or something, I don't know what to do now," her voice trailed off and she put her face in her hands and sniffled.

Jill pushed the tissue box to Leah who blew her nose. Sensing her sadness, Buck sauntered over and rested his soft muzzle on her leg. Leah smiled through her tears and dropped her hand to caress his velvet ears. Jill regarded the girl sitting in front of her; vulnerable, confused, and fragile.

"Leah, this is crazy, but I have something to tell you. I'm actually still trying to process it. I'm not sure, but there is a good chance I might know your father." Leah's eyes widened. "I know a man named Evan Bates. I don't know if it's a crazy coincidence, or fate, or what, but he was who I was going to see yesterday when we got stuck in the elevator. I'm dating him." *And pregnant with his child, maybe his second child.*

Flickering emotions played on Leah's face as the information absorbed. "I was going to see the next Evan Bates I had on my list. Floor 18. The plumber."

Jill nodded.

"Oh my God. Does he seem like he could be my dad?"

"I can't tell you that, but he is about my age and has dark hair like yours."

"Do you have a picture of him?"

Jill picked up her phone and scrolled through her

pictures. "Yes, I have a couple."

She found a picture of Evan with Buck. Leah grabbed her phone and stared at it. She zoomed in on his face. Emotions overcame her. She buried her head in her arms on the kitchen table holding Jill's phone and sobbed. Jill knelt on the floor beside her, rubbing her back. "It's pretty heavy news."

"Do you think it could be him?" She searched Jill's eyes through her tears.

"I don't know, but we're going to find out. Evan will be coming here tomorrow night."

"I can't believe this is actually happening. What do you think he'll say? Is he going to freak out?"

"This is a pretty big thing. I think anyone would freak out a bit. He's really nice though. I care about him a lot."

Jill shared how she met Evan and what kind of a person he was. They were interrupted by the sound of Leah's cell phone, which was finally charged. Leah grabbed it from the counter. "It's Mom." As Leah answered it, Jill left the room so they could have a private conversation.

She went to her room and laid on the bed. She had planned to tell Evan about their baby but now she would have to wait. This was going to be enough of a shock. If you compared Evan's picture to Leah, there was a resemblance. If this girl wasn't Evan's daughter, she certainly *looked* like she was.

How would he react when he found out that he had a teenage daughter and a baby on the way?

She heard Leah finish up her call in the kitchen and then heard her footsteps coming down the hall.

"Jill?"

"Yes, in here."

Leah poked her head around the corner of the doorway. Jill patted the bed beside her. She came in and plopped on the bed like they were having a slumber party.

"How did that go?"

"Good. She said she was sorry for freaking out and asked me to come back home. She was crying a bit. She suggested we could go to counselling together. I agreed on the condition she tell me everything she knows about my dad."

"And?"

"I think it's him. He should be thirty-nine, dark curly hair, a carpenter. Mom said he is tall and played football in high school."

"Does he know about you?"

"Nope. They had sex once, then mom got scared and wouldn't talk to him again. He didn't know about the pregnancy, a few months later he left for school in a different state. She said he didn't do anything mean to her."

They lay on the bed side by side, letting the information sink in. Finally, Jill spoke.

"Leah, can I call him to let him know so he can prepare himself? It's a pretty big thing to spring on someone. He might have a better reaction to meeting you if he has a heads up on what the situation is."

Leah pondered for a moment and sat up. "I am going to go let Buck out. I can't bear to listen. What if he's mad or doesn't want to see me?"

Jill reassured her she would handle it carefully. She got her phone and went back to the bedroom to call Evan.

#

Leah's mom, Lydia cradled the phone in her hands and sank into her living room chair. She bent over with her face in her hands. Hearing Leah's voice and finding out that she was safe made her feel weak with relief. The stress from the last week drained from her shaking body.

She had never imagined she might lose Leah, but now she had found her father, Evan. The unknown terrified her. She had never seen anger in Leah's eyes like the night she had left. Her body heaved with a sigh as she caught her breath. She sat in silence and recited a prayer of gratitude to herself.

She went to the bathroom and washed her tear-stained face, then with purpose, straightened up and strode into her bedroom. The closet doors were flung open and clothing was pulled from the rod and tossed in a pile on the bed. After a frenzied scramble, Lydia stood on her tiptoes reaching with her hand until she found the corner of an old box. Unable to reach it, she got on a kitchen chair to pull it down from the closet shelf.

Kneeling on the floor, Lydia peeled the lid off and began rifling through the books and papers. Her fingers grasped a book sitting at the bottom and she pulled it out onto her lap. Her hand ran over the glossy cover of her high school yearbook. Flipping through, she turned to the senior year class. She knew the position on the page, she had looked at his picture frequently over the years, but it had been a while.

Her finger traced the outline of the photo of Evan Bates. Under his photo was written, *Likes: Vintage cars, football. Dislikes: Dishonest people, onions.* She sighed. Well, she wasn't a dishonest person, but not telling him that he had a child was a bit of a doozy.

Her heart still fluttered at the thought of Evan. The school-girl crush had always lingered. She wondered if he ever thought of her. She allowed herself to think of his boyish grin, his dark curly hair that was just like Leah's. She had no idea the night of that dance seventeen years ago would change her life forever.

She had foolishly believed that Leah would never find out about her father. Pandora's Box had been opened. Leah had no idea what Lydia had gone through or the sacrifices she had made for her.

Lydia had developed a crush on Evan Bates in high school. He was like her: he didn't talk much and stayed on the periphery of the action, taking it all in. He was also really good at sports though and didn't seem to be shy at all when he was competing.

Evan had dated a few girls, but never for a long time. Lydia never received any special attention from him, but she felt her face flush if he gave her a nod and smile in the hallway. She always watched for his #33 on the field when the games were on.

One day after school during a practice, Lydia was walking by the football field and heading home when she heard yelling. She turned to see the coach was calling in her direction. She quickly looked around realizing that he must be addressing her. He strode over and met her on the edge of the field.

His face was red from the effort and he addressed

her with authority as spit flew from his lips. "We've got a player down. Go get some ice from the First Aid room." He pointed a meaty finger in the direction of the school, hitched his pants over his large belly, and turned on his heel before she could even respond.

Lydia had no idea where the First Aid room even was. She ran into the school gym and looked around, spotting the First Aid sign above the door under the 'Go Crusaders' logo emblazoned on the wall. The room was unlocked so she stumbled inside and found a little freezer with ice packs. She grabbed two. She jogged back to the field where the group of players were gathered. She wondered who was hurt and what had happened. As she approached, the crowd parted and she could see #33, Evan, sitting and rocking back and forth holding his ankle. A couple of guys lifted him and helped him walk over to the bench. He sat down slowly to avoid jarring his ankle, wincing in pain with each move. Lydia followed behind like a little lamb, not exactly knowing what she was supposed to do.

The assistant coach crouched down and looked at Evan's ankle, then back to Lydia. "Better get that ice on there. It looks like a pretty bad sprain."

All the players returned to the field to continue practice and left Lydia and Evan alone. She felt awkward and self-conscious, apparently thrust into the role of caregiver. She broke into a nervous sweat despite holding the wet ice packs.

"So, I guess I'll put these on your ankle…"

His eyes were half closed as he continued to groan in pain. Lydia knelt down, grabbed her backpack, and gently propped up his injured leg. She put the ice packs on Evan's ankle. It was growing in size by the minute. He winced again.

"I'm so sorry, that must really hurt," she said, cringing and biting her lip. "Should I take your shoe off?"

"No, I may not be able to get it back on again. Thanks, the ice feels really good. My ankle is on fire right now." Evan opened his eyes and acknowledged her with a weak smile. She felt embarrassed and unsure about what to do next, but she couldn't just walk away. They sat in silence as the practice continued on the field.

He looked down at his ballooning ankle. "It doesn't look like I'll be finishing practice. I'll have to call my mom to come get me." She nodded. "Can you help me to the locker room?" Lydia nodded again and grabbed her bag.

She assisted him to a standing position, and it seemed like the best way to help him walk was to put his arm around her shoulders for support. Her heart pounded as he leaned on her and they slowly limped back to the school doors. She had never been close to a boy like this before, especially one she had a crush on. She stopped at the locker room door with him.

"Thanks, I got this now. I didn't catch your name." Evan propped himself against the door and removed his arm from around her.

"Lydia Armstrong. We don't have any classes together." She looked down at her feet. They stood in silence.

"Well thanks, Lydia, for patching me up." He chuckled and began pushing the door open.

"No problem," said Lydia, but already the door had closed behind him.

She saw Evan around school on crutches for a few weeks and then he was back on the field with the rest of the team. They spotted each other in the halls sometimes and they would smile at one another. Occasionally, he would wave, but they didn't have much contact after that.

When Lydia graduated, she attended college. The usual traditional occupations were encouraged by her parents. She took a business course so she could end up doing office work. It would be an honest living that would support her until she got married and started a family. Even though she had moved into her own little apartment, she still met her family every Sunday at church and helped her mom, Joan, organize fundraisers for different causes; someone was sick or just had a new baby; or a new family had just moved to the community.

Lydia was always delighted to help her mom and their work was appreciated by the parishioners. She still felt detached though. Because she was shy, it was difficult to meet new people, so she continued doing what she always did. Following the same routine was the easiest way to exist.

The church's youth group decided to organize a dance. Lydia was both thrilled and nervous. She looked forward to going to a dance with people her age. She was also terrified because she had never been to a dance alone before. She didn't usually go to college parties either as she didn't feel sophisticated enough. What should she wear? For days, she turned on the radio and practiced dancing in front of her bedroom mirror. She wanted to fit in instead of being the odd one out.

She spent the afternoon getting ready, a pile of outfits

cast off on her bed. Since moving out, she had been a bit more daring and put on light makeup. It usually seemed too dark and she would rub most of it off. It felt good to give herself a little colour. She had cut her long hair to shoulder length and it curled around her face in a flattering way.

When she arrived at the dance, she was surprised to see so many different people there. She approached a group of familiar girls, who surrounded her, peppering her with compliments on her hair and outfit. This was the "new" Lydia. She felt unusually confident as she danced with a few guys she knew and then accepted offers from guys she didn't. Everyone was bobbing along to the music, so she just followed suit. She had never been to an event like this without her parents. The freedom was liberating. She soaked in her surroundings.

She felt a tap on her shoulder. "Wanna' dance?" a male voice behind her asked.

Lydia swung around to see Evan Bates standing right behind her. She couldn't believe her eyes. She momentarily gaped at him, then regained her composure. Evan Bates was at her church dance and asking her to dance. Her face flushed as he gestured to the dance floor. They danced to a few upbeat pop songs before a slow love song began. He smiled at her and naturally pulled her into his arms. Her heart was pounding in her chest and she was worried he would notice. As his arms encircled her, she melted into his embrace.

"You look familiar," he said, gazing down at her.

She stared into his blue eyes. "We went to the same high school." She blushed and quickly looked away, worried her emotions were written all over her face.

He raised an eyebrow in thought, studying her face. "Linda Armstrong, right?"

"Lydia, my name is Lydia," she said and smiled, flattered that he was mostly right. "You're Evan Bates."

"Yes, I am." He grinned and thought for a moment. "You helped me that day when I trashed my ankle in high school."

She felt pleased he remembered. She had thought of their encounter many times over the last two years.

"Yes, that was me." She beamed.

"Well, I am as good as new! Although you wouldn't know it by my dance moves." He shook his head and shrugged. As if on cue, he stepped on her toes.

"Ow!" she blurted and began laughing as he blushed and looked down.

"How come I didn't see you very much back then?" Evan asked.

"I didn't go out much in high school," Lydia said, looking straight forward into his chest. "My parents were pretty strict."

"I didn't either. It was either studying or doing sports," said Evan. "My cousin invited me to come tonight. I haven't been to a dance in a long time."

They danced with other people through the evening, but at the end of the night they found themselves dancing together for the last song. Someone had dimmed all the lights and couples on the floor embraced a little bit closer.

Initially, Evan's hands hung loosely around her waist, but then gently pulled her against his chest as her hands wrapped around his broad shoulders. She was in awe. She had never felt this way before. She could smell his scent of Polo cologne mixed with a bit of sweat. Her body tingled and she felt a giddiness she couldn't understand. As the song ended, she turned her face up to his. He smiled and planted a hesitant kiss on her mouth.

"Can I give you a ride home, Lydia Armstrong?"

She felt breathless as she smiled and nodded. "That would be nice." She had walked several blocks from her apartment to get there.

Lydia anticipated having an experience like all the girls she knew from high school. She remembered the giggled stories about getting kissed and letting a boy get to second base. She always wondered what second base was or even what any of the bases meant. She wasn't a complete idiot though; she knew what a home run was. The deed. Going all the way. Losing your virginity. Sex.

Now, she was going to have a story. It seemed like she could expect to be kissed again. She felt heady at the notion. Not that she would tell anyone, she would have it just for herself. All the echoes of her mom's talks about not letting guys take advantage of her, waiting until marriage and sinning were silenced. She stared at her high school crush driving her home in his beat-up vintage Nova.

They idly chatted about what they had done since graduating. Evan was working for his dad's construction company. The white dress shirt he was wearing with sleeves rolled up to the elbows showed tanned, muscular arms. Lydia tingled inside, wishing she could savor this moment forever.

When they pulled up to Lydia's apartment, Evan got out and walked up to the steps with her, his hand on her back. They hesitated at the door. He bent down and gave her a gentle kiss on the lips and stepped back.

"I enjoyed myself tonight. Maybe we could go out sometime. Can I get your number?" asked Evan.

"Yes, come in. I will grab a paper and write it down." They stepped into Lydia's apartment and over to her desk in the corner. She scribbled down her number and turned to hand it to him. He reached to grab the paper but then gently grasped her wrist and slid his hand into hers.

"I don't want you to leave," Lydia whispered. Evan's face mirrored the same youthful desire as they embraced again. Lydia stepped back and led him into the living room.

They sank down onto the old, slightly musty couch and kissed each other tentatively. They talked about high school and the different people they both knew. He made her laugh with his comical impressions of some of the popular kids.

"I have to admit, I had my eye on you in high school for a while," Evan said as he kissed her neck. "But I never had the courage to ask you out then. You seemed different from the other girls, more serious and mature. I liked that."

Lydia felt her heart swell at the thought of him actually being interested her. Emboldened by his confession, she returned his kisses with fervor and felt herself letting go of her inhibitions. She hadn't drunk a drop of alcohol, but she felt intoxicated.

She could feel his groin throbbing against her thigh as he pulled her onto his lap and tentatively undid her blouse.

Her plain white bra was soon discarded on the floor as he cupped her bare breasts.

She hesitated and he looked up into her eyes with concern. "Are you okay?" he asked. She smiled and nodded. Her whole body had awakened under his touch. He pulled his shirt off and she felt brazen as she ran her hand over his tanned chest. It was if they were the only people in the world at that moment, like Adam and Eve.

They found themselves on the floor and his hands moved to push her skirt up and slide off her panties. His hand ran over her bare buttocks and then moved to unzip his own pants as he kicked them off beside them. They both lay fully exposed, exploring curves and valleys of each other's bodies. Their own little world. All Lydia wanted to do was be with him. Her body was asking to be touched in ways she could never have imagined.

She knew *how* sex was supposed to happen, and despite girls saying it hurt the first time, she embraced the momentary pain. There was nothing she wanted more at that moment than to take this step. She was amazed at the overwhelming spiritual feeling she felt. She couldn't be closer to another human than this. How could it be wrong?

It was over quickly, and he moved off her and gently kissed her lips. "Lydia, that was incredible," he whispered. "That was my first time." He seemed sheepish, but she felt pleased he revealed something so intimate.

She kissed him back and said, "Me too."

"Did it hurt?" he asked. "Are you okay?"

She nodded and looked down as the magic of the moment washed away like a wave lapping the shore.

She felt self-conscious and she began to feel around for her clothing.

Her emotions were mixed as they got up from the floor. Both were embarrassed now, as they turned their backs and quickly got dressed.

He gave her a hug at the door and awkwardly kissed the top of her head as he left. "You're so pretty, Lydia. I'll call you," he said and gave her another squeeze.

Lydia closed the door and watched him walk to his car, get in, and drive off. She had never been so confused in all her life.

She showered, put on a fresh nightie, and shoved her clothes into the washing machine. Shame was already seeping into her mind. She felt for a moment like she was normal, fitting in, but did all girls feel bad after they had sex? *Yeah, but most girls don't have sex on the first date.* Her conscience mocked her. *It wasn't even a real date.* She felt sick and went back into the shower and showered for a long time until the hot water ran cold. She had sinned. She had given into her urges. She was weak. She had acted like a whore.

Over the next couple of weeks when her phone rang, she wouldn't answer it. Her answering machine took all of the calls. Most times it was telemarketers. Sometimes it was her mother, and then she would quickly phone back, but sometimes it was Evan. In the first few messages he had left, he sounded upbeat, calling to invite her out for an event. When she never called back, his messages became less frequent, asking why she never returned his calls. His last message said he had been accepted to an out-of-state college and he might not be back for a long time.

Lydia was embarrassed and disappointed by how she handled herself. Evan didn't seem to be bothered that they had "been together." She couldn't imagine speaking to him again. She felt ashamed she had let herself get swept away in the moment. Her body had completely overruled her mind; she was out of control. She wasn't mad at Evan. He had been so kind and gentle. She had wanted it, like a whore.

Lydia had never prayed as fervently in her life. She was a sinner. Somehow, she managed to act normal around others, but she still felt self-conscious, like she had a label on her forehead saying what she had done.

Then the stomach flu came. She was exhausted and just couldn't sleep enough. After school, she would come home and nap until supper and then not want to eat. Everything made her stomach clench with nausea. Why couldn't she kick this thing?

She went to the pharmacy and filled her basket with Pepto, Gravol, and every other stomach medication on the shelf.

"Can I help you, miss?" a woman in a pharmacist coat inquired. She had noticed Lydia spending a long time searching for something, reading the labels.

Lydia shifted and quickly glanced around to see if there was anyone near them. As she disclosed her problem, her voice fell to a whisper. "I've had this stomach flu for a couple of weeks. It won't go away."

"It's not usual for the flu to last that long. Are you sure

you're not pregnant?" The blood drained from Lydia's face as the realization hit her. She froze, clutching the basket to her body.

By Lydia's reaction, the pharmacist realized how inappropriate the comment was and immediately apologized. "I'm sorry, miss. I've been in the business for a lot of years. I have seen many tired women come in thinking they have the flu when it's a baby on the way." She peered into Lydia's basket. "If you have the stomach flu, those items are probably going to help you. If they don't, you should probably go see your doctor." She smiled, patted Lydia's arm, and walked away, leaving her in the aisle.

Lydia set the basket down and ran out of the store. Was she pregnant? How could this happen to *her*? She had never even kissed a boy before Evan. They had only done it once. She flopped on her bed, balled up in her blankets, and cried until the tears wouldn't come anymore. Had she even had her period lately? It was always unpredictable, and she was so busy with school.

Her blankets were twisted into a pile by the next morning as she tossed and turned and brooded about the possibility. The thought of breakfast was repulsive, so she skipped it completely.

That evening, Lydia found another pharmacy in a different neighborhood. She filled her basket with a bunch of things, slipping a pregnancy test into the pile. When she got home, she read the instructions several times to ensure she correctly understood how to take the test. The kit advised waiting until morning to ensure better accuracy of the results, so she decided to wait.

Beyond the 14th Floor

Again, she fitfully slept as nightmares danced through her subconscious. Lydia was walking through her old high school. People were pointing and laughing as her belly was swollen like a large balloon. They chanted, "Whore, whore, whore." She panicked and ran out the doors. She was carrying something. She looked down into her arms to see a bundle. *My baby*, she thought. She gently pulled the blanket back, revealing a writhing snake. She screamed and woke up covered in sweat. The warm summer morning had made her bedroom stuffy and hot.

She forced herself to get out of bed and go to the bathroom, even though her bladder had felt ready to explode for the last hour. She dreaded this, afraid of the possible answer. The pregnancy test was waiting for her on the sink. The smiling woman on the package mocked her, with her hand displaying a wedding band.

She perched on the toilet with her knees wide apart so she could pee on the little stick. She set it on the counter and flushed the toilet. She curled in a protective ball on the floor, setting the timer on her watch for three minutes as the instructions recommended. She waited five minutes. She couldn't bring herself to check the result.

Finally, Lydia forced herself to stand and carefully study the test. Bile rose in her throat and she scrambled to the toilet. Hanging over it, she retched until yellow froth came. She grabbed a washcloth and ran it under the ice-cold tap and washed her sweaty face and neck. She was pregnant.

She spent the day praying and envisioning how she could tell her parents. All she could imagine was her father's angry face and her mother's lips pursed in disappointment.

They would be so ashamed. Frank and Joan Armstrong saw their family as one of the prominent families in their church, a family that others looked to for example. The priest was at her parents' house every week for a meal. What would he think of her? She was a whore. Any other girls in the church that had a baby out of wedlock had been judged, pitied, and whispered about forever. She would be that girl.

Her family lived for the Church and held her to high regard. Sex was for after marriage, and even then, it was for procreation, certainly not pleasure. How would her family understand it had been a mistake? They would think she was weak and immoral. The thought of telling them and seeing the disgusted expressions on their faces was far too much to bear.

To Lydia, the situation was hopeless, and she could only come to one conclusion. They couldn't know. She couldn't live with ruining their lives. Rifling through the drawers, she found what she was looking for. She shook the blue bottle, the rattle confirming there were enough pills left. She had had her wisdom teeth removed and was given a strong prescription for pain relief. The dentist had given her such a stern warning on how to properly take them, it had scared her. She had put them in her dresser and suffered through the pain instead of taking them. She didn't want to get addicted to anything.

She took a warm bath and got dressed in some of her best clothes. Tears wet her face as she straightened her apartment. Lydia didn't want anyone to think she was a slob. When they found her, she would be sleeping in her bed like an angel. No one would ever have to know she was pregnant. Everyone would remember her as the good girl that helped out at church. Yes, that was what she wanted. Her parents wouldn't have to be embarrassed by her. The shame would disappear.

She prayed, "Dear Lord, forgive me all of my sins. I have tried to serve you in every way. I have failed you. I am not worthy. I cannot see any other way. I can't put my family through this. If you can see any way for me to stay, please send me a sign. I will face the truth and whatever that shall bring. Amen."

She sat in prayer for what felt like an eternity. No sign came. She choked out a sob, clutched the pill bottle, and swallowed the bitter, chalky pills one by one.

Chapter Twelve

"Hey Babe."

"Hey Evan."

"Is everything okay? I just got back to my place and you wouldn't even know anything had happened here last night. The elevator was working fine. What crappy luck you guys had."

"Yes, everything is good. We've made a bit of a discovery here this afternoon. This may be a big shock for you. Apparently, Leah, the girl that was with me in the elevator, was on her way to see you. She was searching for her dad."

There was a confused pause on the other end.

"Me?"

"Yes. She has some information and it seems like it could be true. I'm not sure if you know about this already and didn't want to tell me…"

"What information? I don't have any kids. Remember, Sarah and I were trying…"

"Leah found her birth certificate in her mom's things, and for the first time, saw the name that was listed as her father. It said Evan Bates. Her mom's name is Lydia

Armstrong. Does that name make any sense to you?"

"Whoa..." He paused and exhaled. "Yes, I remember Lydia. She was from high school and I went out with her once in college. I haven't seen her since then, though."

"Leah thinks you might be her dad. Could that be possible?" Jill held her breath.

She could hear a clatter on the other end and then some fumbling. He had dropped his phone.

"Sorry. We were kids fumbling around after a dance. I was twenty and a virgin. It was only one time. I told you I wasn't much of a player when I was young, but I do remember Lydia. It's possible. I am stunned she never told me. I called her after that, several times. She wouldn't take my calls, so I stopped trying. I didn't want to be a creep that couldn't take a hint. I felt bad, like I had taken advantage of her."

"You took advantage of her?"

"No, I didn't force myself on her by any means. We were definitely in the moment together."

"I'm glad, I didn't think you would be that kind of guy."

"I can't imagine what you are thinking right now. Does the girl look like me?" he asked.

"Yeah, she kinda' does. But you can do testing just to make sure it's true."

"Damn. Why wouldn't she have told me? I might have been a dad all these years but didn't even have the chance to be involved. I wouldn't have left her to do it on her own."

"If this is true, you're going to have a lot of emotions to work through. It's a real shock."

"Wow. I can't believe it. I need to find Lydia. I have a

lot of questions for her. I have to see this girl. Can she be there tomorrow night when I come over?"

"Yes, she'll be here. Maybe it will be a bit easier if I'm here, because I know you both."

"Yes, I appreciate that a lot. I hope this won't change how you feel about me. I really care about you, Jill."

"I care about you too. Sometimes life gives us unexpected surprises." She unconsciously put her hand to her stomach. "We'll figure this out. She's a good girl."

"I wish I could come sooner, but I'm booked solid tomorrow."

"We'll be here. I have to work for a while tomorrow morning, then I'll take the afternoon off to be with Leah."

"Okay, perfect. I'll come after I get cleaned up from work. I'm sure I won't sleep tonight. Thanks for everything, bye."

Jill put her phone down and went to the living room, where Leah was pacing. She looked up at Jill, waiting for the response.

"He was definitely shocked but admitted it's a possibility he got your mother pregnant."

Leah squealed. "I've found my dad!"

"Honey, we have to get your mom involved and we should also do a DNA test for definite proof. We'll be able to find out for sure though."

"I'm excited and nervous. I have so many things to ask him." Leah's eyes went wide as the realization overcame her. "Jill, you're pregnant!"

Jill nodded as the puzzle fell together in Leah's mind. "Yes, it's Evan's baby."

Melaney Bossaer

"Wow!"

"I know. I haven't told him yet."

"He doesn't know?"

"No, not yet, and I need you to keep this secret for a while longer. The poor guy is going to pack up and leave the country if we drop all of this on him at once." Leah nodded.

"Jill, this is crazy, but I could be a half-sister to your baby."

"My baby is going to be pretty lucky then." Jill smiled at the thought. It was all she could do; it was so surreal.

"I guess you and my mom have something in common."

Luckily, she was okay with handling a pregnancy with or without Evan. She felt prepared and mature. She couldn't imagine what Leah's Mom had gone through. When you are young and afraid, it is a different story. Jill hadn't expected to get pregnant either. Evan probably assumed she was on birth control of some kind. It was both of their faults that they didn't have a responsible talk about it before they made love.

They discussed what was going to happen and they agreed after Leah met Evan, she would return home to her mom's. She needed to go back to school and do her best in her last year.

The next morning, Jill went into work to take care of some appointments. By the time she got back to her house, Leah was wound up like a top.

"Okay, I took Buck for a big walk because I couldn't sit still. I have tried on the three outfits I had in my bag and they all look terrible. When I left my mom's, I was just shoving random stuff into my backpack." Leah paced the living room liked a caged animal. Weepy eyes betrayed her as she tried to keep her emotions in check.

Jill's heart softened as she put a hand on Leah's arm. "Hey, listen, we have a couple of hours before supper. Let's go shopping and we'll get you an outfit. I know this is a big day for you."

Leah exhaled and her face relaxed with relief. "Thank you so much. I just want to look half decent when I meet my dad for the first time. I have some money to pay for it."

They headed out to the mall and discovered a great little shop. They found a perfect pair of pants and a blue button-up top that matched Leah's eyes. Jill found some cute boots that completed the outfit. Leah shook her head. "I don't have enough to buy those."

"Don't worry, Sweetie. This one is on me." Jill smiled and insisted on paying for the clothes.

They both picked at their supper with nervous anticipation. The meeting tonight would affect both of their lives moving forward.

Soon enough, Buck was at the front door barking and jumping. Jill smiled at Leah. "Evan is here. Buck loves him."

Jill and Leah stood in the hall as Evan walked up. The door swung wide and before they could even greet one another, Buck launched himself at Evan so hard he staggered backwards and almost fell down. "Okay Buck, whoa buddy. I missed you too."

"Buck, my goodness. Calm down. You can always be guaranteed a hearty welcome when you come here." They all laughed as Buck's wild behavior broke the ice.

Jill grabbed Buck by the collar and scuttled him off to the back yard. Evan and Leah stared at one another, soaking in every detail. Jill returned. "Evan, this is Leah."

Now, as they stood two feet apart, you could see the many similarities. Jill felt in her heart it was true, this *was* Evan's daughter.

Leah tentatively stepped forward and Evan reached for her, enveloping her in a crushing hug. Leah began to cry as Evan stroked her hair. He closed his eyes and they clung to each other. Jill teared up witnessing the raw emotion of the meeting.

After a few moments, they pulled apart and stood in awkward silence.

"Let's go have some hot chocolate." Jill herded them to the kitchen table. She asked if they wanted her to leave, but they both shook their heads happy to have her as a friendly third party.

They peppered each other with questions about the important details.

"Leah, I never knew your mom was pregnant. I admit I didn't know her well, but I am not the kind of guy to run."

"Mom never talked about you unless I asked and then she would only say you had died. She would get really upset, so I never asked her much about you."

"I think your mom's family was very religious. I can imagine they wouldn't have taken the news very well."

"They disowned her, or she chose to cut them off. I'm not really sure anymore. Because of me, she's been alone for a long time." Evan reached over and patted her hand.

Leah continued. "She's never even dated anyone all

these years, or at least not that I know of."

"I have to admit I'm frustrated that I missed the chance to know you all these years. I am sure this hasn't been easy for your mom, but you didn't have to grow up without a dad in your life."

She shrugged, not knowing what to say.

"Does your mom know you're meeting me?"

"Yes, I told her I was going to. She was really upset. She is afraid she'll lose me."

"I know I have questions for her. Pretty big ones. After all these years, this is shocking news."

"I know. I am confused too."

"I've got to ask you for one thing." Evan looked serious. "I'm feeling like this is true, but for both of our sakes and legally, I think we should do a paternity test." Jill nodded.

"What's that?" asked Leah.

"They can confirm using a blood test or saliva that we're related, that I'm your dad."

Her face clouded over with a mix of confusion and disappointment.

"Sweetie, it's not bad. You may both feel this is real, but others may question your relationship. This way you will have proof," Jill explained.

Leah shoulders relaxed and she nodded.

"I'm going to ask you to keep this a secret for a while longer. We'll do the testing, and then we can share our good news with the world. I would also like a chance to talk with your mom."

"That's fair," Leah said.

"The good news is you can take your time and get to

know one another now," Jill said.

"You're right. We can get to know one another. Once the results come back, I will take you to meet my family—your uncles and aunts and my dad, your grandpa." He smiled at Leah and then Jill. "Of course, I want them to meet you too, Jill."

"Yes, I'd love that." Jill smiled.

They continued to talk into the evening. Evan told stories about his first wife, Sarah, sharing his heartache at her passing and how they had tried to have a baby. He reached out and patted Leah's hand. "Maybe that has changed now."

Leah didn't reveal she was gay. Jill took her cue and didn't say anything. That was up to Leah, when she was comfortable with sharing that with Evan.

They talked about the elevator and Evan couldn't believe how Leah had done CPR to save Martin. "That is a pretty huge deal. You're a real hero."

Leah beamed with pride. "It was so crazy. My mind was blank, and I was so scared. I couldn't remember what to do, and then it all came back to me."

"I'm anxious to phone the hospital to see how Martin is doing. Hopefully, we can find out," Jill said.

Leah yawned, covering her mouth. Evan looked at his watch. "I'm sorry, girls. This has been an amazing evening, but I have a really early morning tomorrow. It looks like you're both tired too."

They walked to the door and Evan turned to Leah. He gave her another hug. "I'll keep in touch, Kiddo. We'll get this all figured out. I'm not going anywhere."

Jill walked Evan out to his truck.

"Wow. Thanks for helping me with this. I appreciate having you there," he said.

"I'm glad to help. The world sure works in mysterious ways. I think you're right about the testing though. My gut instinct says Leah is your daughter, but it's best to know for certain."

"I feel the same. She's a sweet kid, this could be pretty exciting."

Jill felt uneasy, as her secret was still waiting for the right time. *Was there a right time?*

"Jill, can you give me a hand figuring out this paternity testing stuff? I'd like to get it done as soon as we can." He pulled her close and hugged her

"Yes, I'll help you. It will be good to find out for sure."

"I need to talk to Lydia. I'm angry she kept this from me all these years. I would have liked the chance to know my own kid."

"I can't imagine what she was going through that she chose to hide her pregnancy from you, but I'm sure it will help to talk to her."

"Can I see you this weekend? Are we still okay?" Evan's eyes searched Jill's.

"Yes, we're fine. Leah is a beautiful young woman. I still can't believe how this all worked out." She shivered, and he kissed the top of her head.

"Better get inside, it's really getting cold out."

The next morning, they rose early. Jill planned to drop Leah off at home, and she also called the hospital to check on Martin's recovery. The receptionist advised her that she couldn't reveal any information about a patient. Jill was disappointed and told the receptionist how Leah had saved Martin's life in the elevator and they just wanted to know if he pulled through. The woman was touched enough by the situation she revealed that Martin was currently a patient at the hospital. Jill and Leah were thrilled; Leah really had saved his life.

As they drove Leah blurted out "I think Evan will take your pregnancy news okay."

"I hope so, but I want to make sure I tell him at the right time. I want to let your news sink in for a bit first."

"He seems like a pretty good guy. If he's my real dad, which I think he is, I'm pretty lucky."

"I think you're right about being lucky, he is a really nice guy."

"Jill, I have to admit something. All my life I have wanted a dad and to be a normal family. When I discovered my dad was still alive, I thought if I could find him, maybe my mom and him would get back together. Like, maybe they've both been missing each other all these years. Then I would finally have the perfect family." She shrugged. "But it's more complicated than I thought. When I see Evan with you, it's obvious how much he cares about you. Plus, if you're having his baby, how could I want him to leave you to be with my mom?"

As they pulled up to Leah's apartment, Jill turned to her. "A perfect family can take many forms. If you are surrounded by people who care about you and support you, that's what matters the most." She leaned over and hugged Leah.

Beyond the 14th Floor

Jill waited as Leah got out and ran up the steps and she turned to wave. The door opened behind her and Jill could see a woman waiting. Leah turned and stopped on the top step, then tentatively met her mother at the door. Jill could see Leah's mom crush her in a hug as her face was contorted with emotion. It was clear she loved her, but they needed to find a path to understanding one another now.

Chapter Thirteen

The first night in the hospital was a blur for Martin. He had been in diabetic distress when he arrived, and the doctors struggled to get his blood sugar levels under control. He drifted in and out of consciousness, thinking he was in the elevator one minute and then lying comfortably on a soft bed the next.

By the next day, things had improved for him and he woke to see his daughter and her family sitting by his bed. Their faces were pinched with worry, but they were relieved he would recover.

After being discharged from the hospital, he took a few more days off work and then returned to the school on the following Monday.

"Glad to see you back, old chap," said Principal Schmidt, clapping him on the shoulder. "Sounds like you had quite an adventure last week."

Martin nodded. He was relieved to get back to some sense of normal again. He still felt tired and a bit weak, but happy to be feeling better. His hip was still terribly sore, but he talked to the doctors about it when he was in the hospital and they thought they could help him. His health benefits through work would cover most of it.

After school, Martin heard a page over the intercom calling him to the office. When he arrived, there was a gentleman in the office talking with Principal Schmidt. They were having what appeared to be a somber conversation while Martin waited. He could see Principal Schmidt look up and notice him.

He opened the door to his office gesturing the man out the door. "Here, Martin is our custodian. He'll be able to assist you." The man nodded and looked at Martin. His face was etched with pain and sadness.

Who was this man? He looked familiar somehow, but Martin couldn't understand how, he'd never met him before.

"Martin, this is Scott Tatum's dad, Phil. He's here to collect the contents of Scott's locker."

Martin nodded and extended his hand. "Sir, I'm so sorry for your loss." Scott's dad gazed back with black circles underneath his eyes.

"Thank you. It's been a difficult couple of weeks."

Martin knew where the locker was because the police had been through it already, looking for evidence. Luckily, they had left it in good order and had been respectful of Scott's things. He opened the locker and stepped back to allow Phil to gather the items. As the man leafed through the binders and books, Martin realized he didn't have anything to carry the contents of the locker with.

"I'll find a box for you," Martin mumbled as he shuffled off to the janitor's room. His supplies came in large boxes and he could empty one to use. He found one and as he pulled the items out to put on the shelf, he looked up to see the running shoe. Scott's shoe. He picked it up and placed it in the box.

Pain from his hip shot down his leg with every step as he made his way back down the hall to the locker with the empty box. "Sir, I have a box for you. I'm also returning Scott's shoe. I found it in the hall after they took him away to the hospital. I was going to return it to him."

"Thanks, I appreciate that." He took the box from Martin. He coughed, clearing his throat. "It has been a pretty difficult time for us. They still haven't found out who did it."

"I'm sorry. That must be really hard." Martin's stomach was in knots. He felt guilty for the hardship he had caused. He should have told the police the truth at the start. They stood in awkward silence.

"They have a grainy video, but it was dark, and they couldn't be sure..." Phil cleared his throat again, choking back emotion. "I just want to get this done. So, thanks again."

Martin turned to leave and then hesitated. "Sir, for what it's worth, Scott was a good boy. I seen lots of kids through the years, but he really had somethin' special about him."

Phil studied his face and nodded. "Thanks. That means a lot to me. We felt he was pretty special too." He turned back to the locker.

Clearly, he wanted to go through Scott's things on his own. Martin nodded in understanding and limped off to the janitor's room to give him privacy. He put rolls of paper towel up in the space the shoe had occupied, filling the void.

Martin got home that night and saw his answering machine flashing with a message. He pressed PLAY and a familiar voice came on.

"Hey Martin, it's Jill from the elevator. I called directory assistance and found your number. I guess you aren't home right now. I just wanted to give you a call to see how you are doing. Leah and I were worried about you. Maybe we can all get together for coffee sometime soon. Take care. Bye."

Martin smiled. The elevator had been difficult. Leah and Jill had been so kind to him. He needed to thank them for all they had done. They had saved his life. He had been shocked to discover that the girl, Leah, had performed CPR on him. Yes, he wanted to see them again.

Despite resting in his comfortable chair, his hip throbbed and the churning in his gut would not go away. He knew what the right thing was but that didn't mean it was the easiest. He owed it to Scott to come forward, but he couldn't imagine living with the pain his hip was giving him for much longer. The doctor who saw him in the hospital gave him encouraging news about getting it done. He needed his insurance. Scott was dead; he couldn't change that.

Chapter Fourteen

Lydia had dreaded the day Leah might discover her dad was still alive. *What would he say to her? Would he try to take Leah?*

When Leah ran out the door into the night, Lydia had fallen to the floor and cried. She didn't deserve this. Her whole life had centered around protecting Leah and being a good mother to her. She had never dated. She worked and then came home to Leah every day for seventeen years. How could that be wrong?

Now, she was losing control. Leah was growing into an adult and wasn't her little girl anymore. Was she really gay? Now that she had met her dad, what was it going to mean? Leah would be welcomed into a whole other family that Lydia wouldn't be a part of. What if she had told Evan about being pregnant? No, she still thought she wouldn't have. She wouldn't have wanted anyone to stay with her out of pity. She did the right thing, keeping it a secret. It had worked best for her, until now.

Lydia was so relieved and thankful having Leah back. It had been terrible not knowing where she was. She hardly slept the days Leah was gone and paced her apartment every night wondering what to do. The occasional text from her saying she was okay kept Lydia from going to the police.

Leah told her about her search for Evan and how she ended up trapped in the elevator for the night. She cried telling her mom how Martin had stopped breathing and how she had been so scared having to do CPR. Lydia was shocked and proud that Leah had saved his life.

She was grateful that the people trapped with her had been good to her. She couldn't believe Evan's girlfriend was with Leah in the elevator. Fate worked in crazy ways.

Leah told Lydia that Evan would be contacting her. She was nervous, but she knew she owed him an explanation. She was filled with anxiety about being confronted by him. Would he be angry? She was sure he would be.

The following day, Evan called her. The conversation was short. He suggested they meet somewhere neutral and they chose a coffee shop they both knew. Lydia didn't tell Leah; she didn't want any extra questions or pressure.

She arrived at the coffee shop early. Her hands were ice cold and she was nervous. She had dressed carefully. She wanted to look pretty, despite the years since seeing one another. She began to scan for an empty table when a man stood up, catching her attention. Evan.

He still looked like the boy she remembered but fuller and manlier. His dark, curly hair was shorter than he wore years ago. He looked at her and then recognizing her, smiled and extended his hand.

She tentatively reached out and shook his large, warm,

calloused hand. Her heart jumped a bit. He was still very attractive. He gestured her to a chair, and they sat. Neither said a word as a waitress arrived to take their order then left them alone.

Lydia's eyes watered and her voice quavered. "Evan, I'm sorry."

He exhaled and leaned back in his chair, disappointment on his face. "All I can ask is, why? Why didn't you tell me you were pregnant?"

She picked nervously at a napkin unable to make eye contact. She felt so guilty. She had expected him to be angry; that may have been easier.

"You don't understand. I was so scared."

His face softened. "Listen, I can't begin to pretend what it must have been like for you, but you didn't even give me a chance."

"I felt embarrassed. I should have never let things get as far as they did that night. We barely knew each other. I thought you would think I was a whore."

"I never thought you were a whore. Not for a moment." He shook his head. "I was disappointed that you never returned my calls. I wanted to see you again. I'm sorry, that we hadn't been more careful. I had no idea about Leah all these years. You could have found me to tell me." He raked his hair in frustration. "What happened when you found out you were pregnant?"

Lydia trembled and supressed the urge to cry. This was so difficult. "I was sick. I thought I had the stomach flu. It wouldn't go away. I ended up in the hospital and my parents found out. They were so mad. I thought they would kill you, so I never told them who Leah's father was."

She didn't want to tell him about her suicide attempt. That was something no one would ever find out about. Of the mistakes she had made in her life, that was the biggest. She shuddered at the thought that she almost ended up killing them both. She prayed for forgiveness every day and thanked God for giving her the second chance to live and have Leah. Evan could never understand how terrifying it had been for her and as she thought about it, there seemed like no words to explain to him what happened.

#

Lydia's head pounded and her body felt leaden. Her eyes fluttered but she couldn't keep them open. She could hear weeping and then voices murmuring—her parents, Frank and Joan Armstrong. She was alive.

"I don't understand why she did this. She didn't say anything was bothering her. When she didn't show up for church, I knew something was wrong right away, and then we found her." Her mother blurted out another sob and the nurse nodded with sympathy.

Her cloudy mind began to clear, and her eyes opened. She was in a hospital. A nurse was by her side. "Lydia, Lydia Armstrong. Can you hear me?" Lydia nodded, too groggy to talk. "Do you know where you are, Lydia?"

She glanced around the room—the white walls, the curtains, the monitors by her bed. She nodded to the nurse. A doctor moved into place beside the nurse.

"Lydia, you are at Bellevue Hospital Centre. Do you know why you are here?" the doctor asked in a quiet voice.

Beyond the 14th Floor

Lydia looked down at the sheets and nodded as her eyes squeezed shut and silent tears slipped down her cheeks. The doctor rubbed her arm. "You're safe here," said the doctor as she patted her arm.

She turned to Lydia's parents, who stood near the bed. Joan looked tearful and was wringing her hands. "She will be fine. Her vitals are all stable and it looks like she was found quickly enough. The baby should be fine as well." Joan continued to sob and shook her head as the doctor walked out of the room.

The nurse finished up with the vitals check. "Sweetie, I'm going to get you some toast and juice. That'll make you feel a bit better." She squeezed Lydia's hand and left the room, closing the door behind her.

Her parents protectively gathered on each side of her bed. Joan leaned in close and looked deeply into her eyes, searching. "Honey, who was it? Who forced themselves on you?" Her voice quavered and she clutched Lydia's hand to her heart.

Before she could respond, Frank chimed in. "We'll find the filthy, despicable bastard and he'll pay for what he did to you."

Lydia curled in a ball and wept. Joan looked at Frank over the crying girl and said, "Maybe Lydia doesn't even know who it was. Maybe it was a stranger. Honey, you should have come to us. We love you, we'll get through this. We'll make a plan for this baby. We'll find a good home through an adoption agency. I'm sure they have dealt with rape victims before. You must have felt so awful and worried for you to try to commit…" Her voice trailed off and she couldn't finish her sentence.

Lydia felt terrible and her stomach churned. For the first time, she spoke. "I'm gonna' be sick!" She bolted upright, throwing up into her lap and down the front of her white gown.

Frank paled. "I'll get the nurse." He rushed from the room.

Joan found a washcloth beside the sink in the room and rinsed it under the cold water. The nurse came in with a fresh gown and a stack of fresh bedding, followed by Frank. "Maybe we should let her rest. I will help her get showered and we'll get her back to bed," she said, sensing how distraught Lydia was feeling.

"We'll come back after supper, Honey. You need some rest." Joan rubbed her shoulder and then turned to go. Frank forced a weak smile, put his arm around her mother, and herded her out the door.

The next day, Lydia was resting in bed. She felt a lot better. They had pumped her stomach and she had pretty much recovered from the effects of the overdose. The doctor prescribed some medication for the morning sickness as well. They would keep her one more night and she would be discharged the next day.

A nurse softly knocked and came into her room. Lydia was surprised to see the nurse was followed by a Philadelphia police officer. She stiffened and held her breath. *Was she in trouble? She hadn't done anything wrong, only to herself—and the baby.*

"Lydia, this is Officer Baker from Philly PD. He would like to have a few words with you."

"Miss Armstrong." Officer Baker nodded and pulled a chair up to the bed. "Is it okay if I ask you a few questions?"

Lydia pulled the covers up around her neck and looked at him with wide eyes. He pulled out a clipboard and wrote a couple of things down. He looked at his watch and recorded the time.

"So, Lydia, I know this has been a difficult time for you. I wish I didn't even have to ask you to talk about this. Your parents have reported you were the victim of a sexual assault and we want to see that the person is arrested." He nodded with reassurance. "Can you tell me exactly what happened? Please take your time, I know this is hard."

Lydia's mind was racing. She hadn't even known her parents had called the police. She was humiliated. The situation had spun out of control. She wanted to lie. Her mind was racing, but she didn't even know what to say. She wanted to be left alone to go home.

She looked into her lap and took breath. Her words came out as a mumble and the officer leaned closer. "I'm sorry, miss. I didn't quite hear what you said."

"I wasn't raped."

"I'm sorry, Miss Armstrong. I'm a bit confused. Your parents called the station and said you had been raped."

"I never said I was raped. I never said anything. They just assumed." She bit her lip and put her head in her hands fighting back tears. "I'm sorry for wasting your time. I had no idea they were going to call anyone, or I would have tried to convince them not to."

"So, you weren't sexually assaulted?"

"No."

"Did you know the person whom you had sex with?"

"Yes."

"Was it against your will?" Officer Baker asked.

Lydia looked out the window and whispered, "No. I was okay with it. I liked him."

"Okay. So, it was consensual," Office Baker confirmed, scratching more notes on his pad.

"Yes."

"Is there anything else I need to know? We're here to protect you."

Lydia shook her head and this time made eye contact with Officer Baker. "I was not raped. I'm sorry this has wasted your time."

Officer Baker stood and tucked his clipboard under his arm. "Okay, Miss Armstrong, this case will be closed. I hope you're feeling better soon."

The door closed behind him as he left and she crawled under the covers and curled in a ball, wishing she could disappear.

She could hear quick footsteps coming down the hall and the door to her room flew open as her parents came rushing in.

"Lydia, what's going on? The officer just left, and he said the case was closed. He wouldn't tell us any more about it." Joan stood by the bed, her forehead creased with concern.

"Are you afraid to tell? Is that what it is? Are you scared?" Frank asked. "We won't let the rapist get away with this."

Lydia sat up in bed and pulled her knees up to her

chest. She put her face in her hands and began to cry. Joan moved over to her and rubbed her back. Finally, she wiped her eyes with the back of her arm.

"I wasn't raped."

Shock resonated in the room as her parents struggled to absorb the information. Joan's hand stopped rubbing her back and lifted away. She could tell her parents were looking at one another over her head.

"Are you dating someone?" Joan asked. "Why haven't we met this boy?"

"Who is it?" Frank asked, his voice gruff.

"It was a mistake," Lydia replied. She put her head back down, not knowing what to expect from her parents.

"How did this happen?" Joan asked incredulously. "We didn't raise you like this."

"I don't want to talk about it."

"Listen Lydia, we *are* going to talk about this," Frank said, leaning over her, his eyes flashing with anger. At moment, a nurse entered the room. *Good timing*, thought Lydia.

"Is everything okay in here?" the nurse asked. She could likely hear the voices getting louder outside Lydia's room.

"Yes," Joan replied too quickly.

The nurse made eye contact with Lydia. "I need to go over a few things with Lydia. Would you mind giving us a little while?" The nurse smiled at Lydia's parents and began writing on her clipboard.

"Yes. Yes, we will go." Frank looked at Lydia, straightened his tie with an air that said *this isn't finished*, and grabbed her mother's arm.

When they were out of earshot, the nurse leaned a little closer. "Are you okay?" she asked. "They don't seem very happy. This must be difficult for you."

Lydia nodded and a tear quietly trickled down her cheek. "I don't know what to do." She shrugged and looked out the window.

"Listen, Sweetie. We have some people you can talk to here this afternoon. They can give you some support to help you with what your options are. It may feel like you are the only young woman dealing with something like this, but it happens way more than you could imagine. This may not have been your plan but now it is something you will have to plan for."

Lydia met with a social worker that afternoon and dreaded her parents return. She actually had had no visitors at the hospital besides her parents and she wondered if anyone else even knew where she was.

The next morning, she was up and dressed to be ready for release when her parents swept in, her mother carrying her jacket and a pair of shoes for her. She braced herself for what was coming and felt stronger than she had for a while.

"Okay, Lydia. We have decided what to do with you," Frank said.

"Yes. We were up all evening making phone calls and we know what to do now," Joan explained. "You will go live with my Aunt Rosalie in Detroit. People won't know you there. We can tell everyone you got a job there. When the baby comes, you will put the baby up for adoption then your future won't be ruined by this. Many folks will be happy to have a baby from a good family like ours. Then you can come home and live with us. We don't want this to happen again."

"I think you will agree this is for the best," Frank offered. He nodded and looked at Joan.

"What?" asked Lydia, her mouth agape. "I am going home to my apartment. I'm not moving anywhere." Anger brewed in her heart. "There are single girls that have babies all the time. This isn't the 1950s."

"It's not like that. How will you meet a nice man if you have someone else's child?" Joan said, trying to touch her arm. "Besides, what will the parish think of this? We are role models for many of these people. We have a reputation to uphold. Your father is on the council."

Lydia jerked her arm back and for the first time in her life took a defiant stance against her parents. "I will not move away. I will have this baby. If I'm so embarrassing, I'll stay away. I can't live like this anymore." She grabbed her jacket and shoes and stumbled past her parents out of the room.

She heard her mother begin to call out and follow her and then heard her father say, "Let her go." Her heart broke as she replayed the words over and over in her head. *Let her go.*

She got outside and realized she had nothing with her. No purse, no money, just the outfit she had been wearing when she was found. She felt hollow and realized her life as she knew it had changed in that instant. She turned in the direction of her apartment and trudged fifteen blocks home, her landlord would have to let her in.

#

"They didn't take it well, I'm guessing." Evan's voice interrupted her.

Overwhelmed by emotion, Lydia began to cry. "You have no idea. They wanted to send me away and force me to give up the baby. I refused and they didn't want me to be around their church. They were so ashamed of me. I didn't want to get you in trouble."

"That must have been really hard." He couldn't help but reach over and pat her arm and hand her a napkin.

"I have hardly spoken to them in years. My mother sends birthday cards and gifts at Christmas for Leah, but really hasn't had much contact. It seems easier for them that way."

"I'm sorry you had to do this alone, but I'm not the kind of guy that walks. I would have stayed. You didn't give me a chance." Anger crept in as he tried to keep his voice even.

Lydia put her face in her hands. "That is always something I have struggled with. I didn't know what you would do. We hardly knew one another. I was so embarrassed; I didn't want you to reject me. I know I didn't give you the chance to decide."

"I feel like this is the real deal, that Leah is my daughter—she even resembles me—but I want us to do a DNA test so it's legally proven. If she is mine, I need to have official rights as her father. I wanted to let you know that I will be planning to do that."

"I understand." She looked at him in earnest. "You don't know me well, but I can assure you - you are Leah's dad."

"After the results come back, we will have to meet again. I want to have her in my life too. I have missed seventeen years I can't get back."

Lydia nodded. "Just... just don't turn her against me. She is already so furious that I kept you from her." She sniffled and dabbed her eyes. Despite being angry, he softened toward her.

"No, no, I could never do that. I'm not that kind of person. I want to try to have a relationship with her, however possible. I only want what's best for Leah."

"I'm so sorry," Lydia said. "I didn't handle it as well as I should have. I have many regrets, but I've never regretted keeping Leah. She's the reason that I live."

"How did you manage all these years alone? It must have been hard."

"Hard work, sacrifice, and good neighbors who you help in return."

"Did she ever ask about me?"

Lydia averted her eyes and gazed out the window to the busy street. "I have made mistakes. I told Leah you had died before she was born. I knew deep down she yearned to have a dad. I stole that from her childhood. I will live with that guilt forever."

"I would like to make arrangements to pick her up to get DNA testing done."

Lydia shifted nervously in her chair. "Evan, I need to know more about you before I send Leah off with you. I haven't seen you in eighteen years."

He sighed. "I work for my father's plumbing business. I have since I returned from college. I haven't had many relationships in my life. I thought about you a lot after we... well, after that night. You didn't return my calls, so I thought you didn't like me. About ten years ago, I met the woman of my dreams, Sarah, and I married her. We tried to have kids but instead Sarah had multiple miscarriages. We were both depressed and Sarah took it especially hard. She died from an accidental overdose. So, for the past eight years, I have lived in a crappy apartment because I couldn't bear to be in our house alone. I dated a bit, but I never met anyone special."

"But what about the woman in the elevator with Leah? The place she stayed?"

"Jill. Yes, Jill. She is the first woman that's made me believe happiness could be possible again. I care for her very much."

"She was really good to Leah."

"Yes, she has an amazing heart. Her husband passed away a year or so ago. She doesn't have any kids either."

"Did Leah tell you about her friend that died?"

"No, I've only met her the one time, a couple of nights ago. We talked for a long time, but she didn't mention anything."

"Oh."

"Why, what happened?"

Pause. "I'm not sure what to say about this. I'm hoping it's a big mistake, but I guess you should know."

"About her friend?"

Lydia shifted nervously and picked at the napkin in her hand. "Leah was going to an after-school meeting every week. She was having a hard time at school. I should have asked more questions… It all came out the night she ran away."

"I thought she ran away to find me," Evan said.

"That was part of it." Lydia searched for words. "She came home really upset because her friend was killed. He got beat up and ended up dying from it."

"That's terrible, poor kid. Leah must have taken it pretty badly."

Lydia nodded. "She was devastated. I don't know if they caught who did it. She didn't really say."

"Why would that make her run away?"

"The club she was with, the one she didn't tell me about, was the Gay Alliance group."

She let it sink in. He blinked, registering the information. "So, her friend was from the Gay Alliance group? Her friend was beaten because he was gay?""

"Yes, those were the meetings that she was going to. Leah told me that she thinks *she* is gay."

Evan exhaled and sat back in his chair. "That's pretty heavy for a seventeen-year-old."

"I know, I couldn't believe it. She came unglued and started screaming at me about you. She found her birth certificate and some newspaper clippings that mentioned you. She realized you were alive. That's when we fought, and she ran out. I haven't talked to her about it since. I'm just glad she's home safe. I was sick with worry."

Evan nodded and Lydia continued.

"I want her to go into counselling. I don't know where she got those crazy ideas from; maybe it was my fault. She didn't have a male influence in her life. I'm paying for my mistakes. She's really a good girl. I'm hoping that this gay notion is just a phase and that she's just confused."

Evan didn't know how to respond. He looked at his phone. "I've got to get going. I have an appointment soon."

Lydia gathered her things and they split the bill. They stood on the sidewalk together outside the coffee shop.

"Lydia, just so you know. I will be in touch with Leah, but I'll keep you informed as well. He handed her a business card. Here's my number. You can call or text me anytime. I have nothing to hide."

They parted and headed to their vehicles, both wondering how different the future was going to be.

Chapter Fifteen

It had been over a month since Phil Tatum had collected the contents of Scott's locker. Martin thought a lot about Scott and Leah. He was so ashamed he hadn't come forward. His only solace was his doctor had now scheduled him for his hip replacement. He could hardly sleep at night, it throbbed and burned like an ember ready to burst into flames. Maybe once he got his hip fixed, he would go to the police. He couldn't afford to lose his health benefits now.

"Mr. Sanderson, please come to the office. Mr. Sanderson, to the office, please."

He looked up at the intercom. Seemed like the only times he got paged, there was trouble. He put his cleaning supplies in his room and limped to the office. He wasn't sure how much longer he could manage at work.

He could see through the window, even before he entered, that the police were back. He should have known this wasn't going to be easy. They still hadn't found out Sebastian and his thugs had beat up Scott.

Betty looked up and smiled. "Guess they want to talk to you again, Martin. I'm not sure, but best I could hear them say," her voice lowered to a whisper as she finished the sentence, "they are still investigating that Tatum boy's death."

He grunted in reply and lowered himself into a chair. Soon, the door opened, and he was invited into Principal Schmidt's office.

"Martin, seems like they have more questions for you." He gestured to the two officers, who nodded. "They would like to use my office to speak with you alone." He brushed past Martin and closed the door behind him.

Martin and the officers sat at a meeting table in the corner of the office. One of the officers flipped through his notes and addressed him. "So, Mr. Sanderson, I guess you have a bit more to tell us about the night Scott Tatum was beaten to death here at the school."

Martin fidgeted in his chair and he suddenly felt warm as perspiration broke out over his body. "Why do you say that?"

"We've had something turned in at the station. A running shoe with blood on it."

Okay, he could explain that. "Yes sir. After the ambulance took Scott away on the night he got beat, I found his shoe left behind in the hallway. Was gonna' return it to him when he came back."

The police nodded and one of them wrote as Martin spoke. "Mr. Sanderson, you found the shoe and what did you do with it?"

"I put it on the shelf in my janitor closet. I wanted to save it for Scott. Nowadays, those shoes are expensive. Thought he would have wanted it back."

"Scott's family turned it in to us. They said you had

given it to Scott's dad, Phil Tatum."

"Yes, that's right. He came in to clean out Scott's locker and I remembered I had the shoe. I put it in a box and then gave the box to Mr. Tatum."

"How did you know it was Scott's shoe?" asked the officer.

"I didn't know for sure, but I guessed it must have bin. It had some blood on it."

"Why didn't you turn it over to the police?"

"I... I... forgot about it, then I heard Scott had passed, so I knew he wouldn't need it anymore." Martin's voice broke and he hung his head.

"The family brought the shoe to the station because they said it wasn't Scott's. We found two different blood types on the shoe. We believe the shoe might belong to the perpetrator."

"We are going to ask for a DNA sample and fingerprints from you, Mr. Sanderson. You handled the shoe, so we need to rule you out. Were you bleeding, or did you get blood on your hands from helping Scott?"

Martin felt cold although his palms were sweaty. He was afraid he was in serious trouble. "No, I wasn't bleeding, but I had blood on my hands from helpin' Scott. There was so much blood, when I picked up the shoe, there was already blood on it."

"Officer Weston is going to take your prints and a swab from your cheek, if you agree." Officer Weston picked a briefcase up from the floor and opened it on the desk. It was like a mini laboratory in the case, with swabs, slides, and vials.

"Got nothin' to hide," Martin said, although his shaky voice didn't sound confident.

"Is there anything else you can remember that you may have forgotten about since the first time we talked?"

Martin shrugged and shook his head.

They processed Martin and soon he was out in the hall again. Principal Schmidt was waiting. He felt bile rise in the back of his throat, but he quickly swallowed the lump down again.

"They seem really interested in you. Is there something you need to tell me about this?" The principal tried to sound like an old friend but to Martin it sounded like an interrogation. He just wanted to go home.

"I found a shoe the night Scott got beat. I gave it to Scott's family, and they turned it over to the police. Guess it wasn't his." He tried to sound nonchalant, but the police seemed to think it was a big deal. He didn't want Principal Schmidt to know that. He seemed to mull over Martin's answer and then, satisfied, he turned and walked away.

He was just hoping this big mess would go away. He didn't ask to be involved. He just wanted to work until he could get his hip replacement, then retire.

Chapter Sixteen

At some point in Jill's life, she expected she would have kids. She could never have imagined the situation she found herself in. Brad's sperm had been saved, so if she wished to have Brad's baby without him, she could. She might have seriously considered it, had she not been in the beginning of a relationship with Evan.

Now, she was pregnant with Evan's baby. She was shocked and nervous at first. She knew she was certainly ready to be a parent, with or without the father involved to raise the child. She wanted to tell Evan she was pregnant, but she felt she needed to give him time to absorb the news of having Leah. Thankfully, he had reacted well to discovering he had a seventeen-year-old daughter.

Her and the baby's health had been coming along well. She had gone to a couple of appointments and things looked fine. She had been able to manage her morning sickness with only a few tough mornings. She wanted to tell Evan right away. It would soon be difficult to hide and with Leah knowing, she didn't want it to slip out.

She couldn't stop thinking about Martin these days.

She had left a message for him with her phone number and had left it up to him to respond. She hoped he was okay. It had been terrifying in the elevator as they tried to resuscitate him.

A few days later, her phone rang and she was relieved to hear his voice echo on the other end.

"Martin, I am so glad to hear from you. How are you feeling?"

"Not so bad, pretty tired. How are you feeling?"

She laughed. "Good, pretty tired too. Leah and I were really worried about you, so we've been thinking about you a lot. We have a lot to catch up on. Do you think we could meet you for coffee sometime soon?"

Martin paused. "I would like that. Yes, I would."

"That would be great. We'll plan a date." They chose a time and meeting place. Martin was glad Jill had reached out to him.

Her phone rang again. She could see it was Evan calling.

"Hey Babe."

"Hey, I got the results back from our DNA test we sent in." He paused.

"Well, is Leah your daughter?" She held her breath.

"Yes. There's a 99.99% chance she is."

"How do you feel about it?"

"I feel like I prepared myself for this, but I'm a bit freaked out. This is real now, no 'what ifs' anymore."

"That's huge news. She is an amazing person. I'd say you're very lucky."

"Would you help me tell her? You've been a part of this

from the beginning. I would like you to be there."

"I would be honoured."

"Why don't we have supper at your place on Saturday? I can pick up some take out or bring something over."

"That would work well. Leah and I are planning to meet Martin for coffee on Saturday, then we'll just come back here."

"Please don't say anything. I want it to be a surprise." He laughed. "I'm terrified, but part of me has always wanted to have kids. I didn't imagine I would start with a teenager."

"Life goes in unexpected directions sometimes."

"Hey babe?"

"Yeah?"

"I really miss seeing you. Before I got to see you every day, only seeing you on weekends really blows."

Jill laughed. "I agree. We'll have to figure something out."

She hung up and wondered how she would tell him. It had to be soon. It wasn't fair to him to hide it much longer.

On Saturday, she picked up Leah and they chatted on their way to meet Martin. It was beginning to snow. Jill was glad it wasn't too far of a drive.

Leah complained about Lydia being hard on her. Since running away, she was grounded and not allowed to do a lot of things. Leah was happy to be home, she felt scared and alone when she had run away. She had to get her mom to understand how she felt.

Jill hugged Martin when they saw him. They had lost him and then gotten him back in the elevator. It was a miracle to see the spark in his eyes and a smile on his weathered face.

When it was Leah's turn, Martin held her at arms-length and choked up as he thanked her for doing the CPR that saved his life. She smiled through tears and hugged him.

"I was so scared. I have never had to do CPR before. I'm glad it worked."

Martin pulled a hanky from his back pocket and wiped his wet cheeks. "You two are my angels."

Now in the comfort of a cafe, having snacks and drinking coffee, it was a different world. Jill and Leah updated Martin on their situation and how Evan could possibly be Leah's dad. Jill didn't say anything that would ruin the surprise later in the day.

"Well, I'll be." A grin spread across his face. That's something else. Your baby is related to Leah." He pondered the information and shook his head in amazement. "How we all came together in that elevator is some kind of a miracle."

"But Evan doesn't know about the baby yet. I'm going to tell him soon. He needed to meet Leah first."

Martin shifted in his chair and grimaced as the pain shot down his leg. Leah looked at Jill.

"How's your hip?" Jill asked.

"Not good, although going to the hospital after the elevator was a blessing in disguise. They looked at my hip and I'm scheduled for a replacement soon. I just have to keep working for a bit more so health insurance will cover the cost."

"Did they find out who killed Scott yet? Have you told

them?" Leah asked.

Martin looked down into his lap, defeated. He shook his head.

"That's unfair to Scott," Leah said with disappointment.

Jill gave him a sympathetic look. "Is there anything we can do to help you with this?"

"I'm not sure what. The good news is I gave Scott's family a runnin' shoe I found that night. I thought it was his. Turns out the police think it was whoever beat Scott. I'm hopin' it will put them on the right track. They must be close to solvin' this."

Leah frowned but didn't say anything. Jill changed the subject and soon looked at her watch in surprise. "This visit has flown by. We'll keep in touch, Martin. We should get going. I'm bringing Leah to my house for supper tonight with Evan." They hugged again and headed their separate ways.

The snow had whipped up and Jill drove with caution as her car slid to a stop at each intersection. "I'm going to need my winter tires put back on." She grimaced looking over at Leah. What a night this would be for her. To find out for sure Evan was her dad would be just what Leah had been hoping for. She had gone out and picked up a couple of balloons that said 'Congratulations!'. Her baby was also going to have a beautiful half-sister.

"How have things been at home?"

"Not great. Mom is the queen of not talking about hard stuff. I can't even bring it up. She refuses to talk about my sexuality." Leah looked out the window. "I still haven't gone back to my group."

"That's too bad. Do you have anyone you can talk to?"

"I can talk to some of the people at the Alliance group, but without Scott, everyone there seems a bit lost." She paused and turned to Jill. "I can't even act like myself around my mom anymore. She thinks there's something wrong with me, like I'm a freak. She wants me to go to counselling." She rolled her eyes.

"That must be tough. You and your mom should go to counselling together. Maybe that would help her understand you better and help you talk about things." Jill reassured Leah, "But, you can always talk to me if you need to."

"I wish you were my mom," said Leah, looking out the window at passing cars.

"Awww Honey, that is such a sweet thing to say but your mom loves you very much. No one is perfect. Your mom just doesn't understand what you're going through. Parenting isn't easy, especially single parenting."

"Yes, but she chose that, not me. She is punishing me for her mistakes." Leah defensively crossed her arms.

The traffic crawled along in spots where the snow was beginning to collect. Everyone was driving slowly until they turned off to head out to Jill's place. The traffic began to speed up and it looked like trucks were already out salting the highway.

"I am looking forward to a nice, cozy meal tonight with two of my favorite people." She patted Leah's leg.

Jill approached her turn off the highway and slowed down. Neither she nor Leah saw the large truck coming up quickly behind them. The man driving tried to stop but when he slammed on his breaks, it caused the back of his truck to fishtail wildly. He missed hitting them directly, but his truck slammed into the side of Jill's car.

Leah felt the jolt of the impact and suddenly the car was plummeting down the ditch and over onto the roof. The contents of the vehicle flew around them and then they were still. She was upside down, looking through the cracked windshield. Her mind was clouded and when she moved slightly, rockets of pain shot through her shoulder where her collar bone had broken from the force of the seatbelt.

She looked over to Jill whose eyes were closed as she hung limply from her seatbelt. Blood dripped down from Jill's head onto the roof below, making an eerie pattern on the light roof fabric. "Oh my God! Jill, Jill, Jill!" She shrieked as pain radiated through her shoulder. She could see upside down people running toward their car.

Jill moaned and moved her arms, which were dangling above her head. A wave of relief came over Leah. She had been scared Jill was dead.

People surrounded the car and Leah could hear sirens in the distance. Both doors were jammed as the car frame had bent when the car landed on its roof. People were talking to her through the window, asking her name and letting her know help was on its way.

Jill remained semi-conscious as firefighters sawed the doors away from the car. Leah cried and prayed Jill would be okay. As they began pulling them from the vehicle, the paramedics stepped in. An agitated man on the edge of the crowd nervously watched and called out to her, "I'm sorry. I couldn't stop in time. The road was too icy." Leah presumed he was the driver of the truck that had crashed into them.

When Leah was freed from the wreckage, the paramedics helped her up the slippery embankment to the waiting ambulance and had her sit in the back while they assessed her. Another paramedic came to the door to ask questions about Jill—her name and anything else Leah knew—before they left for the hospital. Satisfied with the information, the paramedic turned to go back to Jill.

"Wait, I just remembered something really important!" Leah cried out with urgency. "She's pregnant."

The medic nodded and said, "We'll take good care of them both." As he stepped away, another figure moved into the space. Evan.

Leah looked in disbelief at Evan standing there and burst into tears. She was so glad to see him. He leaned into the ambulance and took her hand. "Are you okay?"

"I think my collar bone is broken. It hurts so bad."

The paramedic added, "Yes, it seems like we might have a break, we'll take her to the hospital to get checked over and do some x-rays, though."

Evan thanked the paramedic and turned back to Leah, "Did you say that Jill is pregnant?"

Leah nodded. "I'm sorry, you weren't supposed to know yet." His mind struggled to process the information, so he focused on Leah, looking at her tear-streaked face and puffy eyes as the paramedics were carefully securing her arm for the ride to the hospital.

"I was headed over to Jill's for supper with you when I saw a bunch of emergency vehicles and Jill's car in the ditch. What happened?"

She wiped tears away with her good hand and she carefully cradled the other to her body. "I don't know. All of a sudden, something hit us from the side and pushed us into the ditch and we flipped. Jill was knocked out and her head was bleeding. I hope she's going to be okay." She sniffled.

"I will follow you two to the hospital. I'll be right behind you." He squeezed her good hand. "Everything will be okay, I won't leave you."

He approached the other ambulance and hung back as the paramedics surrounded Jill and loaded her into the ambulance and closed the door. He held himself back from pushing through them to hold her and speak to her. He climbed into his truck and followed as the ambulances pulled away heading to the hospital.

Pregnant. What did that mean? Why did Leah know, and Jill hadn't told him yet? Had she decided to have Brad's baby and didn't have the heart to tell him? His mind was churning with worry for Jill and Leah and full of questions about the baby.

The hospital was a flurry of activity. They triaged Leah and sent her for x-rays. She was very lucky; despite being in shock, she only had a broken collar bone. Evan waited while they tended to her arm.

Evan had enquired about Jill, but they said she was being assessed and he would be notified when they could see her. Evan bought a drink from the vending machine for Leah, a coffee for himself, and they reluctantly went to the waiting room. Evan intended to ask Leah about Jill being pregnant when Lydia burst into the room in a panic.

"Leah!" she exclaimed as she saw her across the waiting room. She dashed over to Leah and, seeing the sling, carefully pulled her into an embrace. Leah cried and felt comforted in her mother's arms. Lydia wiped tears of relief away as well and after a time they sat down with Evan.

"Mama, how did you know I was here?"

"Evan called me. I came as soon as I could." She looked past Leah at Evan and her look of gratitude spoke volumes. "Are you okay?"

"Yeah, Mom. My collar bone is broken, and I feel like someone beat me, but I'm really worried about Jill. She got hit really hard. She was knocked out." Leah's voice sounded like a little girl and emotion choked her. "I hope she'll be okay."

They sat together in the waiting room as medical staff bustled by in the hall. Lydia sat on one side of Leah, holding the hand that wasn't in a sling. Evan sat on the other.

Evan cleared his throat. "This is probably as good a time as any. I think we could use some good news right about now." They looked at him waiting for him to continue.

"I'm not surprised, but the test results came back. Leah is absolutely, one hundred percent, my daughter—or at least 99.99%." He smiled and his lip quivered with emotion. "And I couldn't be happier with that."

Leah let out a squeal and jumped up, then quickly grimaced at the pain it caused. "I am so glad. I was hoping so much it would be true." Evan stood and hugged her. He let go and she took her seat and looked at Lydia.

"Don't worry about me, I knew for sure all along."

Lydia gave her hand a tender squeeze. Leah's face darkened and she stiffened. She snatched her hand back from Lydia's grasp like it had been burned by fire. Lydia was taken aback. "What is it?"

"Because of you, I have missed all these years knowing my dad!" Nurses turned to look as her voice became louder. She sprang to her feet again and stood stiff as a board. The tears that came coursed down her face. "You didn't even give him a chance."

"I was scared, and I didn't know what to do. You have no idea what I went through."

A security guard approached the waiting area. "Excuse me, is there a problem here?"

Leah wiped her wet face on the back of her hand. "Yes, I want her to leave," she said through clenched teeth, and pointed at Lydia. Evan stood up and put his arm protectively around Leah. Lydia looked helpless and miserable.

"I came here to pick you up to take you home," Lydia said, stepping toward Leah.

"Don't touch me." She shrank away from Lydia.

Evan's arm tightened on Leah's shoulder. He held up a hand to Lydia. "I think we all need to cool down a bit. It has been a difficult day and we're still waiting to see how Jill is." He looked exhausted. "I think she was going to stay at Jill's tonight anyway, or she can come home with me. I will look after her and we'll let you know how Jill is tomorrow."

Lydia was defeated. She looked at Evan, her faced creased with worry. "Please call if Leah needs me." She stood in front of Leah. "I will call you tomorrow." Leah shrugged and looked away as Lydia left.

They sat in the waiting area quietly, each processing the information.

"So, what will this mean for us?" Leah asked. "I mean, I want you to be in my life, but how can we do that?"

"I want you in my life too. We'll have to sit down with your mom to work out an arrangement. I would like to see you regularly and have you with me for holidays and things like that. Not to mention, helping your mom financially so you have what you need and soon, college."

"I don't even want to be with mom. I want to stay with you."

"It seems like we have a lot to figure out." He patted her leg. "Tell me more about Jill. When did you find out? How far along is she?"

"Martin and I found out in the elevator when we were stuck. Jill was throwing up, it was so gross. She said she had morning sickness. At that time, we had no idea you were my dad. How crazy."

"She never told me."

"I know. She was worried you would be upset finding out she was pregnant. She was planning to tell you soon."

Was Jill worried about telling him because it was Brad's baby? His mind raced as he replayed their conversations back in his mind. There was no indication she was going ahead with having Brad's baby. Was it his? They hadn't used protection; he assumed she was on birth control and hadn't asked.

A nurse poked her head into the waiting area. "Leah Armstrong?"

"Yes, that's me."

"Jill Jones has been asking to see Leah, over and over again. I said I would come find you."

"Yes, that's me. I'm so glad. Can we see her?"

The nurse led them to Jill's bedside. Jill was pale white against the sheet of the bed. Her hair was still stiff with dried blood and she had a bandage on her brow. She weakly smiled when she saw Leah and then a look of surprise as she saw Evan behind her.

"Evan," she whispered.

They both went to either side of the bed and held her hands. The doctor stepped over from the nurses' station. "Are you both with Ms. Jones?"

They nodded. The doctor asked if it would be okay to discuss her results and with Jill's agreement, she proceeded.

"You are very lucky. We have done a battery of tests on you and the baby and everything is perfectly fine. Despite being banged around, the womb is a really safe place and the baby looks unharmed. If you have any pains or bleeding, please come back to the hospital right away." Jill's eye darted to Evan, but it was apparent by his reaction it wasn't a surprise. "You have a mild concussion and some stitches in your scalp. Please come back to see us if you have worsening symptoms like dizziness, a severe headache, double vision, or memory problems to name a few. I will include a concussion information sheet with your discharge instructions. We can release you, as long as someone can stay with you tonight."

"We'll both be with her and we'll take good care of her." He smiled at Jill tenderly and caressed her fingers with his thumb.

"Okay, we'll observe her for about an hour more and then she can go. Does that sound okay, Ms. Jones?" She patted her foot.

Jill gave the doctor a thumbs-up and said, "Yes, sounds good."

She turned to Leah, noticing the sling, "Are you okay? I don't even know what happened. We were driving along, I was slowing down, and next thing, I am in an ambulance. I was so afraid. I didn't know what had happened to you."

"I'm okay. My collar bone broke, probably from the seat belt. I have my wing in a sling." She laughed, showing Jill her blue fabric sling. She teared up and her voice grew solemn. "I was so worried about you. You were unconscious, I didn't know if you were alive or dead."

Evan nodded as well. "I panicked when I came upon the crash. I was coming for supper and all I saw were emergency vehicles at your turn-off and then your white car upside-down in the ditch. I never want to have those feelings ever again." He choked with emotion and blinked back tears. Jill squeezed his rough hand.

"Luckily though, it looks like you're both going to be okay and getting back into trouble in no time again," Evan said to lighten the somber mood.

"Yes," Leah agreed and smiled.

Jill turned to Leah. "Honey, I'm really thirsty. Could you go get me a bottle of water or something from the vending machine?"

"You bet." Evan dug in his jacket pocket and handed Leah some change and she left on her mission.

He pulled a chair up to the bed, struggling to find the

words to ask. "Why didn't you tell me about the baby? Is it Brad's or mine?"

Jill's face registered surprise at what he must have thought.

"The baby is yours. I never would have gone ahead and planned to have Brad's baby without talking to you first. It's my fault, I wasn't using any birth control. I guess I'd had so much trouble trying to conceive before, I didn't expect it would happen so easily." She wasn't angry at his question. There were so many surprises lately, he probably didn't know what to expect anymore.

"It isn't anyone's fault. I was there and wasn't acting responsibly either."

"I'm sorry you found out like this. I was coming to tell you the night we got trapped in the elevator. Who would know I would discover your daughter in that elevator?"

"I guess that made it a bit complicated."

"I didn't want to ruin her finding you. I thought you needed some time to get used to the idea of one child before I sprang another on you."

"I'm shocked, but I'm also pretty excited at the same time. I guess I assumed you were on birth control or that you struggled with fertility like Sarah and I had."

"For us, it was Brad that couldn't have kids after all of his cancer treatments. I got caught up in the moment and I didn't even think of it that night."

"But we made love a few more times after that."

"Yes, after the first time, I was already pregnant."

"I want to be with you and a part of this baby's life every step of the way. I hope we can do this together."

Jill nodded and tears shimmered on her lashes. "I would love that."

"I love you, Jill, very much. I'm glad you had a broken water faucet." They chuckled together.

"Me too. It changed my life. I met the most amazing plumber."

He leaned forward and kissed her softly. Leah arrived with a cold bottle of water. They helped Jill sit up and take a drink. The nurse came in and after doing Jill's vital signs and asking her some questions, they were free to go home.

Evan led his injured women to the front door, where they waited for him to bring his truck up to the door to pick them up. It had stopped snowing and with all the crews that were out, driving conditions wouldn't be much of a problem anymore. They headed home to Jill's. Her car wasn't in the ditch at the turn off anymore; the emergency crews had hauled it away.

Buck launched himself at the door when they arrived. After jumping all over Evan, he was quickly ushered out the back doors into the yard. The girls got settled on the couch while Evan brought the groceries for supper in from his truck. He whistled softly in the kitchen as he made them a delicious lasagna, with salad and fresh garlic bread. By the time they sat down to their late supper, they were all ravenous.

As they had dessert, Evan pulled out a small box for Leah. She looked at the package with surprise and then excitedly tore the wrapping off fumbling with her one hand. She squealed to see a beautiful necklace with an amethyst pendant. Evan looked on with pride.

"Hey, it's my birthstone. Cool!"

Beyond the 14th Floor

"Yes, I wanted to give a gift to my daughter and promise that I will not miss another birthday of yours, ever again."

Leah and Evan got up and squeezed one another in a gentle hug.

Evan insisted they move back to the couch to rest. Buck collapsed on the floor in a heap by their feet and almost instantly began to snore. Evan cleaned up the dirty dishes in the kitchen and soon joined them in the living room. He carried a warm mug of hot chocolate for each of them.

They relaxed, unwinding from the stressful day. Jill yawned and rubbed her eyes. "I'm sorry, you two. My body, and baby, are telling me I need to go to bed. How are you feeling, Leah? I imagine you will be sore and stiff all over by tomorrow."

Leah cradled her sore arm. "Yes, I am already feeling tender spots, for sure."

"Sweetie, if you need anything in the night, come and wake me up." Jill put her hand on Leah's cheek and gave her a tender smile. "Have you ever broken a bone before?"

"No, I've never been injured before." She was tired too. Evan hugged Leah again.

"It has been a terrible day and the best day all in one," said Leah. She wished them goodnight and headed to the spare room with Buck trotting along beside her.

Evan ran a bath for Jill and helped her rinse the dried blood from her hair, avoiding the bandage covering her eyebrow. "You're one tough cookie."

"I sure don't feel like one. I thought I wasn't going to be too bad off, but I can already feel my body getting stiff and sore."

"So, if you got pregnant in late September, that puts you due in May sometime, if my calculations are correct."

"Yes, I'm pretty sure. I have an ultrasound booked in the next two weeks. I was hoping you could come with me."

"Do you think you could keep me away?" Evan chuckled. "I'm really excited."

"I'm so happy and relieved. I was hoping you would want to be involved."

Evan grabbed a fluffy towel and gently dried Jill off. He marveled at her flat tummy, knowing it would soon change. He softly kissed her shoulder as he held up her robe to slip on.

"Are you feeling okay, can I get you anything?" Evan asked with concern.

"No, I think I'm okay. I just need a good rest."

"I want to sleep with you to keep an eye on you, is that okay? Or if you need the space, I can always hit the couch."

She grabbed his hand and held it. "I want you with me."

"Good, I was hoping you'd say that."

That night, as Leah laid in bed at Jill's, she thought about the crazy day. Her body was aching all over and her collar bone throbbed. There didn't seem to be a comfortable spot to position herself in. She wished she was home in her own bed, but she was still angry at her mom for so many things, so she was glad she'd stayed at Jill's.

She wondered what she would do now with Evan confirmed as her real dad. Would she move in with him? What about Jill and the baby? Maybe they could all move in together. Leah thought about her mom. She would be devastated if Leah moved out now. In seven months though, Leah would graduate and then she would move. She was so confused about her life. She should begin applying for college too. It made her long for the simple days when she was a child.

She drifted off as the pain medication gave her relief.

The next morning, Leah was up early and let Buck out. She sat at the table with a bowl of cereal when Evan appeared.

"Hey early birdy, how are you feeling this morning?" he asked. He walked to the counter and began making coffee.

"Like a truck hit me. My shoulder feels like someone karate chopped it."

He brought her a couple of pain relief tablets and a glass of water. She smiled. "Thanks." It felt nice to have him caring for her.

He gently patted her shoulder. "I think Jill feels a lot like you do today. She didn't sleep well last night, but she is quietly snoring now, so I snuck out."

Evan sat down at the table with Leah. She looked up at him. "I'm not sure what to do. Do I call you Dad? Do I call you Evan? How often do I get to see you? What happens now?"

"I know, it's kind of confusing. For starters, I would be happy if you called me Dad, but you can call me whatever feels comfortable to you. I want to see you lots, because I want to get to know you and be in your life."

Her heart brimmed with joy. "What about Mom?"

"That's a little bit tougher. We may have to go to a lawyer and work out some agreements. I'll want to help with college or whatever your plans are after graduation. We will have to sit down together to figure out some things. Your mom has been in charge for all these years, I don't want to barge in and take over. We'll do what's best for you."

"I feel so lucky to have found you. I had always thought you were dead, and it could never be a possibility to meet my dad."

"I feel lucky too. It was a shock, but I look forward to you seeing the rest of your family. You have a grandpa that can't wait to meet you."

Leah's eyes shone. "That's awesome, I can't wait either."

They sat in silence, enjoying the sun streaming through the patio doors.

Leah shifted in her chair and closed her eyes and took a deep breath. "The last thing I want to do is ruin this moment, but I have something hard to tell you." She put her good hand to her face, covering her eyes. "I hope you will still want me as your daughter. This is so hard." She paused and found it difficult to choke the words out. "I think I'm gay." Her eyes met his, almost as a challenge to see what his reaction would be. "I'm so sorry." Her face crumpled and tears came fast as she buried her face in her arms. Evan got up and went over to her chair. He wrapped his arm around her and put his face to her hair.

"Shhh, it's okay. Shhh." He said over and over. "There is nothing to be sorry about. It's okay, I already knew. I will always love you, it doesn't matter. You're still my daughter."

He felt her body stiffen momentarily, then relax. She pulled back and looked at him with her tear stained face. "How did you know?"

"Your mom told me. It's okay. I don't care who you think you are as long as you're safe and happy with your life. I'm just excited and proud to have you as my daughter."

Relief washed over her, and she began crying even harder. "I'm so glad," she whimpered. "I was so afraid you wouldn't want to be my dad."

"Sweetie, nothing will stop me from being your dad ever again."

Jill appeared in the doorway of the kitchen in her bathrobe looking rumpled. "Hey, what's going on out here? Is everything okay?"

Leah smiled through her tears. "I've told Evan my secret. He said it's okay." He hugged her again and sat down.

Jill walked to Leah's side and patted her shoulder. "You've got a pretty good dad there."

"I know, right? After all the stuff we've dumped on him in the last month, I'm surprised he's still here."

"Yes, amazingly we haven't scared him off yet." Jill put her arm around him, rumpled his hair, and kissed the top of his head.

Evan chuckled. "I've gained a beautiful daughter, girlfriend, and baby on the way. My life couldn't be more amazing."

Chapter Seventeen

Martin couldn't erase the look of disappointment on Leah's face when she had realized he hadn't told the police all the information. He was a coward and he knew it.

He wished she could understand his feelings of anxiety were getting worse. His hip was sore, it always was, but now he was having trouble sleeping. The lights would shut off and his mind would race. He kept seeing the boys pummeling Scott and finally the last fatal punch that took him down. He had nightmares about mopping up the blood, never being able to get it all as it just kept reappearing every time the mop wiped it away.

Maybe this wasn't about him anymore. Maybe they wouldn't believe him. Maybe he would get fired. It would certainly be difficult to work at the school with Principal Schmidt if the full truth came out. Scott didn't do anything wrong. As a matter of fact, he was putting himself in harm's way to help other kids. He died for what he believed in.

How would this affect his daughter? Rosa couldn't afford to support him or pay for his surgery. He wasn't a religious man, but that night he stiffly knelt by his bed. He clasped his hands and buried his face in them. He thought of Phyllis. What would she have thought of this? He thought of Scott. Poor Scott.

He tossed and turned. Phyllis came to him in his dreams. She reached out with a warm hand, smiled, and caressed his cheek. He was filled with love. Then her face clouded over, and a tear slid down her beautiful face as her eyes searched his. Not a word was said and then she disappeared. He woke in the darkness, his face wet with tears.

He came up with a plan.

His surgery date was fast approaching. A mixture of feelings swirled through his mind: panic, fear, relief, and resolve. It was time.

He sat at his kitchen table for hours. The pile of crumpled papers grew beside him as he wrote. He ripped and crumpled them, and then began all over again. Finally, in the late evening, he had the copy he felt satisfied with. He carefully folded the paper and slid it into an envelope.

He lapsed into a relaxed sleep and rested better than he had in weeks.

#

"Good afternoon, Betty." Martin nodded as he walked into the office. Betty looked up and cheerfully smiled.

"Hey, how are you today?" she asked, looking over the glasses on her short round nose.

"I'm fine." He shifted his weight back and forth as he stood. He wiped his damp hands on his pants. "Is Principal Schmidt in his office?"

She looked back over her shoulder. "Yes, he's here. He's

had his door closed all day. I'll phone in."

"Principal Schmidt, Martin is here to see you. Are you available?" She looked at Martin, rolled her eyes, and hung up the phone. "Take a seat. He'll be a few minutes."

Martin chose to stand, it was too painful to sit. Soon. Soon this will all be over. Ten minutes passed, feeling like an eternity. Martin practiced his speech in his head going over and over what he was going to say, like an exam.

The office door opened, Principal Schmidt nodded at Martin, and then disappeared back into his office. Betty shook her head with sympathy as he hobbled past her.

Principal Schmidt was seated at his desk. He looked disheveled and tired as he raked his hand through his hair and gestured to the chair across from him. Martin closed the door and lowered himself into the chair, trying to hide his discomfort.

"That hip still bugging you?"

"Yes, Sir."

"Martin, what can I do for you today?"

"I've made a big mistake. I can't live with it hanging over me anymore."

Principal Schmidt nodded for him to continue.

"I saw who beat Scott Tatum that night. It was three boys from our school." He noticed Principal Schmidt didn't react to this information. He cleared his throat. It was difficult to say. "One was Sebastian. He knocked Scott out. He punched him real hard."

Schmidt leaned over his desk, so close Martin could smell stale sweat. "Are you behind what happened last night?" Principal Schmidt's eyes were bloodshot and watery.

Martin shrank back in his chair subconsciously. "What, what do you mean?"

"Don't take me for a fool. When did you go to the police?"

Martin held his breath and could feel his armpits had made his shirt damp. "I found the boy and then the shoe." He said in an even voice. "You saw the times they came to talk with me. I never told them that I saw who did it."

Principal Schmidt stood and leaned forward with his knuckles pressed against the desk. "The police came to our house last night and arrested Sebastian." He waited for that to sink in. "They said he murdered the Tatum boy." His voice was filled with contempt.

Martin was confused. "I never went to the police, Lord help me. How did they find out it was Sebastian?"

"The running shoe you gave to Tatum's family belonged to him. The police claimed it put him at the crime scene."

"He killed the boy. That last punch did it." For the first time, he challenged the principal. "You know it too."

Principal Schmidt stood and paced with his hands in his pockets. "It went too far. They were only supposed to scare him. My boy didn't kill Scott Tatum."

Martin's mouth gaped at the frank admission. "Why were they supposed to scare him?"

Principal Schmidt threw his hands in the air in disbelief, like Martin just wasn't getting it. "Do you really think we need people like that in our school, much less organizing support groups?"

"You sent Sebastian and his thugs to scare him off?"

"I admit, it went too far."

Martin hung his head. "You were there," he said quietly. "You didn't help." The image in the shadows wearing the green jacket flashed through his mind. "He was just a boy."

Principal Schmidt shrugged and sat down. "Martin, you have to understand, this was just a big misunderstanding. A school yard fight that got out of hand. My boy has lots of big things waiting for him. Three colleges have approached him with football scholarship offers. Unfortunately, the Tatum boy died. It was an accident. I'm sure you'll agree we don't need to destroy two lives here."

Martin lowered his gaze and gave a slight nod. They both stood and Principal Schmidt came around the desk to shake Martin's hand, as though they had concluded a business deal.

Martin turned and left, closing the door. He straightened up, smiled, and giving Betty a wave, he walked out of the office. He kept walking out the front doors of the school and ambled to the city bus stop. The heaviness he'd carried had lifted. Even his hip didn't feel as sore. He rode for a while then got off the bus, which incidentally stopped right by the police station. He paused for a moment, looking at the large building. He raised his eyes to heaven, said a silent prayer, and then went in.

After Martin left, Principal Schmidt saw the letter on his desk. It had his name on it. He sat and sliced it open. He unfolded the handwritten letter. It was Martin's resignation.

#

At the police station, Martin met with the detective who was investigating Scott's murder.

He explained all he knew and why he had been reluctant to come forward. They asked a lot of questions and he was at the station for three hours. At times, he sensed he might be in trouble based on the intensity of the questions they peppered him with. He just kept seeing Phyllis' sad face and knew he was doing the right thing.

Later, Martin sat at the kitchen table as he read the paper. His fork clattered onto his plate as he read the headline of the Tribune. Sebastian Schmidt was to be charged with involuntary manslaughter. He would remain in custody until the trial. It was stated that he would be tried as an adult. Martin pushed his plate full of breakfast away. He had opened the gates and whatever came forth was out of his control.

Martin was called by the prosecutor's office and met with them several times to review his testimony. He would be integral to a conviction in this case. Meeting with Jill and Leah for coffee reinforced his determination to see it through. They were so proud of him for coming forward and their support helped him as the trial date was looming.

A faint aroma of moth balls emanated from his suit as he pulled it from the closet. The last time it had been worn was at his wife's funeral. He would do this for her, and for Scott. He would make sure Scott's death wasn't in vain. He also felt he owed it to Leah. He sat in the living room fully dressed, his eyes closed, feeling his heart beat in his chest. He took a deep breath, opened his eyes, and left for the twenty-five minute taxi ride to the court house.

Principal Schmidt and his family sat behind Sebastian

in the court room. Martin could feel the heavy burden of their stares as he truthfully answered questions about the night Scott had been beaten. His stomach was churning and his breathing shallow as he carried out the huge responsibility of sharing what he had witnessed.

After being questioned for forty-five minutes, he was dismissed. Nothing felt better than the large breath of fresh air that filled his lungs as he emerged from the courthouse. To avoid the throng of reporters, the prosecution team arranged for him to be taken away in a taxi from a rear exit of the court house. His relief was short-lived as he pulled up to his brownstone to see three or four reporters milling around his front door.

With a raised hand, Martin passed by the reporters muttering, "No comment." He was assaulted with a barrage of questions. He slammed the door and twisted the lock, then finally exhaled and slumped against the hallway wall.

After two weeks of trial and then deliberations, the verdict arrived. Sebastian was convicted of involuntary manslaughter. Reporters pondered what his sentence would be, with the minimum sentence being one year. It was a small price to pay for the loss of Scott's life.

The local news spooled the story for hours on the TV beside Martin's hospital bed. After a successful hip replacement, he was amazed to be up cautiously walking within days. He was discharged to Rosa, who went home with him to arrange his care for the next couple of weeks.

Principal Schmidt hadn't been charged with anything despite his role in the attack. They couldn't prove beyond a reasonable doubt that he was the one who sent Sebastian to rough up Scott. Perhaps, Sebastian would never have attacked Scott otherwise.

As the details of the case emerged, parents came forward, angry that their children might be harmed with him still at the school. Finally, the school district felt it had no other choice and fired him.

Martin felt better than he had in a long time. He was recovering from his hip surgery very well. Rosa stopped in frequently to help, despite his objections. He appreciated her family's care and attention. They discovered his health benefits could be extended after his resignation, so he had been pleased his surgery was covered. He felt he deserved that much after all of his years of service.

While he was walking every day to strengthen it, he was relieved he didn't have to go back to work. He was exhausted but he finally felt at peace again. In fact, he had had a dream about Scott walking down a path and then Phyllis appeared and reached out to take Scott's hand. He watched them walk together and then disappear. His heart ached and felt full of love at the same time.

Epilogue

"Dad. Jill. Over here." Leah called, waving at them as they were getting out of their truck. Leah and Lydia were on the school sidewalk nears the doors. People filtered in past them as they waited.

Evan smiled and waved at her across the parking lot. He helped Jill get the car seat out of the back seat. They joined hands and walked together.

Leah was standing in her graduation robe with Lydia, who was beaming with pride and wiping away the tears. "I'm glad you got here early. I want you to have good seats. How's my little brother doing?" said Leah as she leaned into the car seat and caressed the sleeping baby's fuzzy, little head.

"Still not getting a whole lot of sleep, and Buck is still not sure what we brought home with us." Jill laughed and shrugged. "We're figuring it out."

Evan hugged Leah. "You look wonderful. We're proud of you." Leah's face flushed but it was apparent she enjoyed hearing the compliments.

"Leah, we have a special surprise for you. He asked if

he could come," said Jill, nodding to the truck.

On cue, Martin appeared. Leah squealed with excitement. "Martin!"

"Look at you. You're rockin' that new hip." She gave him a big hug and he pulled back to arms-length, appraising her blue graduation robe.

"Ain't you a sight for sore eyes? Your parents must be so proud." His eyes glinted and he gave her his tobacco-stained smile. "I hope it's okay, but I asked Jill if she thought I could come." He turned to Lydia. "I hope it's okay with you too, Ma'am."

Lydia held out her hand. "Mr. Sanderson, we're glad you came. Leah hasn't stopped talking about you all spring. You've become her hero, helping convict the boy that killed her friend."

"Your daughter is an amazin' young woman. It was 'cause of her that made me decide I should come forward. Sometimes the right thing to do isn't always the easiest." He smiled and patted Leah's shoulder.

"We're proud of you, Martin. How have you managed?" Jill asked.

"Rosa helped me figure out my benefits, so when I got my hip replacement, it was covered. Pension ain't great, but it's all I need, plus, my grandkids get to see me more."

"I'm so glad Scott got justice. I can't believe Principal Schmidt put his son up to that."

"Yes, I'm glad they have a new principal now."

Baby Matthew let out a squawk and they laughed. "Looks like you have your hands full these days too, Evan." Martin nodded to the car seat.

"Yes, my life is completely different from last year at this time. Really, the changes that can happen in a year are incredible. I went from being a bachelor, eating on the couch in front of the TV, to a father of a newborn and a college kid." He nodded toward Leah.

"I am still stunned that I got in. Plus, I got my grades up enough that I qualified for a scholarship into the social work program. I was really lucky," said Leah.

Martin nodded. "Like my pa always said, 'People ain't lucky, they's prepared for opportunity.' That's what happened to you, Leah. Your hard work prepared you for this." Leah beamed.

"It's out of state, but Leah has assured me she will phone me three times a week, at least," Lydia said, putting an arm around her daughter.

Leah rolled her eyes with a smile. "I will, Mom. I'm sure I'll need someone to chat with until I make some friends there. I'll come home often too."

"You'd better. Your little brother will want to get to know you." Evan smiled as baby Matthew let out a squeak then began to loudly wail.

Jill held up her left hand and a new diamond sparkled on her ring finger. "Martin, I hope you can make it. We're getting married this fall. We'll plan a small celebration when we find out Leah's schedule."

"Wouldn't miss it for the world," he grinned.

Acknowledgments

I am grateful for my pen wielding editing team, Katrina Swan, Tim Huber and Shirley Huber, who helped clean up my manuscript.

I wish to thank my husband Keith, and my daughters Tia, Chantal, and Jolie who read my drafts and provided feedback on my numerous questions about the characters and plot.

To Tia Bossaer, who pulled out her acrylic paints and with every brush stroke, created an original book cover even better than I could have imagined. I'm pleased to share this experience with you!

I am surrounded by amazing, friends and family that have been fabulously supportive of this dream of mine. I appreciate all the kind words and encouragement that I've received.

Feel free to send me an email with your thoughts on this book at **melaneyboss@outlook.com** or follow me on **Instagram @melaneybossaer.**

CPSIA information can be obtained
at www.ICGtesting.com
Printed in the USA
LVHW051217251119
638398LV00009B/220/P